WHEN STARS BECOME SHADOWS

EMMIE HAMILTON

CONTENTS

Innulum Press is an imprint created and owned by Emmie Hamilton. For more information, please visit www.emmiehamilton.com

Paperback: 978-1-7366994-9-2
Ebook: 978-1-7366994-8-5
First paperback edition July 2022.

Developmental Edit by Quinn Nichols
Line and Copy Edit by B.N. Laux
Cover design by Franzi Haase: www.coverdungeon.com
Book design by Nicole Scarano Formatting & Design
Siren Song written by JP McDonald

Printed in United States of America.

Also by Emmie Hamilton

Chosen to Fall

Fated to Burn

Destined to Rise (Winter 2022)

For those who feel trapped and are longing for freedom – rattle that cage.

A Note to the Reader

Dear Reader,

Thank you so much for deeming my book worthy of any minute of your time. Out of the millions of novels you could have chosen, I feel honored that you chose mine.

As always, I feel it is necessary to be honest about what you are about to read. I came up with the idea for this story when I felt my life was at a precipice, and drafted it during a time of extreme grief and healing. There are emotions among these pages that run deep, and as such, darker elements are woven throughout this story.

While compared to others books, this one may seem mild to some, but make no mistake: this is a Dark Fantasy, layered with explicit sexual content with BDSM themes, references of sexual assault, abuse, violence, PTSD, body image issues, depression, anxiety, and death. Some or all of these may be triggering, so I urge you to make your best judgment before reading.

I value you more than anything, reader, for granting me

the opportunity to continue doing what I love and allowing me the freedom of expression I've withheld for far too long. Thank you for coming on this journey with me.

Yours,

Emmie

"But her sweeter song
It is foretold
Will soothe the soul as death takes hold"

— -FROM THE TULLYHOUSE'S MOST
POPULAR SEA SHANTY

PART ONE

T he ship docked at midnight.

Like clockwork, the current carried the behemoth along until it gently nudged against its assigned space, where it would stay until after the morning market. I knew this because I'd watched it every night since I signed my contract. Every night since my family was murdered. Every night since I was forced into something akin to slavery because I had nothing else to offer.

Because my body was worth more than my mind.

My fingers gripped the lace curtain covering the soot-stained window, its glass casting a shadowy sheen against the sails, making it appear as though it were an apparition rather than my salvation.

Thick cuffs chafed my wrists as I strapped a thin dagger to one thigh and a pouch containing a worn seashell and some loose coins against the other. Remnants of a life I once lived had become my ticket to freedom.

The sounds of late-night debauchery seeped under the cracks of my door along with the scent of spilt ale and day-old roasted meat. I hated that tavern. Hated the room I was locked in until a caller felt my curvy frame would be worth thirty seconds of their time. But through each encounter of old men stinking of unwashed bodies, whose teeth were half-rotted and tempers were even worse, I earned one more coin that ensured I could buy out my servitude.

Stomping footsteps clunked down the hallway, the worn carpet doing nothing to mask their approach, and paused just outside the door, blocking the thin strip of light from underneath. Heavy breathing muffled through the thick wood, but I knew it was Julian listening in to see if I was occupied. He liked to listen, sometimes.

"Briar," he yelled as he pounded the door with a thick fist. "Where's your client?"

Bile rose as I glanced over at the blood trickling out of the corpse cooling on the bed. I'd never killed a man before. I swallowed against the sour feeling creeping up my throat. "He fell asleep. He paid for two hours with me."

"Well wake him up and get on with it. We've got a line of people waiting out here."

I scoffed to myself. There was always a line of men and the occasional woman waiting for me. Always someone else to take their piece of me while I slowly withered away inside.

Not anymore.

"I will," I responded. I worried he would wait to see if I complied, but a moment later I heard his heavy gait slam against the stairs.

The ship outside my window swayed in a light breeze,

mocking me, waving its fingers in a beckoning dare. *Aren't you coming, Little Red?*

My chest nearly cracked under the pressure of what I was about to do. Though I'd starved myself for three months in preparation, I hadn't planned on that night being the one I'd squeeze through the window in an attempt at freedom. The cuffs clasped around my wrists would make the jump difficult, but I studied the eaves in the walls every morning on the way to the market, and knew every crack in the cobblestone road under my window. I was certain I could make it.

I patted the body down, looking for any spare coin or weapon, but the drunk had nothing except for half a tablet of *cassov*—a drug that put one in a hallucinogenic state. It was addictive, unpredictable, and often resulted in death to those who didn't know when they'd had enough. My father used to peddle *cassov* in its powdered form, often masking it under the spice trade he was known for along the southern coast of Carnithia. I should have recognized my client was high from the moment he stepped into my room, but it wouldn't have made a difference. The second he wrapped his hands around my throat he was a dead man, anyway.

Boisterous music blasted from below as yet another sea shanty filled the tavern. I used to love them. A younger, more naive version of me used to beg my parents to allow me to stand outside our local tavern just so I could peek in at the dancing and revel in the laughter of the patrons as they hopped and clapped along to the music. Their shadows would pour out of the doorway and for a few moments, it would be as if they were dancing with me and I'd be a little less lonely.

The same setlist played every weekend, allowing me to devise each part of my plan down to the second. I counted the silence between songs and I wrapped my arm in a spare bit of fabric, and when the crooner belted out the opening note I'd been waiting for, I swung my elbow back through the pane of glass of the window. Twice, three times. The crackling of broken shards was drowned out by the stomping and clapping of the tavern's patrons. I forced a smile against the sting of pain where the glass cut through my shoddy cloth protection and savored the scent of crude oil mixed with the salty ocean breeze as it billowed against my face. I could taste a hint of rain on the back of my tongue as I gulped in the fresh air, ridding myself of the copper tang of the cooling blood that leaked onto the wood floor. My ship of salvation creaked steadily as if waiting for me to make my next move.

Nothing but painful memories lurked from the darkness as I glanced briefly around my assigned room one last time: empty dressers housing the only undergarments I wore, the closet where few skirts and dresses hung, the hole in the wall barely covered by a hastily draped tapestry, its door that hung off its hinges from when a particularly voracious client thought being rough meant slamming me against it until he could see the evidence of his strength, and the threadbare bed I slept in for seven years, now occupied by the man I'd just killed.

It was a grim sight—one that I was not sorry to miss. Seven years of indentured servitude, stuck within those walls until Julian deemed it necessary for me to strut about town, dolled up exactly the way he wanted me in a tight corset and deep red lip stain, as if to entice potential buyers to his wares. To him, I was a product for sale and nothing more.

My fingers gripped the edges of the windowsill, barely able to hold on with the chain held tightly against my wrists. Wriggling my body through the small opening was only the first challenge; finding a way down without breaking my back was the next. I shimmied through, ignoring the sharp slicing of skin against the jagged glass still clinging onto the sill, and sucked in a deep breath as I raised first one foot and then the other onto the narrow ledge.

For a moment the burst of freedom I desired clung to me like a second shadow in the night. Up there, I was a nightingale ready to take flight—to see lands unknown and dive into oceans unexplored. It didn't matter that my body was used like a well-oiled machine, or that I shamed myself so deep within a well of darkness I wasn't sure I would ever feel sunlight kiss my skin.

And for once, I was unafraid of where the road would lead me.

The deserted, dusty street below me beckoned for my shot of bravery. It would be unwise to leap two stories and risk breaking my leg, or worse, especially when on the run for murder while trying to escape my gangster owner and break from this indentured servitude. The wrist cuffs would do little to aid me, though I might have been able to scale down the uneven brick wall. A light drizzle misted from the clouds, as if the gods thought I needed another challenge—another way to prove I was worthy of freedom. My dark red hair clung to my chest like rivulets of blood in the foggy night. I hoped it wouldn't be an omen for things to come.

The banging on the door to my prison echoed in the death chamber, reminding me how short on time I was. A shot of adrenaline danced in my veins.

"Briar!" Julian's muffled voice yelled through the door. "You have three seconds to open this gods-damned door before I do it for you."

Three seconds? I glanced down at my right wrist, the ink of the tattoo Julian branded on me shimmering against the dim lamplight from my room. He would kill me as soon as he found out what I did. A sharp gust of wind pushed against me, risking my ability to get to the ground safely, or at least as safely as I could with metal cuffs around my wrists and a death threat attempting to break down my door.

A fear of heights was never something that was ingrained in me, nor was the fear of danger. I relished the feeling of knowing I walked the line between right and wrong. I thrived on the knowledge that I held a little secret, my own piece of control, no matter how fleeting.

The greater the danger, the more I craved it.

So, I did the only thing I could do.

I jumped.

2

There's freedom in falling.

Freedom within the act itself, in the dance with the wind as it tosses your body in a skilled pirouette, in the way inhibitions are torn just as a scream threatens to escape your lips. Freedom in caring about little else other than what comes next.

The unexpected.

My unexpected came in the form of a large male body, grunting as he took the brunt of my weight. The scream I wanted to release squeaked out of me as my skirts tangled around his shoulders. Something small and metallic fell to the ground as his arms whipped around me. His balance teetered precariously until he shoved me off him, but not before the sharp end of my cuffs dug along his cheek, leaving a thin trail of red.

"What in the seven hells!" he shouted as he braced his hand along the cut, now bleeding in the dim lamplight. "Where the fuck did you come from?"

My chest threatened to cave in as I took stock of the sludge-covered brick buildings, the rain slicked road, and the boisterous crowd from not just The Tullyhouse, but other taverns and brothels that lined the seedy back alley. The scent of ripe bodies and heavy floral perfume drifted through the air, with the occasional ocean breeze doing nothing to give a reprieve. Bodies hunched along the brick walls and next to dumpsters, mumbling to themselves and rocking back and forth. *Cassov*, no doubt, coursed through their veins.

What absolute luck to land on a brute of a male. Perhaps the gods appreciated my boldness and decided to favor me or maybe he had been hidden in the shadows with his metal trinket just for a moment of sheer divine intervention.

"What the fuck!" a gravelly voice echoed down into the alleyway, silencing all but the mumbling of those on *cassov*. "Where the fuck is she? What the hell is this fucking body?"

"Fuck," I said under my breath, willing myself to melt into the darkness. Perhaps no one had seen me leap two stories out of a window.

"There are more colorful words you can use, you know," the male I landed on said with a wry smile. "I'm happy to teach you."

Adrenaline resurged as my eyes skimmed over my surprise savior. He was in the middle of picking up his metal instrument, the needle of which spun wildly until it landed in my direction. The man's eyes shot up at me under furrowed eyebrows, then toward the sound of a bellowing Julian. I hadn't made it nearly far enough before he discovered what I had done. I needed to get out of there, quickly, before any of Julian's thugs left their posts around the tavern and streets.

"Did he just say there's a fucking body up there?" the man asked, his voice harsh after his attempt at playfulness. He stood from retrieving his trinket slowly, his body unraveling to its full height. The lamplight did little to lessen the severity of his dark features as shadows bit across the planes of his face. A thick scar ran through his left eye, giving him a cruel appearance.

"What was that about knowing more colorful language?" I was surprised my voice held steady when everything in me was screaming to run away. I swallowed against the fear. He didn't look familiar and he hadn't recognized me, which meant he wasn't a previous client or one of Julian's thugs. Escape was still an option.

"Maybe we can chat about it over a drink." His voice was flat, threatening.

The scarf I wore around my shoulders loosened in my fall, and I slowly raised my hands to the knot around my neck and finished untying it before allowing it to drape over my wrists like a shawl. Distracting the man would be a challenge if it weren't for the echoing stomps of several sets of feet hurrying toward where we stood. I wouldn't look a gift horse in the mouth. My salvation was down the road tied to the edge of the furthest dock, and I would find my way there.

As if we were one unit, we backed into the recesses of the alley. I inhaled sharply at the bite of pain accompanying my swollen ankle before melting into the shadow of the building behind me.

"And where are you off to now, Red?" His voice was laced with danger. The man with his strange instrument watched my silent retreat, and it was all I could do not to cringe at the nickname he set for me—the same one my family used to call me before they were all murdered.

It was a rule to never turn your back on an enemy, wasn't it? Not that I knew if the man who caught me and saved me from any broken bones was an enemy, but something told me not to turn away and start running towards the docks like I wanted to. Instead, I felt my way along the craggy wall, side stepping over the prone bodies of drunks sleeping off their liquor, keeping an eye out for any of Julian's thugs who were undoubtedly on their way to see what his incessant screaming was about.

The man with the scar didn't pursue me, though his cunning eyes seared me, targeting me. Somehow, no matter where I went, I knew he would find me.

Boots pounded against the slick stone road as more shouts accompanied Julian's. "I will fucking kill her!" His shrieks clanged against my skull and urged me to move quicker before someone caught me lurking in the recesses of the alley.

Wasting more time wasn't an option. I allowed my internal compass to guide me as I heeded the pull of the ocean. The crashing of the waves against the stone cliff upon which this cesspool of a town sat upon called me like a lost lover begged to be returned to my arms. I was minutes away from ridding myself of Skarsrowe, the lowest dregs in the country of Carnithia, or at least hiding myself for long enough to reassess what my plan was.

"She has to be down here," a gruff voice reached me. "Spread out. If you find her, keep her intact for the boss."

A pool of unease fluttered through me. The voice belonged to Viktor Sinclair, Julian's sadistic right-hand man. He was the cruelest person on Julian's payroll, whose infamy laid with the women he had tortured, not hesitating to take it too far if the mood served him.

Several sets of footsteps echoed in the alleyway, making it impossible for me to determine how many of Julian's cronies were after me. Doors to the other brothels and taverns slammed shut, not wanting to be involved in the danger they knew Julian posed. The rain pelted on, and the wooden signs to the closed shops creaked in the wind. I gasped for air as I made my way swiftly down the twisting alley, taking care to avoid the puddles as rain came down in sheets. The road curved for a brief moment away from the sight of the ocean and my clothes hung heavily from my body as a chill settled into my bones. Street lamps flickered to life.

Where was the man with the scar? Did he join the others in chasing after me? It was a wonder that I'd never seen him before, given my familiarity with countless others in this godsforsaken place.

A body slammed against mine, tossing me backwards to the ground, a muddy puddle seeping into the bottom of my skirt. A rush of cold flooded me, both from the water and from the dread that I had been caught unaware. The silhouette of a man covered the lamplight behind him. I forced myself to take a deep breath, ignoring the stench of oil and bodily waste that hung thick in the air. My sprained ankle prevented me from running away, my cuffed wrists prevented me from properly defending myself.

"You okay, ma'am?" a deep voice said. It was one I didn't recognize. Relief slowly inched through me, though I remained on guard. He might be working alone, wanting to get on Julian's good side to call in a favor somewhere down the line from one of the most powerful players in Skarsrowe. "Let me help you up."

His face cut through the light, and I could see a young man standing before me, concern in his eyes. Nothing within their deep green depths was recognizable, thank the stars, though I did find the halo of gold surrounding his pupil to be curious. "No, thank you," I said, struggling to stand while trying to keep the cloth covering my wrists. "I'll be fine."

Angry shouts and sounds of barrels being overturned made their way toward us, hastening my need to be away from this man and on to freedom.

"I can escort you wherever you need to go." He looked in the direction of the ruckus then reached out his hand, waiting for me to take it. The sleeve of his shirt lifted, revealing swirling tattoos glowing in the lamplight.

"I'm fine," I said as I stood, careful to keep the scarf over my wrists. "I'll be fine." I turned the corner, facing him until I was sure he wouldn't follow.

A sob threatened to escape me when I could finally smell the briny ocean again, the tang of seaweed coating my lungs. It seemed almost too easy to escape a life of indentured servitude, but if Eosa, the goddess of Fate, decided to look my way, I wasn't going to question it.

The bite of pain speared through my ankle and it throbbed as I shuffled my way onto the large dock, throwing a glance over my shoulder every few steps. There was nothing to hide me now. Though the rain slowed to a trickle, the lampposts lining the dock still lit the path enough for it to be obvious I was there.

It didn't matter, though. Just being so close to the Baronian Sea gave me a breath of life I hadn't experienced in years. I craved the open water and fresh sea air. My mother once said that I must have been blessed by Eos, Lord of Sea and Storms. She said I was born of the sea, how

I needed to hear its waves crashing against the shore to know I was alive, and it called to me more than any other.

A stone fell to the pit of my stomach at the thought of her. The love she shared was infinite, and to know I'd never feel the warm embrace of it again filled me with something deeper than the ever-widening chasm of longing that persistently grew in my chest.

The ship's mast was silhouetted against the light of the moon, its alluring presence like that of a courtesan. It was beautiful and commanded attention, yet I knew it could hold secrets the way a chalice could hold the elixir of life—quietly, unassumingly, reverently. The ship called to me because we were very much the same; we beckoned those we wanted, promised a night of freedom, then were forgotten to the depths of darkness like an anchor dropped to sea.

Gold-embossed lettering on the side read *Vox in Ventum* —the Voice on the Wind. A deep sigh escaped me as the words and their meaning nestled inside my bones as if they belonged there and I'd only just realized they'd been missing.

The ramp leading up onto the ship lay ahead, like a friend reaching their hand out, watching, waiting to see if I would accept their help.

Nervous energy flooded me at the thought of finally sneaking onto the one ship I knew would deliver me from the hell I had been a part of for so long I barely remembered the name I was born with.

Emersyn Jane Merona, the ship whispered as it rocked side to side, swaying with the current. *Welcome home.*

3

There is beauty in forgotten things.

A baby's favorite toy, left in the narrow space between the bed frame and the wall. A photograph of a holiday long past, its familiar scents drifting away with time and memory. The whispered words of a former lover in the intimate hours before dawn.

Starlight, to me, was among the most common forgotten things. It was lost within the shine of the moon's glow, hidden beneath a cover of storm clouds, and only remembered if one thought to look up.

Looking up was all I could do to survive.

The ship seemed forgotten when I stepped onto it, but I wasn't fooled. The gangway was left in place, so someone was out and due back soon, or would depart shortly. It wasn't an overly impressive ship, though its magnitude was evident in its length rather than its width. Ropes were piled haphazardly on top of crates stacked against the railing. A small opening among the wooden boxes beckoned to me.

At least I could hide to get my bearings. I'd have to approach the captain of the ship cautiously. He wouldn't be likely to trust someone bold enough to sneak onto his vessel, especially someone with blood dried under her nails and bound in handcuffs with a serpent eating a daisy—the mark of Julian's prized whore—tattooed on her wrist.

The cold drizzle that soaked through my clothes finally let up and the breeze stirred, bringing with it a spicy undertone of something familiar that made me feel heady with nostalgia. I knew that scent, could taste its flavor on the back of my tongue like a memory long past beneath the kerosene-and-salt-soaked wooden planks. I added it to my list of forgotten things.

As the clouds cleared, starlight fell upon the deck and illuminated the crates encasing my hiding spot. A dark symbol was revealed on the boxes, fuzzy at first but soon I was able to see the outline of a fire and the shape of a round gemstone. A pit opened in the bottom of my stomach. *No.* There must have been some mistake. I couldn't possibly have been dumb enough to sneak onto the ship of Julian's main rival.

Captain Killian O'Donnell was notorious in the dregs of Skarsrowe. He was rumored to be charming, wealthy, handsome, and ruthless when it came to what he wanted. His name was whispered in The Tullyhouse as if he were the Lord of Lost Souls himself. Of course, no one alive had seen Lord Malakai Barron, ruler of Vallah, the realm lost souls travel to on their journey to the afterlife. And if they had, they didn't speak about it, so for all we knew, Killian *was* the Lord of Lost Souls. Sweat dripped down the back of my neck and a sour taste crept into my mouth. I risked every-thing leaving one monster only to find myself potentially in the hands of another.

Julian was dangerous because his language was in streets and back-alley deals, not the promise of unknown adventure waiting on the current. He couldn't control the ocean the way he could with men. But not Killian. The ocean was his orchestra, and he the conductor.

The cursed stars illuminated my hiding space, my crimson hair an instant beacon to any who would walk onto the deck. I needed to get out of there, I needed—

"Well, if it isn't a stowaway," an amused voice cut through the darkness. I nearly toppled over as I suppressed a shout of surprise. "Come out, kitty cat. Slowly."

The glint of a thin, sharp sword gleamed inches away from my chest. My mouth ran dry, but that was nothing compared to the way I felt. Craving danger was one thing, but being well and truly fucked was another. It wasn't something I could explain myself out of. There was no reason for me to be on a ship belonging to any rivals of Julian's. There wasn't a reason for me to be on a ship at all.

"Lift your hands away from your body," the woman said. I could see her clearly now that I stood. She was beau-tiful, with gorgeous blond hair and piercing hazel eyes that looked down on my shorter frame. Her grin sparkled with amusement but there was something cutting behind it. Ruthless. She wore a pair of loose linen pants and a dark chemise tucked in the front. One wrist had a cord wrapped around it and tattoos lined her fingers.

Lifting my hands would mean the scarf I held in place would fall to the ground, revealing both my mark and the cuffs around my wrists. The sword moved closer to me, nipping at my cheek, its sting so similar to the ones I bore on my thighs from the cut window glass, reminding me of all it took to get me here. What other choice did I have, though? I slowly raised my hands before me, careful to keep the scarf covering for as long as possible.

"What are you hiding under there, girlie?" she asked.

"Nothing." My voice came out strong, and I was thankful at least that I didn't have a weak constitution. "My hands are empty."

"What have we got here?" A deep voice cut through the darkness. He shifted until he stood underneath a lantern hung on the mast of the ship. His chestnut-colored hair gleamed the color of fire in the light. "You're a doll, aren't you?"

"Fuck off, Sven," the woman said. "We don't need your sleazy commentary."

The man named Sven laughed but raised his hands and backed off. He wore dark pants and a pressed white shirt, the sleeves rolled half way up his forearms. It was strange attire for a shipping vessel, though it probably meant he was conducting business in Skarsrowe. "I was just making an observation, Clara. No need to get so feisty."

"She's a trespasser, not a piece of fucking meat. Take a step back."

Sven gave Clara a crooked smile but did as she said, folding his arms as he leaned against the mast.

"Please," I said. "I just needed to get away...I didn't mean to—" I cut myself off. There was no point in lying. "This ship was my salvation. I can pay. I'll give you everything I have, and I can work. I just can't go back."

"And where is it you can't be going back to?" The deep familiar drawl sent shivers crawling down my spine. "Don't be shy, Red. Tell us all about it."

Eosa, the Goddess of Fate was fucking with me. There

was no way that the six-foot tall, thickly muscled man standing in front of me was the same man I fell onto when I jumped from the window. Captain Killian O'Donnell. His wavy brown hair blew in the light ocean breeze, the longer locks sweeping across his forehead. The shadow of his jagged scar was just visible in the starlight. He had a cruel smile on his face, like a cat that finally caught its elusive mouse. He stood casually, as if he were ordering a rye or mead at a local tavern, but movement behind his shoulder let me know that two others joined the group. I was surrounded. They waited for me to say something, to say anything.

Squaring my shoulders, I said, "I am Julian Murphy's prize whore. And I will not go back to him."

The woman called Clara, still standing in front of me, bared her teeth in disgust and took a slight step back, though her sword remained inches away from my face. Sven looked at me with renewed interest, a lewd smile gracing his lips, but I focused my attention back on the captain.

The corners of his mouth twitched but he quickly schooled his face, a look of boredom etching through his rugged beard. His eyes slowly dragged down my body, taking in my frayed bodice, the way my wet skirt clung to my thighs, accenting my wide hips. They rested a second longer on the scarf covering my bound wrists before gazing back in my eyes again. He dragged his tongue across his bottom lip and I felt a pull low in my belly. He was as handsome as the rumors had claimed and I knew I had to be careful not to fall for his charm. I clenched my jaw but refused to look away. I would not back down.

And I wouldn't let another viper get a hold of me.

"The famous Briar Donovan...this is unexpected. Do

what Clara said, love. Show us what you're hiding under there."

The lilt in his voice increased the pulse in my throat. I would rather toss myself overboard before letting him think he affected me. The less cards he had to play, the better. I knew he didn't get to control half of Skarsrowe from sheer luck, but rather through skilled, strategic movements. Guys like Killian, like Julian—they knew how to play the long game, and luckily for me, so did I.

Slowly, I let my arms fall and revealed the proof to my claim. The tattoo shimmered in the night, thanks to a special type of dye Julian liked to use on his girls. It was impossible to remove or cover it up, rendering our identities as solely belonging to him until he deemed he was through with us. By the time that happened, his girls were usually husks of who they once were, barely able to function in society, so deep in their misery they often became addicted to *cassov* or worse—anything that helped them survive the horrors of their mind.

"My name is Emerson Jane Merona," I bit out, needing to establish my new self—my proper self—with them. Briar was a meek girl hiding from an unknown enemy. *I am a woman who survives.*

Captain Killian O'Donnell prowled toward me as if he had all the time in the world and removed a silver dagger from his waistband.

A raspy chuckle rose up behind him. "That's right, Cap'n. Kill her and toss her back to the rats she belongs to."

The captain paused in his advance and whipped the dagger he held behind him, slashing the cheek of the man who spoke, before embedding itself in a wooden beam. "Don't say stupid shit, Kelso," his voice rumbled. "This is a precious treasure that's landed on our ship. Who would give away something so valuable to their enemy?" He shifted back toward me and removed a second dagger from his belt. "Sorry for the rudeness, love. It's been a while since we had any action."

I didn't want to think of the type of action he meant, not with yet another weapon poised at me. He was sorely mistaken if he thought it would be so easy to share my body with any of them. I was out of Julian's clutches, at least for a moment. Anything I chose to do with my body from there on out would be exactly that—my choice.

"Spread your wrists as far as they can go."

I eyed the dagger warily, but considered the weight of the words he'd just shared. I was valuable so it wasn't likely he'd harm me. Not yet, anyway. I did as he said and in another moment he slashed the dagger at the chain, slicing through it as if it were little more than melted butter.

"How?" I spluttered. The chains were solid steel. "What sort of weapon can slice through metal like that?"

"Nuh-uh," he said. "You haven't earned any of my secrets yet. Willy," he shouted at someone behind him. A tall, broad-shouldered person stepped forward. "Take her to my room."

"I will not be locked away again." I stood my ground, panic attempting to seep its way into the cracks of my insecurities. I refused to let it.

"My room has fresh water and food." Killian's voice took on a softer tone. "You will not starve on my ship, but you won't be getting in the way either, Red. Willy won't hurt you." He turned his back to me. "Let's move!" He shouted at the rest of the crew.

"What? Wait, where are we going?" Willy tried to grasp my arm but I yanked it back out of their reach. "This ship never leaves until after the morning market."

"This ship never had you on it. Be a dear, and get out of the fucking way. I'll see to you shortly."

Willy snatched my arm and gripped it in a vise. Their nails, sharpened into points, dug into my cold flesh. My worn slippers slid across the drizzle splattered deck, making it hard to find purchase to hold myself back. The cuffs around each wrist jostled against my raw skin and it was all I could do to not whimper in pain.

"Let's go, *Red*." Willy looked down at me with a smirk. "You'll be secure in the captain's rooms, like he said. I won't lock you in if that makes you feel better," they added as if it were an afterthought.

Perhaps it was some attempt to make me trust them— to allow my freedom, something Captain Killian knew I desperately wanted since he quite literally caught me while fleeing to a new life.

I wouldn't allow it. I couldn't. That cesspool of a city was filled with nothing but lying, cheating, dirty murderers and thieves. I would know. I'd been forced to fuck all who entered into Julian's territory.

Everyone wanted a piece of his prized possession.

"Lock me in for all I care. I need to speak with Captain O'Donnell, anyway."

"Ha!" they barked in response. "Don't ever let him hear you call him that. It's Captain, or if he likes you, it's Killian." Willy took a moment to look me up and down, their eyes lingering for a moment on my curves. "And I'm guessing he's gonna like you a whole lot."

"Disgusting. I would never," I said, feigning offense. I learned long ago never to say never, especially when an opportunity arose that could change my fate.

"They all say they would never," Willy said, their cunning eyes looking at me knowingly. "But then they do."

I had no response to that. No doubt they were right.

The captain's quarters were located three steps down from the main deck of *Vox in Ventum*. A dark stairwell continued down from the landing, but Willy stopped and pulled a key ring from around their wrist. They had the same type of braided cord wrapped around them that Clara had. It was odd to see; my father's crew often got the same tattoos, but I'd never seen anyone wearing similar bits of string before. I could hear the rest of the group call out to each other and work as the well-oiled machine they were as they readied the ship to leave port. The creaking of the swinging ropes and the mast billowing out in the wind felt like a symphony on its own. Regardless of what happened next, I had the fresh air. I had space to move around. I had value, even if it was currently being used against me.

More than that, I had control over what I did with my body, and that was a certain type of freedom I never thought I would know the taste of again.

The door to the captain's quarters swung open, revealing a surprisingly lavish room. A large bed was bolted in place to the left of the doorway, with layers of blankets and pillows piled on top of it. The events of the night wore on me and the temptation of that exquisite set up almost had me tossing myself on top of it, modesty be damned. A flicker of light brought my attention to a large desk covered in maps and papers, with various instruments strewn about. A wardrobe took up the other side of the room, and a small table with two chairs was fixed down in the corner.

t was three times the size of my room at The Tully-house, and much more equipped as well. A tempestuous storm swirled inside me. Anger at how much money was spent to make his bed more comfortable. Relief, realizing I wouldn't be a burden. Exhaustion at knowing I was safe, at least for a moment. Disgust at him thinking I would stay with him in this room. Excitement at knowing I wanted to.

Well, I wanted that bed, at least.

The click of the door as Willy left reverberated throughout the room and my eyes fell upon an ornate golden plate of fresh tropical fruits and spiced meats. I couldn't remember the last time I had fresh fruit. My usual meal consisted of stale bread or day-old soup, when I was remembered.

Much like the stars that were forgotten until they were needed for navigation, I was also a forgotten thing until my body had use.

The door creaked open and I turned around, expecting Willy to be there again to taunt me more. Instead, the man who made the comment about throwing me back to the rats stood in the doorway. He wasn't very tall, but what he lacked in height he made up for in muscle. His burly body took up the width of the doorway, and he toyed with a dagger that he tossed lightly into the air. I saw the threat for what it was. His eyes were dark and soulless. I'd had to service men like him before. They were often the cruelest.

He looked me up and down, but it was nothing like how the captain did it. His hatred gripped me. The longer he stared at me the more I felt like a dirty thing. I kept my back to the desk, my hands casually dropped at my sides to not alert him to the alarm I felt. I didn't dare look for an escape should he try anything; this room had no other points of exit except the window. I'd had enough of chucking myself out of windows for the night.

"I see nothing special," he said, his voice filled with contempt. "Why does everyone want you?"

I didn't understand his animosity, unless he was just offended that a stranger snuck on board the ship, and wasn't sure if I should respond, but he stared at me as if waiting for my answer. "I don't know," I replied. "There isn't anything special about me."

"The boss seems to think there is. He's willing to risk everything just to have you."

"You mean Killian? Why are you telling me this?" It seemed strange for him to reveal any of the captain's desires, unless they wanted to try to trip me up, to get me to reveal something while being caught unaware. If that was the case, this was a strange tactic to choose.

"He's not who I answer to," the man said. He stepped into the room and lightly itched a scratch against his cheek with the blade of the dagger. The rough sound of his beard assaulted the space between us. "It would be easy to kill you. To blame your death on a number of different things. To toss you overboard, to convince them all you offed yourself."

"Killian has witnessed what lengths I would go to survive. He'd never believe it."

"No, not tonight, perhaps. Watch yourself, whore." He spat on the floor before turning around..

My shoulders tensed as I thought of something, anything, that I could do or say to defend myself. To protect myself against being called a whore, when I was one no longer. I grabbed an instrument resting next to my hand and gripped it tightly. It was heavy and gold with strange markings running down the sides of it. It looked like it could have been a magnifying glass, except there appeared to be a clear liquid that stayed within the confined of the gold rim where the glass would have been.

I raised my arm, holding it as a weapon, with every intention of harming him until the one named Sven appeared. "What's going on here?"

He narrowed his eyes between my raised arm and the other man's turned back as he was about to exit the room. I quickly placed it back on the desk and shrugged my shoulders.

"Just letting the bitch understand her situation," the man said as he left the room. Sven stayed in the doorway for a moment longer. "The captain will be in to check on you shortly."

"Can't wait," I said, letting out a sigh of relief as the door snapped shut again.

My body shook as my heart tried to calm itself and I felt tears spring to my eyes. Would I never have a moment to rest? To process and recover? I swallowed against the lump in my throat, wishing I was alone. Wishing for someone on my side. For the first time in years, I longed for a friend, for my sister.

Fresh drizzle melted against the glass window as the ship rocked and lulled. I reached for a fresh slice of mango, its juices dripping down my chin and landing on the edge of my worn corset. It was shabby and threadbare, the boning popping out of its stitching. It once was a lovely pearl color, but had become gray, ripped, and stained. I could barely remember what it was supposed to look like. I couldn't imagine what it would look like if I had been able to properly care for it.

I hated how it propped up my breasts to showcase what the universe thought was necessary for my survival. Like it knew the world would try to forge me into a weapon of pleasure and leave me a broken shell of who I once was.

I will never break.

The clasps of my bodice ripped and pinged off the floor in my haste to tear it off me. My breath became ragged as I choked back a sob, the events of the night catching up to me.

I'd killed a man, because he told me I was only good enough to be a whore as he bore down the brunt of his weight on my throat. Because he insisted on having me in ways that no woman should be had. Because he was not there for pleasure, but for the momentary high from inflicting pain.

Escaping Julian's clutches, tasting freedom while being chased by danger, landing on the ship of his enemy, who in a sense, was also my enemy. Fatigue clung itself to me like a second skin, burrowing into me, twisting me into an evil version of myself—one capable of doing anything for survival.

The plate of fruit and meats sat upon endless maps and notes in other languages, swirls of iridescent symbols woven into the fabric. There was a strange awareness about them. I couldn't decipher whatever code it was, nor did I recognize what culture they belonged to. Given the amount of time I spent in that godsforsaken tavern, I was surprised at how little I knew of the people in the world.

Muffled shouts from the crew came through the door and the ship swayed as it changed direction. The rocking of the waves as they lapped against the sides of the hull soothed me, wrapping me in their embrace.

You did good, Red, they seemed to say. *You made it.*

I threw my ruined corset off to the side, stripped off my slippers and climbed into Captain Killian O'Donnell's bed. The plush blankets and pillows cocooned me as I sank into their sweet warmth. The scent of jasmine and suede enveloped me as I turned onto my side and watched Skarsrowe fade away as I slowly drifted off to sleep.

4

There is power in seduction.

It starts off simple. A heated look. A slow lick of your lip. The caress of your tongue against the nape of their neck. A gentle stroke along the curve of their hip. Then when the gaze turns hungry and the lust nestles into the empty spaces between you, comes the shift. The one where you've ensnared them and with a knowing smile you can begin.

Sometimes it's in the erotic elegance of an arched back, your head thrown back as you chase the need to shatter. Or maybe it's in the weapon you wield as you scratch your nails against their spine, capturing their eyes while they're wrapped in your slick embrace. You're in control now. It's in the bite of your lip as you moan, it's in the exaltation of a harsh curse as they follow you in the high of the ecstatic moment of pure bliss. And when your sweat-glazed bodies are pressed against each other, there's that feeling that consumes you. When you know it was your words, your hips, your moans that made them surrender.

I'd had years of practice in the art of seduction. I learned how to tear secrets from the mouths of men, how to whisper suggestions in the ears of women eager for any piece of information that would get them closer to Julian, or closer to their demise, depending on what my owner needed. I was a pawn in his game to control his territory, and everyone succumbed to me because I had the uncanny ability to make anyone trust me.

Nestled in the heart of Captain Killian O'Donnell's bed, I felt a subtle shift in the air and realized someone was watching me. My skirts were tangled up around my thighs, revealing my measly dagger and coin purse strapped against me. My nearly see-through shift hung dangerously low across my breasts, not having the corset on to keep it in place. I cautiously opened an eye, trying to get a sense of what time it was. I couldn't have slept for longer than an hour.

The adrenaline that had been depleted raised again as Killian O'Donnell stared back at me. His gaze was not fixed upon my exposed body, however, but my neck, where the bruises from my now dead client had undoubtedly started to make their appearance. His mouth tightened.

"Comfortable, love?" he asked, his eyes still trained directly on my neck. "Did you eat enough?"

Rubbing the sleep from my eyes, I sat up on my knees, one hand against my chest, holding up my shift so it wouldn't fall any lower, and cleared my throat. "What are you going to do with me?"

His steepled fingers rubbed back and forth against his mouth as his eyes took on a greedy look. "That is the question, isn't it? What shall I do with my enemy's most prized possession? Hmm."

His eyes raked down my body and back up again and his face took on a predatory look, a cruel smirk lifting one corner of his mouth. I didn't trust him before, but there was hope in knowing I had value. In that moment, I didn't know what to think. Perhaps he did want to murder me. Perhaps he wanted to fuck me.

I hoped it was the second option.

My need to be valuable went beyond wanting to live another day. It was more than just freedom. It was about getting out of the entrapment of those with power. It was about needing to believe I was worth more than a cheap fuck. Needing to believe that I could survive on my own.

No woman should have to depend on a man for survival.

I wracked my brain, waiting for him to answer. There was more to seduction than just providing temptation. It was about waiting for the cues, listening for words to be spoken—something that gave away what the other person desired before they knew it themselves, transforming it into something more.

And if all else failed, I could use the information I had in my favor. The unmarked crates stacked on deck reminded me of the crates and barrels my father would use when he smuggled drugs across the different port cities and regions of Carnithia. Killian didn't become rivals with Julian by playing fair. There was something about those crates they didn't want me to know about, and I intended to figure out how I could use that information to my advantage.

"Are we stopping at Portsmouth?" I asked, wondering if

we were to follow the traditional trading route that my father used to take when he was a tradesman. "I need new clothes."

"Hmm."

He stood and removed his belt, setting it on the chair he just occupied. I sat straighter and readjusted my shift. Did he think he could take liberties with my body without asking?

He removed his pants and replaced them with another pair made of a clingy, softer looking material. The impressive outline of him was visible. I peeled my eyes away to examine his face, getting into that quiet place in my mind that allowed me to do what I needed to do. I felt the tension leave my shoulders, a wave of sudden calm washing over me. It would be like any other job, I decided, except with a better payoff: a real chance at freedom.

Inhale. At least he seemed to bathe. *Exhale.* At least he didn't have any rotten teeth. *Inhale.* At least he, according to the rumors, would treat me kindly, perhaps even like I was something special. *Exhale.* Seducing Captain Killian O'Donnell would be the easiest thing I've done in the past two days.

And yet, even as I settled into the familiar feeling of disassociation I'd learned as a coping mechanism for the trauma of my job, I still couldn't help but think the same words I always did just before meeting a new client.

For once, I wanted to be a true prize, without the word "whore" attached to it.

For once, I wanted to be special to someone.

For once, I wanted to be enough.

A slow smile crossed my face as I shifted my hair behind my shoulder, and subtly spread my legs a little wider, my shift rising up the length of my thighs. I bit my lip, looking up at him from hooded lids. Killian's stare dipped lower and he took his time as his eyes landed back on my face, then again on my bruised neck.

"What do you think you're doing, Red?" Killian's voice was soft, as if he was channeling the very viper I wished to avoid.

It was a precarious line to balance on. Pushing the limits to see how far I could take things with him was something I knew I could do, but he was also a wild card. I'd only known rumors of him. Though he was calm, there was an undercurrent of restless energy, and making my next move might upset the balance I was striding for.

Batting my eyelashes would make me like every other person that pawed after him, so that was out. I was already biting my lip so it wouldn't make sense to lick my lips and draw his attention there. I wasn't wearing any jewelry that I could play with as an excuse to touch some part of me.

Why did I have to do it the same as always? If the rumors were correct, he'd had nearly every female on his side of the dregs and even more besides. Undoubtedly they knew the same tricks.

But I was a prized possession for a reason. I cleared my throat and smiled a little wider, reaching for the ties that held my shift together. Slowly, as I pulled the ribbons apart, a deep, throaty hum left my throat and filled the empty space between us.

Killian froze, his pulse leaping in his neck. His eyes glazed over as my voice held a single note before trickling into another. I swayed my hips to the music, watching as he relaxed, reaching for his waistband.

A tremor went through his hand as he went to pull

down his pants, and he paused, his eyes momentarily clearing. He looked at me with accusation and disgust, as if he'd never seen something more despicable in his life. I'd never had someone give me *that* reaction before. Surprise cut my hum short.

As abruptly as the sound stopped, Killian shook off the trance he was in. His nostrils flared as his chest heaved in precise, controlled breaths. "Really, Red?" His smile was a cruel slash, emphasizing the menacing scar across his eye. For a moment he looked as threatening as the stories foretold, but I didn't have enough sense to care. I was distracted by the way he shook me off. I'd never come across anyone who wasn't affected by me before. "You of all people should know what it's like to have no control over what their body is used for."

His words were a slap to my face. My fingers slipped from my ribbon and my fists clenched in my lap. I wanted to look down, to hang my head in shame, but I would not submit to him, no matter how much his words affected me.

"How did you do that?" I asked, staring into the depths of his blue eyes. They were like the ocean when the sun's rays first hit them in the morning light, deep with a golden hue flecked within their wave of colors. "Everyone enjoys the sound of my voice." I tried to keep the pout off my face, trying not to look like the petulant child he made me feel like.

He toyed with a rope around his wrist, the same as the others I'd notice on his crew. *What is with these people?* What kind of crew needed friendship bracelets? I tried not to let that affect me, either. My closest friends were the shadows that crept into my room each night, silently keeping me company while I did what I had to survive.

"How did I do what, exactly?"

"How did you...never mind." I didn't know why I could do what I just did to Killian. I did it only to those I wanted to feel safe from, but it didn't always work and it never lasted long. I first discovered the ability within my first week at The Tullyhouse. Julian had watched me work the alley behind his tavern, seeing if I could do what he required of me.

A man had lurked in the doorway to La Commode, a brothel next door to The Tullyhouse, seeking out any girls with a pretty voice. I'd always thought I was decent enough, and Julian needed information from him so I had volunteered. I'd already sold myself to that life and I never backed away from my commitments. Even if I had tethered myself to a life of being used.

I had pressed my body against his, inhaling stale smoke and the sickly scent of peppermint or antiseptic. Whispered words of desire stuck in my throat, and I hummed a tune before falling into the lyrics of a song I enjoyed as an adolescent about the nature of love being a fickle beast, impossible to tame, yet making all who dared addicted to try. The second my voice lifted in the first note, the man went slack against me. I had looked back at Julian who uncrossed his arms, his eyes narrowed as he watched what unfolded. I whispered a suggestion into the man's ear, that he should tell me where he hid the *cassov* Julian wanted to intercept, and he complied easily before I continued humming the tune.

That was it, for Julian. No one was allowed near me as I worked that particular power, when the need arose, whatever it was. I wasn't even sure if he knew what exactly it was, but I became his prized whore from that moment on, not for what I could do with my mouth, but with my vocal cords.

"Hmm." Killian slid his hands in his pockets, dragging the material tightly across the length of him. This time I didn't look away like I did before.

I sensed him sidle up to me until the area I was shamelessly interested in was at face level. Finally, I dragged my gaze up his body, noticing the way his shirt molded against his torso, giving me a clear view of what lay beneath. I swallowed hard against the rising lump in my throat. It had been so long since I truly desired a man for myself, rather than survival. Why did it have to be my new captor? The one who all the females wanted. The one who would treat me as just another name to add to his undoubtedly endless list of conquests.

I would not let anyone, not even Captain Killian O'Donnell, conquer me.

Finding a way to take control consumed me. My gift couldn't affect him for some reason, which meant my failsafe was useless. It might work with the other crew but I couldn't risk it. Maybe they all were as immune as he was. Maybe the second I tried, they really would feed me to the sharks.

Or worse—return me to Julian.

There had to be a way to get out of my predicament. Becoming as cunning a mastermind as my father used to be second nature to me, but I'd spent so long doing just one thing that my skills sorely fell out of practice. Manipulation was my specialty, but I was too thrown off by exhaustion and too distracted with the anticipation of what I wanted to do.

Killian towered over me, his expression unreadable. He smelled of cinnamon and leather, its heady scent more intoxicating than I'd realized it would be. I slowly licked my lips, his eyes zeroing in on the movement.

"I know you want me, Captain," I said. The instinct to impulsively call him "sir" overtook me, but it didn't feel right. What did you call your new captor? How polite should I have been?

"You aren't here to bed me," he said. His brogue was thicker, his voice deeper. "You don't need to do that anymore."

"You left me alone in your room, door closed, to wait for you. What else was I to expect? This is all I know." A little truth and vulnerability might go a long way with him. I reached for his waist, my hand gently settling against his hip. Muscles greeted my fingertips. Heat warmed my palms and spread throughout my body, anticipation slowly building.

He could have shifted away, but didn't.

"I left you in here to eat and to rest until we got out to sea. Not to undress. Not to seduce me. I just want to sleep. I came in here to change and take some sheets to the other cabin on this ship. You can stay here tonight."

"You'd leave me with your maps and...trinkets?" I looked past him to scan the various pieces of sculpted metal with an untrained eye. They must have been extremely valuable. It didn't make sense. I couldn't trust him. Why would he trust me?

"You can't go anywhere, Red, unless you plan on becoming awfully intimate with Lord Eos in his kingdom in the deep sea. There is nothing here that you would understand, and if you did, we would be having a more interesting conversation."

"Why can't I understand them? What are those symbols on the maps?" I looked up at him with wide eyes, my hand still on his waist. I needed him closer to me, but I had to wait for the right moment.

He raised his brows, the only change in his expression. "We all will be able to resist you," he said, going back to the original subject. "Don't bother trying it."

Feigned innocence. That's what I needed. Innocence to prove to him—and let's face it, myself—that I was useful. I slid my fingertips around his waistband and dipped them a little further in. I knew he was attracted to me. I could practically smell his natural musk in the air, and I was surprised to find my own mixed in with it. The rush was heady, that moment where I felt in control of not just me, but what might happen to me. It wasn't a client I was forced to satisfy, but the legendary Captain Killian O'Donnell. The spicy sweetness of desire coated my skin, thrummed through my blood. It fueled my boldness.

"I said we can resist you." The veins in his arms stood out as he clenched his fists at his sides as if it were an effort to not touch me. I smirked to myself. *Of course it was.*

"But do you really want to?" My voice was deeper, sultry. I stilled my fingers, waiting for him to pull away. As the seconds ticked on, longing poured from him, fueling my needs, enhancing the fire between us. He wanted me. Badly.

"It doesn't matter what I want. You aren't here to pleasure me, nor any other member of my crew. You're valuable to me. And if you want to make yourself useful, you can stay out of the way while we're at sea."

The scent of desire made my head swim and the need to lose myself in him flooded my body as evidence of it coated my thighs. I was normally much better at keeping myself separated from feeling. That detachment I once felt— where had it gone?

Damn this Captain and his endless ability to catch me off guard.

"Why would you do that?" I asked. "I snuck onto your ship. You know who I am. I know you've heard of my... talents." The word felt like sandpaper in my throat, tearing apart every surface as it forced its way out. "Why wouldn't you punish me? Try to control me? Threaten me, even?" It was almost offensive. There was no way that the goddess Eosa still shone her favor on me.

"Because regardless of what *you* might have heard," he said, leaning closer to me, his breath tickling against my cheek, "I am not as ruthless a bastard as you believe. Especially not with an innocent woman."

He rested his hands on either side of the bed next to my hips. My fingers slipped out of the grip of his waistband, dragging down his thighs before resting back on my lap. I leaned back slightly so I could still look into his eyes, our lips inches apart.

I didn't know him, not really, other than he happened to be lurking outside of my window when I jumped. He had enough scars to make me wonder what his real story was.

"So are you saying you don't want me?" I asked. I hated that my voice came out like a breathy whisper, as if I would be upset if he said no. As if he could affect me in that way. I knew it would be a lie.

"What I want is irrelevant. What matters is that we each choose to do the things we do or don't want to do, isn't that right?"

Was it right? I wouldn't know. I hadn't chosen anything for myself since I signed my life away at eighteen years old.

As if he could sense my hesitation, he straightened himself and took a step back.

"I know you desire me," I said. Was this what the sting of rejection felt like? "Why do you deny yourself?"

"Red, you came on my ship. I didn't seek you out." His mouth tightened and a vein pulsed in along his forehead. His jaw clenched as if he were biting back the words he wanted to say. "Why don't you have a little respect for yourself?"

Anger licked my skin, tearing through the layers as his words whipped through me. "Why do you insist on insulting me?" I was degrading myself *because* of the amount of respect I had. A question reared its way up my throat, pressing against my teeth, begging for a way out. *Why are you rejecting me?*

We stared at each other for several long moments, the tension thick enough to slice with the dagger in his belt. I had enough of this *respect* for myself to not flaunt myself at him anymore. I readjusted my shift and covered myself as best as I could, given that the only clothing I wore was little better than a loose-fitting sheet.

Killian's eyes softened. "You're beautiful, Red. But you don't need to fight all the time. Your body is more than a weapon. It should be cherished."

He took a tentative step closer, his knees brushing against the edge of the bed. Cherished? What did that mean, really? I bathed myself regularly and made sure to get checkups by the healer constantly. Julian had one on retainer just for me. I took care of myself, if that's what he meant by it. One of Killian's hands reached out and fingered my long burgundy locks.

"I'm not denying you because I don't want you. You are caught up in this defense mechanism. Fight for survival or be killed, is that it?" He was exactly correct, though I did nothing but raise an eyebrow at him. "Well, that's not me, despite whatever you've heard. I would never take advantage of a woman who was not in full control of her faculties."

"Ah. That's where you're wrong." I laid back down on that damned soft bed, the blankets curling in around my body as if it were bracing me from the impact struck from the truth of his words. I fixed a smile on my face. "I am in complete control."

We stared at each other again, as if in challenge, but this time I paid attention to the feeling between us. The moment of desire that would tip the scales in my favor. I didn't have to do anything but wait. I was practically laid out like a feast fit for the Lord of Lost Souls himself. Patience would win.

His smirk tugged at the scar on his face, the shadows from the lanterns deepening its groove along his cheek. "Is that truly what you think, Red?"

Still, I said nothing, letting the scent of him wash through me and burrowed a little further into the blankets and pillows, spreading my legs as I settled in. His eyes trailed over my wide hips, my creamy thighs almost completely exposed.

"Is this you making this decision, or your need to survive?"

A lie untold was better than a lie I couldn't take back. I bit my lip and ran my hand down the front of me, grabbing the hem of my shift and lifting it to expose the thin lace panties I wore before dipping my hand inside.

His eyes darkened and his jaw muscle flexed. We both knew I would win the game tonight.

Killian prowled toward me across the bed, his arms on either side of my body, caging me in. My heart raced as the familiar fear I felt so routinely tried to take over. *He won't hurt me. I have value. He won't hurt me. I have value.* I worked on the same patterns as before, allowing my mind to shut down bit by bit until I was completely detached. The only emotion I would allow myself to feel was desire with none of the welts of the whip that came with it.

His mouth hovered just above mine, waiting for me to make the choice to claim him. A frown marred my face, confused once again why he wouldn't take what was clearly being given to him, and hesitantly closed the distance. His lips were soft as they molded to mine and he kissed me, gentle and slowly.

Fuck that.

I pushed harder against him, wrapping my arms around his neck, pressing him closer to me. My tongue sought entrance but he denied me, taking his time.

"Enough of that shit," I said, annoyance lacing my words. "I need more."

"So eager," he said with a small smile. "It's okay to take your time and appreciate the feelings."

"Fuck feelings," I responded as I hungrily reached for his mouth again. He reared back in surprise, but I wrapped my legs around his waist and held him in place, my tongue finally finding its way into his mouth. He met me stroke for stroke and that encouraged me to move my hips against his, seeking the friction he was intent on denying me.

I fumbled with his waistband, wanting to pull down his pants but he grabbed my wrist and shook his head.

"No. We're not doing that."

"What?" I asked, flustered. I pushed the hair out of my face. "We're fucking tonight Captain. And then I'm going to sleep."

"No," he said again. He gently pushed me back against the pillows and settled himself between my hips. He raised the rest of my shift higher on my stomach, careful not to expose more skin than necessary. I wasn't ashamed of my curvy body. Though I had starved myself for a few months, I was still soft and pliable. I couldn't understand why he didn't want to see it.

"If you insist on playing this dangerous game, then I'm giving you a night off," he said. "You fled that life for a reason, and it wasn't to service the enemy of your owner. But if this is what you're *choosing*, then I'm going to make you feel as good as I can so you can see there is pleasure in wanting and desire in waiting."

A scoff threatened to leave my throat, but I held back, knowing what he intended to do to me. I would probably have agreed to anything he said in that moment if it meant that I could have Killian O'Donnell's tongue on the most intimate parts of me.

I'd had someone go down on me before, but it was always rushed, always half an effort. Always men nipping at me as if I were a piece of overcooked meat they were trying to tear through. Only the women knew how to do it, though that was no surprise. Of course we knew what we wanted. I was interested to see if the famous Captain Killian O'Donnell lived up to the hype.

He pulled my panties down, then fixed his gaze on me as he slowly dipped his head toward the area I needed him most. His blue eyes darkened to a stormy sea and I could smell my desire radiating from me. His tongue stroked straight through my center, and it was all I could do to hold back a whimper. I bit my lip as I silently dared him to do it again.

I knew it could feel nice, or good, even, but he treated me as if he were a man dying of thirst in the desert and only what I provided could sustain him. He moaned and his tongue increased in pressure as I grabbed his head, his silky hair soft beneath my fingers. I tried to remain quiet, unwilling to let him know how much he affected me. It was stubbornness, perhaps. Or a way for me to not give in to his mercy once again. One less thing he could use against me to control me.

But then he pushed one finger inside my core, coaxing me to relax as I stretched to accommodate him and I couldn't help but let out a harsh breath. *More*, I wanted to beg. *I need more*. I needed a memory that wasn't filled with hate and fear. Maybe that was the point he was trying to make, though I had no idea why he would do that for me. He knew nothing about me.

But then I remembered who he was and what we were doing together and I felt hate anyway. Hate for myself, as much as him, for making me feel desire without my life-saving detachment, like maybe I could be different than all the others on his list. I didn't want to feel it, as if I were special, though I knew I was not.

He took his time, leisurely stroking his finger in and out of me and lapped gently against me, his tongue just missing the spot I needed him most.

Frustrated, I tightened my grip on his hair, raising him from me. "Make me cum, or I will do it myself."

He chuckled darkly, evidence of my desire dripping from his chin. He slowly inserted a second finger, and this time he focused on that sensitive spot, relief coursing through me, allowing my legs to spread wider against my control. I raised my hips off the bed and rolled them into him, forcing him to go faster, to lick me harder.

I couldn't recall a time I enjoyed it so much, not even before I was sold into servitude. Killian kept up with the pace I set, watching me and waiting for the moment I would fall apart.

It was tempting to remain silent but soft mewling fell from my lips and he continued with renewed vigor. I moaned as I climbed higher, one hand fisting his hair, the other desperately clutching the sheets next to me, moments from euphoria.

He ceased his movements suddenly, focusing on lapping against that sensitive spot as his finger pressed firmly against the nerves inside me and I crashed as wave after wave of ecstasy radiated from my core to my fingertips.

He licked me clean as I came down from the rush then slowly removed his fingers, aware of how much the stimulation would affect me. I almost wept at the sudden emptiness but then my mouth went dry as I watched him stick his fingers in his mouth, savoring every last drop.

I swallowed hard, struggling to get my breathing under control, waiting for my legs to stop shaking, then sat up and reached for his pants. Again, his hand stopped me.

"Tonight was for you, Red." His voice was rough and he looked away quickly, as if he was ashamed of what he did. I didn't want to ask him if that was what he felt, but I apparently was a masochist.

"Are you filled with shame now, Captain?" I asked bitterly. Now that the high of the chase was finished, regret crept into me as well. He still wouldn't let me touch him, which was the entire purpose of me seducing him, of me trying to prove that I was valuable in my own way, and I was left with nothing.

Why had I reverted back to all I knew? Hadn't I just lamented that everyone wanted my body instead of my mind? And yet, at the first opportunity, I served myself up as if I were an all you can eat platter and he had had his fill.

"Not shame, Emersyn. There is no shame in anything I just did, or in you enjoying it."

"Regret, then?"

He paused a moment too long and I knew that's what it was, or something like it. "You don't belong to me," he finally said. "I should have resisted you, no matter what you had done. I know about you—I know you think I would have succumbed and I proved you right. But I should have resisted, and now I fear the repercussions of when he finds out."

"Who, Julian?" I scoffed. "Since when do you care about that? You were just salivating over the fact that you had his prized *whore* in your possession."

"Don't call yourself that," he snapped. He slid off the bed and readjusted his clothes. "There's a small bathing chamber there," he said, pointing to a slit in the wall I hadn't noticed before. "Feel free to clean yourself up. The water is still warm. And help yourself to more food." He grabbed a few blankets from a wooden chest in the corner of the room. The creaking of its hinges cracked its way through the tension between us. "I will be down one level if you need me. Sven is my first mate, and he's on watch tonight, just in case you decide to wander around. Though I suggest you sleep. We have a big day tomorrow."

"So we *are* going to Portsmouth?" I asked. I suddenly worried about how very little coin I had. It would take at least half of what I had to get a new dress or perhaps pants like Clara.

"Rest, love. I'll see you in the morning."

He left me lying in his quarters, alone, rejected, and dismissed. I took a peek in the small bathing chamber. It was little more than a closet space, but the bronze tub was filled with steaming water. It was clear and pristine, so it hadn't yet been used, not the way Julian's girls often had to reuse each other's water.

I ran over to the table to grab the platter of food, then back to the bathing closet and stepped into the tub. Heat kissed my skin and I welcomed it, allowing it to sear the shame of what I'd just done. The stinging cuts in my thighs were soothed by the warmth of the water and even my ankle that I hurt in my fall stopped throbbing. I balanced the tray along the lip of the tub and nibbled on a piece of sliced meat as I contemplated my next move.

Sex didn't work, and though it was pleasurable, it certainly wasn't the outcome I hoped for: a way to control him before he could control me. I considered I might need to do something more drastic. Something that required more brain power, more manipulation. A scheme.

I spent seven years learning to uncover the secrets of Skarsrowe. I could certainly do that here on Killian's ship.

Though the water was pleasant, I quickly finished and climbed back into bed, dressing in a long shirt I found hanging in a built-in commode in the corner. The bed still smelled of us. He wanted nothing from me except to give me pleasure, and though I wanted to be satisfied with it, I wasn't.

Sleep claimed me, swift and thorough. A haunting song invaded my dreams and a silhouette of a figure too dark to see stood before me. *Oh gods, not again, please not this again.* Though his eyes were hidden, I knew he watched me. It felt familiar, yet dangerous. I didn't know who he was but I knew I didn't want him to watch me, or know where to find me.

Terror seized me, gripping me as much as the darkness

that pressed against my skin. The same dream had haunted me when I was younger, right up until Julian claimed me as his. Searching for a way out was the only hope I had, to find light where there was none. I yelped as I snapped myself awake and stared out the window long into the early dawn hours, wondering why I was plagued with that nightmare again, and why the image of those eyes left me so unsettled.

5

There is satisfaction in destroying.

When I was younger, my father would take me on the schooner he captained when he would go on quick one- or two-day excursions. I used to get sick from the rush of the water and the swaying of the boat in the wind, but he always told me to keep my eye on the horizon and all would be well. He was right. Overtime I came to learn what speed we traveled at, and to estimate how much time it would take to get there based on the number of knots the wind blew. The workings of a ship became intimate knowledge, especially with the way a crew interacted with each other. They were like family as much as a machine, each of them relying on the other to help them through the day. For weeks at a time, sometimes longer, they were all each other had for company. It was imperative for them to operate well together..

But there was always a weak link. Always someone looking after themselves before anyone else. Always someone who wanted to rise through the ranks. Always someone who would do whatever it took to get more.

That was where I would start.

I would seek them out, the way I knew how to snatch secrets from the mouths of men. The way I could feign friendship with the very same women I would later cut to threads with my words, exposing their wicked ways. It needed to happen immediately.

The lack of movement woke me. Gentle bobbing tapped against the hull, but the force of the current ceased, as did the rush of wind through the sails.

Stretching widely, I suppressed a yawn as I dropped my feet over the bed, padding softly against the warm wooden planks to the window overlooking the bay. It was a wonder how toasty the captain's quarters were, especially given how the rain brought an unwelcome chill through the night.

Dawn was not far off, and though the sky was still a deep midnight blue, the stars were dimmer than at full night. I opened the window, letting the rush of the sea breeze pour over me. I could see the sleepy outline of a town along the shoreline. Few windows lit up with the fires burning within. It had been years since I'd been to Portsmouth, but I thought I recognized the shape of the buildings and the hazy outline of hills in the distance.

I looked at my stained and dirty clothes laying against the pristine wood planks of the floor, then back down at the long shirt I stole from Killian's closet. Belts and various pieces of clothing were piled haphazardly on a small armchair under the window, so I cinched one of his leather belts around my waist and crept to the door, listening for the other crew. The door swung open silently. A single lantern was lit on the landing, and I could see nothing but darkness descending down the stairs toward the other sleeping quarters and what I presumed was the storage area below.

The three narrow steps groaned under my weight as I walked onto the deck. It was empty of life, the crates standing like silent sentries waiting for their orders. Sidling toward a stack in the corner closest to me, I tried to pry open the cover off the top one, but it was nailed shut. A long, rectangular crate to the left of me caught my eye. There were no secret markings around the edge of that one, either. I felt along the top to see if there were any grooves or impressions that someone with a trained eye might be able to see, but the dark wood was smooth. It was nailed shut, too. A feeling of unease trickled over me. It felt sinister, those containers. Maybe it was intuition, but—

"...said we aren't allowed to touch her. He would find out."

Hushed voices whispered in the air, the breeze brushing the words toward me.

"I heard them in his room earlier, and she was definitely touched."

I inched closer to the upper deck, careful not to trip over the thick woven ropes coiled on the floor. They were speaking about me. Sven, and the other one. What was his name...Kelly? Kellen? The one I couldn't remember spoke.

"His whore can't find out about—"

"Shh," Sven interrupted. "We don't know what she knows and we ain't askin'. Just listen to the boss."

"I'd rather slit her throat and fuck off with the rest of it."

Slit her throat. Slit *my* throat? But Killian said I would be safe. I was a fool for believing it.

"You aren't doin' shit and you're gonna get us all fucked over if you kill the bitch," Sven said. "Think about what you're saying."

A hand closed over my mouth and I was yanked back against a small, soft body. The smell of jasmine engulfed me, reminding me of the scent embedded on Killian's sheets. My gut twisted as I realized whose scent it had belonged to.

Clara held a finger to her lips as she dragged me away across the deck. I didn't bother fighting her off, not wanting the others to know I was spying on them. Once we were hidden behind another set of barrels and crates taller than the both of us, she whispered, "Why are you eavesdropping, kitty cat?"

I crossed my arms, the fabric of Killian's shirt scrunching up with the movement. There was no way she was going to make me feel like I was in the wrong, not when her own crew contemplated my death. "Why are your crew members discussing my murder?"

Her eyebrows drew down, a frown marring her face. "No one is going to murder you, though you're walking a fine line of our trust at the moment. Sneaking around the ship in the hours before dawn?"

"Am I a prisoner? Didn't Killian say I was not? I thought I was supposed to be valuable?"

Clara looked me up and down, a knowing smile slowly crawling across her face as she took in my appearance. My hair was mussed from a restless sleep, and I was dressed in Killian's things. No doubt his scent was all over me.

"Did he prove to you how *valuable* you are, then?"

Shame and disgust slithered their way through me again, leaving their oily mark as they settled in my bones, a spiral of intrusive thoughts invading my mind.

I had been trained to sleep with multiple men and women every single night. It wasn't my business how often Killian serviced his own crew. It didn't matter that it proved I wasn't special, exactly as I thought, because I knew it all along. I couldn't get upset about perpetuating the idea that I was nothing special because I added myself to his list, the very thing I said I didn't want to do but then I did anyway.

I fucking did it anyway.

Why did I think that my first night of freedom would find me in a place of position, of power, of ownership over my body and my mind? I fell into the same tricks because that was all I knew, all I was conditioned to believe I was good for. The evidence was clear. I smelled her on his sheets, and then I'd spread myself for him on them afterward.

Was that how the men and women at The Tullyhouse felt about me? Had they thought of what my sheets smelled like, what my hair smelled like, whose scent still lingered on my skin, though I quickly washed after each person? Had they wondered what number they were for the night, or were they able to let go of their inhibitions and just enjoy the time they paid to spend with me?

It didn't have to be serious all the time. It didn't have to be about a deep connection. I didn't make connections unless it was carnally, ruthlessly, fearlessly. Did I think I really was someone different for him, just because he decided to give me pleasure? Or was it because of the way he looked at me? Or the way he said I deserved to be treated special and he happened to be the one to do it?

None of it mattered. I knew what my heart told me, what my body told me. He had wanted me to stop fighting, so I would be more pliable, so I could ease his worries instead of defending mine.

No more.

"Yeah," I finally answered Clara. "He couldn't get enough of it."

Her smile sharpened. "You're a clever fox, babe. But you aren't smart." Her face turned serious. "You need to be careful who you sneak up on around here. Killian might be the captain, but he isn't the one in charge."

She gave me a meaningful look, the waves of the ocean the only sound stretching in the silence between us. She started to turn away, but I grabbed hold of her arm. She couldn't possibly think she could say something cryptic without explanation. "What do you mean by that? Isn't Killian your boss, the way that Julian is—was —mine?"

Clara dragged her eyes down my body again, taking in my complete state of undress, save for the shirt, and back up to my frizzy merlot hair. "You'll know more if and when you need to." She chewed on her bottom lip for a moment. "Come with me."

I hesitated. She said I needed to be careful and then expected me to follow her? Was she counting on my ignorance, like she'd just pointed out?

"What are in these crates?" I asked, keeping my voice low, cautiously following her back toward the stairs leading down to the rest of the ship.

"That is definitely not something you need to know. Now, or ever." Her hips swayed as she entered the dark stairwell, the dim light from a lantern ahead giving Clara a blurry silhouette, as if she were an apparition and I were following it into the unknown. "Come on kitty cat, we only have a few minutes to spare."

She led me down into the belly of *Vox in Ventum* and lit another lantern before entering a room on the right of the narrow hallway, housing two large tubs filled with hot water. I had yet to see a fire or stove of any kind to explain how they boiled the water to bathe in. Not to mention, I was fairly certain it wasn't salt water in those tubs. Where did they get so much fresh water? Where was it stored? Why would they waste it on one bath, let alone three? There were so many questions I had, yet I knew they wouldn't be answered if I asked. I added it to the stack of mysteries I needed to solve about this ship and its crew.

A floral scent permeated the air, one that smelled over-whelmingly like—

"Jasmine," Clara said, watching me take stock of the room. "It's the scent of the soap we use on the ship."

Realization dawned on me along with an unfamiliar sense of relief. "I see."

"So everything, all our fresh clothes, our *sheets,*" she raised her brows, "all smell like this. Just in case you were wondering why there was such a floral scent...you know...everywhere."

I feigned indifference. "I wasn't, but good to know. Why exactly are we in here?"

"I assume you want to go into Portsmouth wearing something a little more than that?" She waved her hand up and down at my attire.

"I didn't think Killian would let me off the ship. In fact, he basically told me as much."

"He's protective of what he considers his," Clara said. She stepped closer to me, examining my face with a shrewd eye. I wonder if she saw the echoes of bruises from that particularly enthusiastic client last night, the memory of handprints imprinted around my neck. "I'm willing to take the brunt of his anger so you can have a taste of real freedom. None of Julian's goons will be there, and if word gets back to him, we will be long gone by then."

I was immediately suspicious. "Why would you do that for me?"

Her eyes were downcast as she walked over to a table against the wall, fidgeting with a pile of clothing in front of her. She opened and closed her mouth a few times, as if she changed her mind on what she wanted to say. Finally, she settled on, "We're all prisoners in one way or another. Any chance at pretending we've escaped the cage, we take it."

She couldn't possibly know what it was like to be a prisoner. She sailed the open seas every night. She was able to wear what she wanted, eat what she craved. She had no idea what it was like to be caged. Unless she was referring to life with Killian, or the person who controlled them. Learning more about the crew was paramount in my plan to cause discord among them so that I could either slip away unnoticed or so they'd leave me unharmed until I was better prepared to escape.

Clara tossed a pair of brown pants at me and new underwear, something less lacy and more practical. That alone would have cost more than the money I had. "Who does this belong to? It doesn't seem right to take it."

"Technically they're mine, but we all share everything here. It's all ours and no one's. And there are plenty of extra, so if you were thinking of spending a bit of your coin or whatever on new clothes, you won't need to as long as you're with us."

"I don't exactly want to stay with you," I said, holding the clothes away from my body. I didn't feel worthy enough to be given something so freely, nor did I understand this sudden show of trust. "How do you know I won't just escape when you sneak me into town?"

"Because Julian will be on a wild hunt for you, and Killian will never give you up. He'd bargain his soul for you. I guarantee it."

"That feels dramatic, considering he doesn't know me."

"He knows your value, hun. Believe me, we all do. Put on the clothes. We leave in five minutes."

Freshly dressed in dark pants that felt like butter against my skin, I pulled on a loose-fitting white shirt and a leather corset over it. Clara showed me how to tie the strings in the front in just the right way to hold me in place without suffocating me. It was the most comfortable clothing I'd worn since being signed into indentured servitude. Worn leather boots completed the outfit, and though they were slightly too big, they worked beautifully.

"How do you plan on sneaking me off of here?" I asked. "That one that doesn't like me is right outside."

"Do you mean Kelso? He and the others have a delivery to make," Clara said. "Besides, it'll tickle Willy to see Killian lose his shit over you being gone. But you've got maybe an hour of so-called freedom, tops."

We made our way back on deck, the seagulls greeting us with their caws as they searched for their breakfasts in the early morning light. I still didn't know if I trusted Clara. Actually, I know I didn't, but my body was protected in clothes that weren't provocative and that I felt comfortable in for once, and I was about to walk the streets of a different town as a nobody instead of on display in that godsforsaken piece of Skarsrowe. Maybe I would buy a pastry from a bake shop, or check out what the wares the vendors at the morning market were selling.

Or I could do as my precious owner had taught me all those years ago. Stay quiet, stick to the shadows, listen, and pick up information to use against the crew. There was something amiss with those crates, and with the way Clara wouldn't tell me who was really in charge, if it wasn't Killian.

Sowing a seed of distrust among them was top priority if I couldn't find a way off the ship, but Clara...if it turned out she could be trustworthy, it could be the start of something new for me. Friendship. I hadn't had a friend since the day I lost my sister.

"Will you be following me, then?" I asked Clara, careful to keep my voice low. We crept along the deck but there were no signs of movement besides the creaking of the ship as the water thumped against the hull. The sky had the slightest gray tinge and the last of the stars dimmed as the sun readied its appearance over the horizon.

Clara put a finger to her lips and shook her head. She pointed toward the gangway to the dock and led us to the shadow of the crates closest to us. The outline of Killian's body walked slowly up the ramp, holding something large and lumpy in his arms. Kelso and Sven followed close behind, and the two of them pried open a crate with a crowbar before Killian placed whatever he was holding inside of it. The three of them murmured softly to themselves, then Killian let out a curse on a harsh whisper and walked toward the archway leading down to the captain's quarters.

Clara snatched my arm and ran on light steps down the plank, the other two oblivious to us leaving. We ran as night faded until we reached the first true city block across a vast lush courtyard hedged in by blossoming oleander shrubs.

"What the hell was that?" I asked, slightly out of breath, still whispering, not wanting to be overheard. Though it was early, men carried tables and some sort of small stage onto the large lawn. It looked like an event was getting set up in the courtyard before the morning market.

A burning disgust filled me as I watched them. I hated those large spaces. The deadened grass where the stage was set up so frequently. The makeshift podium that usually came with a gavel used by the auctioneer. The stage. The only times anyone stopped to watch a performance was for purchasing slaves or to witness a death sentence play out. Both were the same, in their own way.

"Answer me this," Clara said, suddenly gripping my arm to get my attention. A deep line formed in between her eyebrows, and I wondered for a minute how old she was and what she worried about so often that such a deep groove would form on a face so young. "I noticed you had blood under your fingernails last night. Was it yours?"

I looked down at the offenders in question, remembering the way I stabbed my client's jugular with the same dull dagger I had strapped to my thigh, as he squeezed my throat. The way his final reaction was to press on the wound, trying to staunch the flow of blood. The way I pried his hands away and held them down, watching as the blood flowed, feeling a sense of satisfaction at the metallic tang filling the room as it soaked the same sheets that clung to my secrets. The way I smiled after, loving the rush of power I received from finally having control over my life. Over someone else's.

How could she tell I had blood under my nails? Were the stars that bright? Was it a lucky guess?

"I, um..." *Should I admit it? Tell her it was self-defense?* If she saw the blood under my nails then surely she saw the bruises against my throat. I could deny it, but I knew the rumors about Killian. I knew he didn't think twice to murder those against him. If I lied to a member of his crew, would he consider that a personal offense? Would Clara look at me differently if she knew that I was a murderer?

Not that it was a secret anymore. Killian heard Julian screaming about a dead body after I flung myself out of my window. Surely, if he trusted his crew as much as he should have, they would all find out eventually, if only so they all had every piece of information when it came to dealing with me. With what level of danger I might pose to them.

"You kill a man last night, kitty cat?" Clara tried a playful tone but there was something sharp and dangerous in it and her face was unreadable as she waited for my answer.

"Yes." I decided she didn't need further explanation. What did it matter anyway? What was done was done.

"Fuck!" she exclaimed. A flock of terns took off in flight from a nearby tree. "No fucking gods-damned wonder he was in such a hurry to leave."

"What does it matter? People are murdered all the time in Skarsrowe."

"Yes, but not by the precious-fucking-hidden-prized-possession. Son of a fuck!" Clara bit her lip as she scrutinized me. "Okay. You need to get back on that ship, pronto. Before Killian realizes you're missing."

There was no way I was letting that ship collar me again after five minutes of freedom on land. "He was walking to the captain's quarters when we snuck out. He will clearly see that I'm not there."

"Shit. Okay. Well, fuck me. You're out here now." She ran her hands through her blonde hair and looked around us, her eyes settling on the bakery we stood in front of.

"Let's get us a treat as a consolation present for the fuckery we'll be returning to. Then we can just stroll back up, casually, and act like nothing happened."

"Nothing *has* happened," I said, my frustration building as I wondered how I got caught up in a den of so many secrets. "I need some answers about whatever the fuck this freak out is you're having right now. What's going on? Why does it matter if I'm on the ship or not?"

"It isn't for me to explain, buttercup."

The bell to the bakery tinkled overhead as I followed Clara inside, the warm scent of honey and vanilla engulfing me. My stomach growled. I was never allowed indulgences such as those that were laid out before me, even in the 'before' when my family was still alive and we were happy.

Display cases were filled with freshly made bread stuffed with cheese and veggies, fruit tarts, mini pies, sticky buns, cookies, cakes and more. A wisp of a man came from the kitchen, his dark face covered in flour and dusting sugar. Clara bought us a large cinnamon bun to share, which I was grateful for as I didn't think I'd be able to eat an entire one myself. I savored the cinnamon sweetness as we walked back out onto the courtyard, moaning as the warm pastry melted down my throat.

Vox in Ventum swayed in the distance, bobbing in the water as the waves lapped against the shoreline. Relief flooded through me at it still being there. I didn't expect them to leave without me, not without Clara, but I was used to watching it sail away each morning. It was a comfort to know that it was still taunting me from afar, only this time I was either brave or stupid enough to return.

Movement in the darkened alley across from the bakery caught my eye, and I recognized Sven and Kelso slink between makeshift shelters of homeless people and piles of garbage piled haphazardly across the ground. They carried a crate of some sort between them, and though it was too far away to make out, I was certain it was one from the ship. They stopped against the brick wall and knocked on it. In the graying morning light, they looked little more than a shadow, but I didn't miss their constant peeks over their shoulders to make sure no eyes were on them. I turned toward Clara, ready to demand that she give me answers on what was really going on with the crew and the ship, until the sharp snap of a gavel slammed against wood. On the far end of the courtyard, a group of girls walked across the grass, chains linked between their waists.

Bile rose in my throat and sweat lined my skin despite the chill ocean breeze on the cold, dreary morning air. My steps felt like lead as I walked closer to where they stood, the cinnamon bun all but forgotten as it stuck in my throat. I watched the girls on display for the seedy men and women of Portsmouth. A line up of men stood behind the girls. Their sellers.

The gavel sounded again and I stopped, the blood pounding in my ears. My breathing increased as I tried to think of something, anything I could do to save these girls from their wretched fate of being used until they were nothing but echoes of who they used to be.

Clara touched my shoulder, her voice softer than usual. "Hey, let's go back. There's nothing for us here."

I yanked myself away from her touch. Nothing for us? There was everything. My past colliding with my present. Me, wondering why I thought I was worthy to escape my contract when these innocent girls were about to enter into one. They looked so young, except for one woman at the end of the line. Dressed in a torn and stained dress, she held her chin high, her shoulders back as if she were proud

—a significant contrast to the girls curled in on themselves beside her. Towering over her from behind was a brute of a man who looked like he had seen better days. His shirt barely contained the belly threatening to burst from it and his pants were dirty with stains near the knees. His hair was disheveled and his smile was a grimace of rotted teeth. He was devoid of any jewelry or any other piece signifying who he was or his position within Portsmouth, save for a thick iron band gripping his finger like a vise. I looked back at the woman. A finger on her left hand held a similar, though slimmer iron band. They were married, then.

My lip curled in disgust. How dare a husband sell his wife as if she were little more than cattle? As if whatever pennies he received for her were worth not having her anymore.

The bidding started and I felt others close in around me, wanting to get a good look at the wares that were for sale. I peered up at them, at these men leering at the girls as if wondering what they looked like without their clothes on. Actually, that's probably exactly what they were picturing. One such man caught my attention. He wore a smart suit, not the usual clothes of the working class of Portsmouth, and his hair was neatly coiffed. He had a goatee and a tiny tattoo of a skull under his right eye.

I gasped and threw myself behind a group of taller men all clambering to get closer to the girls and twisted my hair in a low bun before snatching the hat off Clara's head and fastening it upon my own. Viktor Sinclair would spot me in an instant with my blood-red hair. Clara looked at me in alarm then swiftly scanned the crowd. Her eyes narrowed and her mouth tightened once she spotted him.

"Come on, Em, we have to get you back to the ship

immediately." She grabbed my arm and gave it a valiant effort, but still, I shrugged her off.

"I need to see this. There has to be something I can do."

Sven sidled up next to us, hands in his pockets as he surveyed the scene unfolding in front of him. So far three of the five females had been sold and some of the crowd started to disperse. Viktor would spot me any moment. Sven scanned the remaining crowd, his gaze zeroing in on Viktor as well. The fact that both of them knew who he was only meant danger for me, because it meant he would recognize them as well.

"Hey doll," Sven said, his voice lowered. "What are you doing off the ship?" He shifted an accusatory glance at Clara who gave him the finger in return. Sven shrugged out of his overcoat and placed it on me, tugging the hood over my head. I felt a confusing surge of gratitude, but kept it to myself.

"I'm not going back until this is over," I said. I recognized the fervor with which I spoke and the manic way I kept my eyes glued to the older woman. She picked me out of the crowd and held my gaze back. She was beautiful. Her dark skin glistened, her high cheekbones and bright brown eyes were alluring. Her long hair was braided and bounced at her waist. She would catch a fair penny if she were younger. I wanted to tell her I would free her. I could save her from this life. But I had no money, none that her husband was likely to accept, anyway, and then what would I do with her? Bring her onto Killian's ship? It was bad enough he had one unwanted person there, let alone two.

"And what do you think you'll be doing when it's done?" Sven tried to reason with me. "You can't change anything. This is the way of life here."

"I think I know that better than most," I snapped, turning my attention back to him. His dark eyes and easy smile seemed tense. I glanced around, realizing Kelso wasn't there. "Speaking of things that aren't your business, where's your friend? Done sneaking around?"

"And finally," the man at the podium cut Sven's response. "We have a Miss June Leona, thirty-nine years of age, no children. Bidding will start at three coppers."

Disgusting. Three fucking coppers for a human being. The crowd had almost completely dispersed, so it seemed unlikely she'd get even that. Her husband yanked her back by the hair and though she refused to cry out, tears sprang to the woman's eyes. "Good for nothing." He struck her across the face, leaving an angry welt on her cheek. "Can't even get a copper for yeh."

Fury burned through me. Without hesitation, I reached into my bosom and pulled out my coin purse—the one where I saved every single damning piece of evidence I had from doing any traumatizing thing asked of me, all to earn my freedom one day, and poured out the contents into my palm.

"For the love of the Dracon," Sven hissed at me, referencing the name of the seven demon protectors of the underworld. "What the fuck do you think you're doing?"

I walked up to the podium and thrust the coins, all of them, into the auctioneer's sweaty palm. He quickly unlocked June Leona from the chain around her waist. Her husband tossed her toward me, but I was ready for it. All men were the same, ready to throw aside the person they made a commitment to for something newer, brighter, shinier. In this case, money.

A contract was shoved under my nose, one I was supposed to sign upon purchasing. Disgust mixed with the cocktail of rage and self-loathing that made its home in my veins. Without thinking, I signed Killian's name, took my copy, and dragged the woman away from her bastard of a husband.

"You shouldn't have done that." Her voice was deep, calm, melodic in a way. "Giving away your money like that. I'm not worth it. And he doesn't deserve it."

"That's not how this works," I said through clenched teeth. I whipped around to face her. She was taller than me, and little more than a waif of a woman, but sturdy. I'd guess she spent years on a farm or doing manual labor. Maybe Killian would see that as a positive to have on his ship. "He would have beaten you down until you cried out. And those sick bastards that were left would have witnessed what it took to make you scream. How much you could endure." I looked her up and down. "I gather you would have kept silent until you could no longer."

Her jutted-out chin told me all I needed to know.

"They salivate off that shit. They would have figured out how to break you. And then they would have turned you away when you no longer were of use to them. I did you a favor."

"At great cost to yourself." She yanked her wrist out of my hand. "I have no desire to be owned."

"I don't plan on owning you. You can do whatever you want, but you need to come with us." Clara gave me a look like she wanted to object but I bared my teeth at her. "Fucking try it and I will disappear faster than you can say my name."

Sven, of all people, was the voice of reason. "Okay, look. You don't understand exactly what you just did, but I can tell you the boss don't have any use for another stowaway that don't have a clue how to act on a ship."

"I'll get off in Hammerford," June said. "I have family there. I can be with them."

"Ha," I laughed sardonically. "Is this the same family that clearly never gave enough of a fuck about you that they left you with that vile creature you married?" Maybe it was cruel, but I didn't care. I didn't just spend my entire savings that I meant to use toward my freedom for her to be turned loose to others who would rather see her dead than alive.

"I can make my way myself. Any life would have been better than the one I had."

Her eyes were deadened as surely as mine were. I understood her wanting to get away from the abuse. Trading one form for the other, or sometimes a mixture of both...Was that really the life she wanted to live? "You're coming with us on the ship, and then Killian will decide what to do with you."

Clara walked beside me, chewing her lip nervously. "This isn't what I meant when I said you deserved the illusion of freedom. I don't know how Killian will react...we're in the middle of a job as it is."

"Any chance you'll tell me what that job is?" I marched toward the ship, not really caring to hear the answer anyway.

Sven put his arm around my neck and pulled me close. I looked down at his sun kissed skin and noted the tattoos crawling up his arm. The same string was wound around his wrist as the others. I had the absurd impulse to tear it off with my teeth. "Not a chance, babe. Nice try, though."

I shrugged his arm off of me and gave his coat back as I made it to the ramp with my new slave in tow. *How did I get in this position? Why did I have to give away all my money?* I needed to look out for myself, not a woman who was more than ten years older than me and looked as if she really could have taken care of herself.

What was this need that I had to protect others? I'd been alone for so long, I hardly remembered what it was like to be around anyone else. My father was a tradesman and my mother was a dressmaker. Both were murdered on the sea, the result of a deal gone wrong. My sister, Gabriella, was caught in the crossfire. I didn't remember much of it. I was on shore when it happened, flirting with... what was his name? Thom? Renley? I couldn't remember. I was supposed to be with them, on my father's ship, *The Windmaker*. I only remembered they were waiting for me but I couldn't be bothered. I was so selfish, just wanting a moment to myself to have a bit of fun.

A fierce storm had gathered quickly and another ship, much larger than my father's tiny schooner, approached on a raging current. I don't know what happened. It sounded like thunder crackling through the sky and then the waters were red everywhere. I tried to run to them but someone pulled me back. The face was blurred by the coarse brush of time. I remembered nothing other than they told me to run. And I did.

My home was burnt to the ground and there was nothing left. That's how I knew it was calculated. That's how I knew someone was after my family.

That's how I knew I was on my own, for good.

I had shifted through the debris and rubble and found a seashell I normally kept on me at all times, and a few coins scattered about. Nothing that would last me longer than a few days, if I was going to pay for food. I remember thinking it odd in the moment how relieved I felt at seeing that piece of shell survive. I used to rub it whenever I was anxious. The edges are soft and worn down, and it was the only thing I had left that reminded me of home. No photograph. No trinkets or jewelry.

A broken piece of shell from a broken home.

"Oh, shit."

Sven's voice yanked me back to the dock, back to the sound of waves crashing against the boats anchored along the bay. The seagulls cawed and a low rumble of thunder could be heard off in the distance. The briny air mixed with the scent of food cooking as it trailed lazily over the townspeople. The auction was over and the morning market at Portsmouth was being set up, all an hour after dawn.

I cut my eyes over to Sven at his curse, his wide eyes staring up at the ship laid before us. I knew what I would find if I followed his line of sight—or rather, who I would find.

Silhouetted against the stormy sky, a thick shadow of a man stood proud, the wind billowing off his dark hair. The shape of his scar was etched on his face, and the minimal morning light sharpened his features. Captain Killian O'Donnell stood against the railing, ire coming off him in waves.

"You have to be shitting me," June said through clenched teeth. "Captain Killian O'Donnell? That's who you've indebted me to?"

"Relax, he isn't going to keep you." I hoped not, anyway. "And I'm the one that gave away my hard-earned savings so if you're indebted to anyone, it's me."

I rolled my shoulders back and wished desperately for a napkin or something to wipe the sticky remnants of the cinnamon bun off my face. I had been so distracted by the auction, I had barely swallowed the thing down and didn't think twice about cleaning myself afterwards. I had no one I needed to impress anymore.

Of course, I'd forgotten that I meant to seduce my esteemed captain and spending all my money and bringing home a refugee wasn't exactly seduction material. Judging by the fire in his eyes, I'd say that the situation wouldn't end in an argument and a toss around the sheets.

My chin was proud as I walked up the bridge, maintaining eye contact the entire way. His upper lip was stiff and his knuckles turned white against the wooden banister. It wasn't until I was close enough to him to touch that he changed his position.

Killian turned to face me, his arms loose at his sides and his fingers twitching toward his belt. What was it he longed to reach? His sword? His strange magical knife that could apparently cut through anything? Something worse? His clothes hung loose on his body and he looked as though he hadn't slept in days.

Kelso stood off next to a stack of crates that were half the height they were only an hour ago. They must have been busy unloading whatever unmarked goods were inside of them. My chances of finding out what they were up to were shrinking by the hour.

Killian took his time drifting his eyes down my body, taking in the clothes that allegedly belonged to everyone, noting the way the pants clung to my hips. The impulse to shift my weight under his scrutiny overwhelmed me, but I refused to give in. Swallowing hard, I opened my mouth, prepared to get ahead of the argument that I already knew was brewing.

Instead, his head whipped over to Clara, who stood next to me, her arms around her middle and her eyes downcast. "Care to explain, little dove, why our *guest* left this ship after there were explicit orders not to let her?"

Clara, to her credit, didn't fidget as she said, "She deserved a taste of freedom before—"

"Is it up to you to decide what she needs? Have you taken control of this ship? Does it speak to you now?" His voice was deadly calm.

What did he mean by, *Does it speak to you, now?* Did he mean in the metaphorical way that some people understood their possessions so thoroughly that it felt like a kindred counterpart to themselves? That's how I used to feel with the ocean when I was younger. I knew that I belonged to it, and it to me.

"No, the ship doesn't speak to me now. Gods, Killian. She just escaped last night, and from the look of her this morning, she had finished up one last job." Clara cut him a scathing look. Killian's face remained inscrutable. "We got off and bought a cinnamon bun. No harm done."

"Looks like you bought more than a pastry," he said. His eyes cut over to June now, who was busy fidgeting her hands in her skirts. "And you? Who gave you permission to enter my ship?"

"Well, sir—captain—this woman just purchased me... in your name," June trailed off.

I rolled my eyes. *Is this why I have no friends?* Because women were so quick to throw each other under the bus when they were caught in the intense glare of a good-looking man? *Typical.* "I tried telling her it was a bad idea," Sven chimed in with his arms raised. "I swear, she didn't want to hear anything."

"You're all cowardly fucks," I mumbled. "I gave all my coin to save this woman from being slaughtered within her first week of indentured servitude. Only the grimiest people were left after Viktor purchased—"

"Son of a bitch!" The sudden outburst from Killian

caused a vein to pop down the middle of his forehead. "Viktor fucking Sinclair, as in Julian's fucking incestuous right hand?"

"He didn't notice me," I said. I resented that he spoke to me like I was a child who didn't know what they were doing. I was twenty-five years old. I'd been taking care of myself my entire life. I knew exactly what I was doing.

"Oh really? Your hair is a fucking beacon, Red. I guaren-fucking-tee he noticed you."

"Who cares?" I tried to put on more bravado than I felt. I didn't want Julian to find me, especially not after I killed one of his better paying clients, even if it was justified. He would murder me all the same, and I didn't think my special gift or being his prize would save me this time. "We aren't staying here. I assume whatever sketchy business you're up to here is concluded, so let's go."

"She isn't coming with us," he said through clenched teeth, pointing at June Leona.

I cocked my head to the side, wondering where his rage came from. They had plenty of food, and I knew they had plenty of clothing. She wouldn't be in the way, especially not if they put her on laundry duty or something. I slid the rolled-up parchment from my pocket and shoved it in his chest, ignoring the pulse of electricity that ran through me at the touch of my fingers against a sliver of his bare skin. "Actually, she is. She's yours. Congratulations."

His face drained of blood, his lips white and he clenched them closed. He held the parchment away from him as if he thought it would explode in his hands. "You didn't."

I smiled at him, finding a sick sense of satisfaction at his discomfort. "Relax. She doesn't want to be owned. She wants to get off at the next port."

Kelso coughed as if he were covering up a laugh. I didn't

know why he thought anything I said was funny. Who cared if she spent a night with us until the next port?

"We aren't going to another port," Killian said. His nostrils flared. "We have a week's journey at sea before a quick stop for supplies and then another two weeks."

"What?" I gasped. I looked at the others, who looked guiltily at anywhere but me. So they all knew we wouldn't be at another port, which meant they also knew that I wouldn't have a chance to escape or buy my freedom, either. Not that I could buy it anymore. "That would mean that we're—"

"Leaving Carnithia. Immediately."

"You can't!"

"Listen, Red. I didn't tell you to seek safe haven on my ship. I'm in the middle of a job and I'm already behind by a day thanks to you. The big boss is going to boil the skin from my bones for what I've done and I'd rather not return to him until I've got something valuable enough to trade."

"Who is he?" Gods, he was infuriating. The ship, the ocean—it all called to me, beckoned me to come to it as a siren does to her prey, and for what? For me to get caught up in something far larger than I intended? I only wanted my freedom. I needed to get out.

"Let's hope you don't find out."

Willy, who stood off to the side, stepped forward. "I'll take both of them to my room."

"No." Killian's voice was unrelenting. "June here is with Kelso on the wheel."

"What?" Kelso cut in, shoving his dark curly hair out of his eyes. He was utterly unremarkable with his pale skin and dead eyes. He was shaped like a barrel and looked to be about as intelligent as one as well. "Why?"

"Because all she needs to do is stand there. She can't fuck it up."

"Actually, I can do manual labor," June cut in. She straightened her skirts then boldly held Killian's stare. "I think you'll find I'm quite capable of whatever you need."

I narrowed my eyes at her. Whatever he needs, is it? I knew I didn't rescue her just for her to sleep with the captain right underneath my nose. Not that I cared, obviously.

Killian gave her a scathing look. "You are no slave and you are not a member of my crew so you will not do chores. Go stand with Kelso."

He took a minute to look me up and down, as if contemplating what my punishment should be. I crossed my arms —something that would have resulted in a swift beating back with Julian, and the face I gave him dared him to touch me that way. The corner of his mouth tilted upwards, as if he were amused by my behavior and knew exactly what I was doing.

"You're with me."

6

There is scheming in deceiving.

When I was around nine or ten, my father used to bring me with him on his trading runs. Everyone knew him as the Spice Trader, though *cassov* was his specialty, and he hid it well between the ground black pepper, turmeric, cinnamon, and salt that he would barter. He wasn't exactly "one" with the law, though he paid his taxes on time and that was all the council leaders cared about. Anything else, and they turned a blind eye, unless it caused a problem with them directly.

The trading route ran from Skarsrowe to Portsmouth, then up to Hammerford and around the Black Isle in the Bay of Baronia, just off the entrance to the Baronian Sea. I was never allowed to leave the schooner, especially when he had deals to tender, so I spent my time observing and mimicking. By the end of the year, I could sail the thing on my own if I hadn't been too weak to pull the ropes and turn the wheel.

But I knew what made a ship work: the trust of a dedicated crew, and the right equipment. I knew that Killian wouldn't be tempted by me again, not with how livid he was at me disobeying his orders, almost getting caught, and bringing someone back on board. There seemed to be something else to it, as well. His whole crew acted strange toward me. Sure, I was a stowaway, their rival's prized whore, a beacon for bad news. But it was in the way Sven kept leering at me and the way Clara insisted on a friendship, as if she felt sorry for me. It was in the way that Killian kept me close at hand while constantly sending furtive glances around him, as if waiting for someone to pop out in the night and snatch me away.

Was that what it was? Was he worried that now he had something of true value, he would lose it? He wasn't at a disadvantage when it came to money. The trappings of his captain's room and the fact that there were three but probably more hot tubs of water, magically heated throughout the day, proved his wealth. His clothes were always crisp and they had plenty to spare. And I had the suspicion that no matter how much they deflected, whatever they kept hidden in their unmarked crates was worth more coin than the entirety of the Skarsrowe black market had ever seen.

As I followed the captain toward the stern of the ship, a memory flashed suddenly. The crates my father would use to hide his illegal activities were unmarked as well, save for a series of hash marks on the side of the lids. They always represented what was inside; three slashes for drugs, two for alcohol, one for illegal or stolen goods. I shifted my eyes toward the closest crate but couldn't see any hash marks on it. Though it had been fifteen years, it seemed like it was a method that would still be in use, and I hadn't heard anything different from the current illegal shippers during my time gleaning secrets from the seedy patrons of The Tullyhouse.

Once at the stern of the ship, Killian pulled me closer to him toward the edge of the railing.

"See that, love?" He pointed down at what looked to be schools of fish biting against the wood floating in the water. "It's strange activity, wouldn't you say?"

I was taken aback by the question. I'd spent seven years mostly locked in a tavern room and he wanted to talk to me about fucking fish behavior? "Um, I suppose so."

"Nothing like this happened before you stepped on my ship."

"Okay..."

He snapped at the string tied around his wrist in agitation. "Why do you suppose that is?"

"I don't know," I said. Irritation flashed hot in my veins. First he rejected me, then he pleasured me, then he told me I had to stay on the ship, and then he chastised me in front of everyone else. Did he want me to pant over him? Is that why he insisted I stand so close to him? And why the fuck would I ever want to discuss the habits of fish with him? "Was there a point to this?"

I knew my attitude was shit, but maybe his rejection stung harder than I cared to admit. All I knew was that my body had been wanted—savored in the way that alcoholics savored their whiskey. A sip at first and then overindulged, uncaring of what filled the bottle. Not worried about what pieces of me were spat back out at the end of a long night, leaving me to fester on the ground and beneath the soles of men who couldn't think past their own dicks' needs.

"I'm asking you what's special about you. The thing you attempted last night, do you care to talk about that at all?"

"No." I would sooner throw myself off the boat than explain my gift to him. Not that I knew of a proper explanation, anyway. "There isn't anything special about me."

That cruel smile slashed across his face again and his scar dragged down with the pull of it, making him more menacing than ever. "I know you killed someone, Red."

The change in subject threw me, but I was sure that's what he was aiming for. "Ooh, is this starting to get kinky? Does it turn you on to think of me bathed in someone else's blood?"

"What a mouth you have on you." His hand cupped my cheek then slid down to my neck as he pulled it back, forcing me to look up at him. "Who knew there was such a feisty bitch hiding beneath that mask of innocence you wear."

"Innocence?" I scoffed. "You do understand what my job entailed, right? All the ways I had to perform for men and women. Sometimes both at the same time." I stepped closer to him. His breath tickled the hairs along my forehead. "The things I had to do to them." I trailed my fingers down his chest, allowing my nails to scratch against the softness of his shirt. His muscles tightened underneath but there was no other indication that I affected him. I didn't need it, though. His unique musky scent underneath the normal leather and sea he gave off let me know how much he loved it. I stopped just short of his waistband and lowered my voice to a sultry whisper. "The way I moved against them made them want more of me." His pupils dilated and he swallowed. My eyes trailed down his throat as his Adam's apple bobbed with the movement and I had an intense desire to lick it. "Does that sound like innocence to you?"

He stared at me, his breathing even, though his nostrils flared for a moment. Was that annoyance? Was he annoyed that I got one over on him?

"I would think someone who was so eager to escape their legal place in life wouldn't be this quick to brag about all the things they had to do to maintain their...*value* within their position."

His words lacerated me as if he slid a dagger against my throat. I fought to keep my temper down, locking away my feelings the way I needed to when preparing for the next client. I refused to let my brain process his words, and instead focused on my own breathing. The inhale and the exhale, tucking all the feelings inside and away, deep down where no one, not even I, could touch them.

It wasn't until I was sure that my words would hold no inflection, would give no indication of the tumultuous storm warring inside of me, when I said, "There is nothing special about me. I don't know why you care about fish too small to eat or earn coin from. Give me something useful to do to earn my stay, or let me at least stand with the woman I forced onto your ship."

His eyes softened imperceptibly but I quickly looked away. I would not let him change me. I would not break down and accept his pity. He said what he said, either to hurt me or to make his point, and that was it. He was entitled to his opinion, just as I was entitled to keep my secrets to myself.

"You aren't crew yet, Red. You aren't doing tasks until I know what to do with you."

"Well, apparently I'm only good for one thing. Only *valuable* in one way, as I've proven again and again. So unless you're going to let Sven, or Clara, or even that fuck who wants to kill me have a go, I don't know why you're forcing me to stand here."

His eyes narrowed at that. "What fuck wants to kill you?"

"That dipshit you have manning your wheel next to our new friend. I overheard him telling Sven it would be easier to just kill me or throw me overboard to the sharks. Have you seen the way he looks at me?" I turned my nose up at him as I looked to the stormy distance on the horizon. The rumble of thunder was still in the air, and waves rocked the boat as a swift breeze picked up speed. Were we meant to be sailing out to sea in such weather? "You expect me to believe that I have worth to you? When one of your own is so willing to feed me to these very fish that you're obsessed with?"

His fists tightened against his sides. "There are explicit orders not to harm you. The consequences would be dire."

I had no idea what he meant by that, nor how to respond to it. "Well, this *Kelso* that you're so fond of, that you trust with whatever secrets you're stashing away on this boat, may not give a fuck what the orders are when he thinks it'll be better to kill me and be done with it."

Killian was silent a moment. Willy and Clara sat on barrels on the main deck, speaking quietly to each other while Sven leaned against the mast, watching the two of us as he pretended to clean his nails with the edge of a knife. Pathetic. I could help with his spying technique, but then again, I hoped to leave the ship and be on my own as soon as possible, so what was the point? We were too far away for him to hear anything, but he had cunning eyes. I couldn't decide if I needed to befriend him or keep him as far away as I would with Kelso.

"Sven!" Killian barked. "Front and center."

Sven meandered his way along until he reached us and put his hands in his pockets. He shifted his shoulders and stretched his neck as if he were limbering up for a fight. His foot tapped almost imperceptibly which I quickly picked up on as a nervous tick.

So the crew *did* fear Killian, to an extent, though they often joked at his expense. Interesting.

"Is Red telling the truth? Did Kelso threaten to kill her?"

Sven shot an accusatory stare my way and I lifted an eyebrow in response. Was that a look of betrayal? As if I told one of his secrets? Did he think I owed him some type of loyalty, just because he helped to hide me from Viktor?

"Don't look at her, look at me. Answer the fucking question."

Sven ran his tongue over his teeth and looked off in the distance before meeting Killian's stare. "Maybe, Kelso might have said something. I don't know."

"The truth, Halstrøm, before I toss you to the sharks."

Sven looked as though he would argue that fact, but I felt the waves of fury coming off of Killian, and even I wouldn't refuse to answer him when he was in this mood. His was the face of the killer he was rumored to be, with his cheekbones sharpened and his teeth bared to give him a menacing look. It fascinated me. The danger he presented caused a thrum of excitement to stir in my blood.

My eyes darted between Killian and Sven, unsure of what would happen between the two. Disagreements between a captain and his first mate were common, but it wasn't something I often saw on a smuggler's ship. The crew needed to be in sync, to work towards their common goal. More than anything, they needed to trust each other.

A smile tilted the corner of my mouth and I fought hard

to school my expression. I couldn't believe my plan was working. It wasn't the way I meant for it to happen, but it was unfolding so nicely.

"It's true. He said as much this morning before our drop off."

Killian's eyes trailed over me again, once again lingering on the bruises that marred my neck. I swallowed, the pain in my throat still there, the reminder of the danger I'd been in and what I had to do to get back out of it. Hell, I was still in danger. I didn't know what type of strange situation I got caught up in by sneaking onto Killian's ship, but I knew based on the way the secrets were thick as a tongue swollen with lies that it wasn't legal, or good.

Killian finally tore his gaze away from my neck and stared into my eyes instead. I could feel the leftover lust, the rage blanketing me, warming my skin against the shrill cold of the damned morning. Was all that emotion he felt for me, or because one of his crew thought to go against his orders? Was he just thinking of whatever money he would be giving up, whatever bargaining chip he'd have to do away with, if I were murdered? Or was it something more personal?

I thought I understood men, but Killian was a delicious, infuriating mystery that I wanted to unfold.

In one fluid motion, he removed his shirt along with his sword, scabbard, and smaller weapons. Sven rolled his eyes as if this were a common occurrence, but then did the same. Both men were covered in tattoos: Killian's were a series of symbols and runes all over his torso and arms. They looked remarkably like the type of symbols that were etched all over the maps and trinkets in the captain's quarters. Sven's tattoos were on his left arm trailing up toward his chest and appeared to be mostly nature scenes: a stormy sea, mythical beings, and ocean waves took up most of the images. I spent the next few moments slowly appreciating their bodies, eyeing their muscles and golden skin from years of working on a ship under the sun. I certainly could have ended up with a worse looking crew.

Thunder rumbled again and a light drizzle broke out. I shivered, hugging my arms around myself. I wasn't used to being out in the rain so much, not unless I was on a job, and even then I would at least have some type of shawl. Julian was a monster, but he did what he could to make sure I didn't get a lasting sickness. Couldn't have his prize out of commission.

Gooseflesh rose against Killian and Sven's skin as they both took up protective stances, one fist up near each of their faces, the other slightly lower. Willy walked up beside me, dwarfing me with their height. They held out a coat that was much too large, but I quickly shrugged it on and gave them a reluctant smile back. First Clara gave me a small taste of the freedom I craved, then Sven lent me his coat to hide my hair, and Willy was making sure I was comfortable? I didn't know what to make of it. I trusted no one but they seemed to be working hard to get me to change my mind.

"This hasn't happened in a while," Willy murmured next to me. Their wild hair frizzed and swayed in the rain-drops. "What caused this?"

"I told him I didn't feel safe with death threats hanging over me," I said. "Sven confirmed that your pal Kelso wants to murder me and that was it."

Willy sighed, rubbing their eyes. "Our beloved captain is such a hothead." They half-turned toward the open deck behind us and let out a shrill whistle. Kelso, June, Clara, and three others I hadn't noticed before all climbed up to where we were and stood in a rough circle around the two. Kelso took in the scene then stared at me with murderous intent. I lifted a brow to him and showed him the smirk I failed to hide. *Bring it on.*

"It isn't you I want to be fighting with," Killian said. "But you're the one that allowed such talk to begin with so it's only fair you get the first taste of this."

With that as his only warning, Killian threw a jab at Sven, forcing him to back up two steps. Sven shook his head and bounced on his feet, then barely had another moment to take a breath before Killian came at him with a combination jab and uppercut. Sven landed on his back, blood gushing from his nose. He laughed as he spit blood out of his mouth and he held his wrist to his nose in a vain attempt to bring it to heel.

It didn't go unnoticed that Sven did nothing but defend whatever blocks he could. Though I was positive that Sven could be a fair fighter, he did nothing to further anger the blood in Killian's veins. As soon as I finished that thought, Sven shot his legs out and twisted them around Killians' and jerked him, causing him to land on all fours. Killian's head hung down then he whipped it forward, his eyes gleaming with a silver light as he stared at Sven like he was something more akin to prey than his crew mate. My eyes narrowed as Killian bared his teeth at him. They looked sharp as razor blades and more menacing.

What the hell?

"Fuck me," Sven said, raising his hands to placate Killian. Willy put their hand on the sword at their belt and the three crew members I hadn't noticed previously looked between each other then stepped forward as one. I was startled to realize they were triplets, a rare occurrence for Carnithia. Clara slowly backed to a storage unit and slid open the door, revealing a net that looked as though it were woven from iridescent silk. I straightened, feeding off the intensity of the crew.

What the fuck is going on?

At the sound of my gasp, Killian flicked his head toward me and I watched as the pupil of his eye contracted into a slit similar to that of a snake then back to its normal round size. A sense of deja vu drifted over me. He inhaled and stood slowly, turning to face Kelso.

"You." Killian pointed, blood dripping from the corner of his mouth. Something dark stirred inside me at the sight. His knuckles had cracked open and a bruise was starting to form on his ribcage, but still his eyes were lit up with manic excitement and he showed no signs of stopping. I found myself wanting to see how far he would take things.

Kelso finally looked away from me to address Killian. "You aren't seriously defending her," he scoffed. "She doesn't belong here, and we have a job to do. She's nothing but a distraction."

"Fight me, or you forfeit and I throw you to the sharks. It's up to you."

What was with him and throwing people to the sharks? Were the sharks in the Baronian Sea something different than what I remembered, or was that a code word for something I didn't know? I wouldn't be surprised. There was so much I didn't know about the crew.

Kelso walked toward the blood-spattered ground where Killian stood in the center of the circle and shook his head in disbelief. His long curly hair clung to his forehead and his shirt hugged his chest. "You would fight a member of your own crew over a whore?"

I swallowed against the feeling that threatened to tear through me. The way he spat the word 'whore' was as if I left a bad taste in his mouth, as if he couldn't think of anything viler than who or what I am. What a joke. I could almost guarantee he paid more for women than my best-paying clients, and if he thought he could have me, he would have tried.

Killian closed the gap between them with a swift punch to the gut. Kelso grunted and leaned over his stomach, breathing sharply in and out. Killian hardly waited for him to catch his breath before he barreled him onto the ground and held him in place with a knee. He punched Kelso's face again, then again. A part of me thrived at the sight, while the other was terrified. What did it say about me that I liked to see Kelso get punished? That it excited me?

My time in enslavement must have traumatized me more than I realized.

The deck was slick with raindrops and the wind kicked up salty ocean spray from the ocean, coating us like a briny wet blanket. Movement down Kelso's thigh caught my attention. His fingers curled around something indistinguishable, and then, even as Killian laid punches that sounded moist from Kelso's blood, I watched as he flung a knife straight for my face. I was slow to realize, though I watched it all play out, that a weapon was flying at me until it was too late to move. The point of the knife skimmed my cheek, its sting amplified by the salt in the air. Shock rippled through me as I clapped my hand against my cheek. Had that bastard really just attempted to kill me? In front of everyone?

Kelso's mashed up face was barely recognizable but I still saw a smirk, or at least his attempt at one through what looked to be a broken jaw. Killian's body jerked as though his movements were not his own and he lost all control, and his tattoos took on a strange gleam. *That ink.* It was so familiar, hovering at the edge of my memory.

He punched and clawed at Kelso as if he were a wild animal, while the triplets snuck up behind Killian with the iridescent net that Clara had taken out. Sven plodded over to me, holding his nose upright, and Clara crept in closer as well. It was almost as if they were forming a protective circle around me.

I had never seen a human lose their control like that before. I'd never seen *anything* lose their control like that. Kelso, a bloody mess of a person, was still laughing from his prone position, the gurgling of blood in his cough. He wasn't in any shape to kill me, if he even survived, and though I wanted to cause dissension, I never meant for Killian to lose his shit.

"Hey, Captain," I called out. "You've done enough."

He paused for a moment, then resumed his assault. Kelso had become quiet, outside of the squelch of the slick punches beating his pulp of a body.

Killian's crew each took turns trying to get his attention with no luck.

"Shit, we're gonna have to tranquilize him," Sven said.

"What is happening to him?" I asked. "He's acting like nothing I've ever seen before."

There was a pause as the crew shared a look between one another, then Willy said, "You were never meant to see this side of him. Maybe I should take you down to his quarters while we handle this."

"Are you out of your fucking mind?" Clara said. "If you remove her from his sights he'll go on a killing spree and then we'd all have a lot of explaining and bargaining to do."

"What is that supposed to mean?" I demanded, frustrated that no one would answer any of my fucking questions.

The triplets were almost at Killian's side, the net contraption glistening in the raindrops.

"Killian O'Donnell," I tried again, to no avail. I didn't know what would happen when that net was around him, but it gave me a visceral reaction, like I needed to do anything to prevent him from being trapped within its web. There was one other thing I could try, though he said it wouldn't work, and it would expose me to the crew if they didn't know already. Panic rose in me as my instinct to protect Killian grew. Fuck it.

"Killian," I sang out, my voice rising in tone at the end. "Stop."

Immediately, he ceased all action, his head whipping over to me. Everyone on deck froze, glancing between Killian and myself.

"Stop," I commanded again. To my surprise, he pulled off of Kelso, his breath out of control.

"I thought that wouldn't work on us," Sven whispered.

"Shut up, Sven," Clara said.

The crew were tense, but so was I. Kelso still garbled to himself from the ground, and though he didn't move, he tried hard to speak. It sounded like he kept repeating the same thing over again. We waited, wondering what was so pressing.

"Whore," he wheezed. "You will only e-ever. Be a whore and can't. Help b-b-but to go fr-from one. Master t-to the next, sucking their d-dicks. As. You go."

Sudden ire settled into my bones as I cocked my head at him. What an odd choice of words to use, knowing they would probably be his last.

A rage overcame Killian again, but before he could

deliver another blow to Kelso, I walked the three steps over to him and kicked Kelso in his face. And then I did it again as I thought of every man who only ever thought of me as a whore. And again as I thought of every man who made me a whore. And then once more when I realized that I was the one at fault. It was me that made my life that way.

Something crunched against my boot and through heated tears and freezing rain, I realized that Kelso had long since gone boneless, and the voices in the distance who were begging for me to stop, were now loud and clear. I looked down and saw grey matter and gore against my boots. Kelso's face looked like he had gone through a meat grinder.

"FUCK!" Killian swore over the sound of thunder coming in from the endless sea. "Fuck!" He ran his fingers through his hair, his eyes filled with a crazed type of fear I hadn't seen on him yet. Why would he fear a dead asshole? This was Killian O'Donnell, the meanest boss on his side of Skarsrowe.

I looked behind me at the rest of the crew, my eyebrows drawn down in confusion. Maybe they could clarify the purpose of his tantrum. Clara stood with her eyes wide, her mouth dropped open in shock, or horror. Probably both. Sven was still shirtless and shaking in the rain and Willy, their curly hair wild in the impending storm, looked disturbed. I didn't know why they all had that look on their faces. Certainly, they had seen a dead body before. Okay, so it was a grim sight, but I killed someone who wanted to kill me and clearly was going to stop at nothing until he did it. What kind of psycho still tried to murder someone when their body was as broken as Kelso's was?

Why did he hate me so much that he tried to kill me until his last breath?

"Fuck!" Killian's voice punctured my thoughts. He walked to the side of the ship and looked over the side into the water. "Fuck!" He punched the railing until blood flowed freely from his knuckles and down his arm. I don't know what Kelso meant to them, but he didn't wear that ridiculous friendship bracelet so he couldn't have been part of the inner circle. Maybe I killed off someone extremely important to them. But if that were true, why was Killian just a moment away from killing him, himself? Did I make a mistake and turn the crew against me, rather than against each other, as I had intended?

It seemed absurd, but I felt like I needed to pierce the awkward tension, somehow. "I'm sorry," I said. The words fumbled from my lips and fizzled against the static electricity in the air. "I didn't realize what I was doing. I just couldn't take him calling me a whore." Why was I defending myself and who I was to these people?

Killian shook with rage but kept his gaze averted. After a moment, he turned on his heel and walked away, straight toward the bowels of the ship. Willy was still speechless, but Sven shook his head and said, "You have no idea what you've just done."

I looked between the three of them, wondering if anyone was going to explain that cryptic sentence any further. More than that, I wondered when it would be an appropriate time to get out of the rain, or at least to do something other than stand still in it next to the body of the man I just murdered.

"That's two," Clara said. "Two men that you've killed within two days."

The first man I killed was in self-defense. He was choking me to death and it was all I could do to save myself.

The second man was Kelso and frankly, he didn't deserve to live.

"Shit," Sven said. Once we saw Killian disappear in the darkness of the ship, the triplets quickly got to work to clean up the blood before it stained the wooden planks of the deck.

Something about their behavior was off. June Leona, bless her, stood off to the side and looked at me like I was a freak with three heads. In that moment I almost wished that was the problem I had. I had never felt like I needed a friend or someone on my side more. I wished, for one too many times, that my sister was still alive and with me.

"Look, I don't find pleasure in killing," I started. "I didn't realize I would kill him. I felt like I wasn't even here, but instead just completely removed from everything that was happening. I know none of you are saints so don't act like you've never murdered someone or worse." Sven looked at his blade as if remembering all the throats he'd slit with it. "We both come from the same place. Surely you understand that I needed to hurt him like he did me."

"Well, you sure did that, babe," Sven said.

"Stop calling me babe," I said at the same time Clara said, "Don't fucking call her babe."

Willy looked to the sky, squinting against the rainfall and then at our surroundings. Kelso was picked up by the nameless trio and carried below deck. I wondered why they didn't just toss him to the sharks as that seemed to be the ongoing threat from Killian, but I didn't feel like it was appropriate to ask, given that I was the one who killed him. It weirded me out to have a dead body hanging out below deck. Was he the only one? How many more were there?

Willy cleared their throat. "Well, let's weigh anchor."

Lightning struck, splashing quick flashes of light

against our faces. I didn't think I heard them correctly. "We're leaving? In this storm?"

"It'll lighten up once we get back out to sea."

The clouds were black, ominous, heavy with the rain that still needed to fall. "But it looks like we're about to get pounded by a hurricane." The waves picked up speed as they thrashed against the boat. I looked down at their foamy white caps and noted dark shapes pounding against the hull. Were they the same fish from earlier? I couldn't be sure.

Clara shook her head but went to help Willy raise the anchor, leaving me with Sven. We scrutinized each other. I knew my face resembled something like awkward indifference, and he smirked in amusement. He came over and put his arm around my shoulder. I didn't bother to shrug it off.

"You really put us in a fuck of a spot, letting two souls loose like that."

Two souls loose? Who spoke like that? "What is that supposed to mean? Look, I already apologized for killing him, but if you want me to feel remorseful about Kelso, I won't. He would have killed me once he recovered anyway. If he recovered. I didn't need to worry about his murder attempts on top of everything else there is for me to worry about."

"No one gives a shit about Kelso, sweet pea. He was a loaner from a different crew. It'll cause problems later, sure, but it's fine for now. He was a dipshit, anyway."

"Then what's the issue? Why are you all freaking out over a dickhead you don't even care about?"

"It's the big boss that will be after you now."

"Was he close to Kelso or something?" I didn't need any more bosses to worry about. I was so tired of assholes thinking they could threaten me and do whatever they wanted with me. I'm a person. With feelings and emotions and the ability to think and do for myself. I shouldn't be treated like a piece of steak for the wolves to fight over.

"Nah, but he'll want to be close to you now."

"Why? What the fuck is that supposed to mean?"

"It means he'll be onto your scent, darling. So we better get a move on."

He gave me a gentle nudge down to the main deck toward the others and I helped them crank the lever to raise the anchor while Sven and a few others let the sail drop. Willy took over the wheel, the muscles in their arms straining as they tried to keep it from turning against the current, and led us out to sea.

The thrill of danger was one thing; not knowing if someone would catch me doing something naughty was enticing, like when I ran away from Julian's goons in that seedy alleyway. Being suicidal was another. I might have felt like I belonged to the ocean, but that didn't mean that I wanted its salty essence to be my last breath.

A surge of relief coursed through me. If Killian weren't standing right at the railing when we returned with June Leona, I would have done something to sabotage the sail or even tried to figure a way to release the anchor chain. Something inconvenient, but fixable, that would have put us to Hammerford, the next port town, where I knew I could have gotten away if I wanted to. My plan was to create distrust and tension between the crew, and then swoop in and fix things so that I could prove that I was valuable and needed, just in case things hadn't gone my way. I wanted to manipulate the entire operations of that godsforsaken savior of a ship of mine.

Imagine what kind of state we would have been in, then, if I had given in and done just that. Sailing into the heart of a stormy sea, with a dead body in the hull of a magical ship, and a captain who looked like he wasn't even human but instead entirely unnatural—then, bam! Mast breaks. It was too much, even for my sick mind.

After raising the anchor, I stood around, unsure of what to do. I felt a pull toward the captain's quarters and Killian. I should have been afraid of him, of what he was capable of. I saw a piece of the ruthless, crazed bastard the rumors said about him. In a sense I was afraid, but perhaps that was what enticed me to him. I stepped toward the stairs when a hand on my shoulder held me in place.

"Hey, doll," Sven said, his mouth a little too close to my ear for comfort. I looked down at his hand then back up at him, waiting for him to remove it. He gave me a half smile and rolled his eyes, but complied with my unspoken wishes. "I just wanted to say, what you did to make Killian stop..."

He trailed off and panic swarmed my skin like bees working in their hive. It was the moment I feared when I had decided to use whatever gift I had to attempt to calm Killian. I swallowed, waiting for him to say anything, because I was, for once, filled with nothing but dreaded silence.

His eyes searched mine and the cocky smirk he wore disappeared. "Look, I don't know what you know about... anything." He wiped his forehead from the drops of rain falling into his eyes. "What you did, what you could do—"

"How did you know about it?" I asked him, suddenly curious. "Did Killian tell you about last night?"

"No..." Sven said. "It's complicated and I really couldn't explain even if I wanted to. I just wanted to say that it shouldn't have worked, but I'm glad it did. Confused as fuck, but glad. If we needed to subdue Killian...it wouldn't have been good for any of us."

"When am I going to get some sort of explanation?" Two days. I'd been on the ship for two days and already I was exhausted and at my breaking point. "I am so sick of everyone knowing more about everything than me. What are these crates for? I know you're smuggling something illegal. How does this ship constantly have hot water baths? Where does all the food come from? Who is this bigger boss you're all so afraid of?"

Sven turned me to face him, holding his grip on my upper arms as he tried to stare in my eyes between the pounding rain. "I can't answer those questions, Emersyn. Not even Killian can. You'll find out soon enough. As soon as the boss calls us in, you'll see."

It worried me that he called me by my real name rather than a nickname he'd come up with. "I'm going to check on Killian."

"I won't stop you, but you probably don't want to do that."

"Make sure June Leona is settled," I said as my parting words as I headed to the stairs leading below deck.

I paused just outside the door to Killian's room. I could hear the rustling of papers and what sounded like furniture being tossed about. I'd had experience with all manner of men who blustered and pomped their supposed strength about, trying to prove they were something to be admired or feared. I was done dealing with those types of men.

I didn't bother to knock as I shoved open the door and came face to face with the mysterious captain of the *Vox in Ventum.*

7

There is strength in becoming.

My mother was a dressmaker for our little shipping village out in the country on the outskirts of Hammerford. When I was around seven and Gabriella was ten, my mother would watch us in her shop after school lessons. If it was a slow day, which it usually was because not many people could afford new dresses, she would let us play with the different fabrics and when she was in a particularly good mood, she would pin swaths of material around us so we could see what we would look like if we were like the wealthy families who wore fancy dresses every day.

One such afternoon, my mother sat me down on her lap and ran a comb through clumps of burgundy, spilling over my shoulders like waves in a storm, fitting a decorative pearl clip above my right ear. I thought I looked like a mermaid from one of the sea shanties I loved to listen to at the tavern. I glowed at my reflection, expecting my mother to look pleased with a job well done, but her beautiful tan skin paled as she looked at me. Her mouth was tight and her amber eyes were lined in silver. I glanced down at the cerulean fabric she pinned onto me, the silver sequins reminding me of the crest of a wave as it crashed against the sand. I felt as though I belonged to the ocean itself.

"Mother, don't you like the dress you made for me?" I jumped off her lap and twirled, setting the sequins on fire from the sun's rays shining through the window. "Why do you look so sad?"

"Oh, my child, I just never want you to come of age. One day you will leave a powerful imprint on this world that even the gods will be forced to bow to. I just want you to stay with me, always."

"But where else could I possibly go? I only want you and Papa for all times."

She had burst into tears at that and ran to the stockroom, citing the excuse of it being her moon time and she just needed a moment.

"She gets sadder every year," Gabriella had commented. "She doesn't look at me the way she looks at you." The resentment was clear, as was normal between siblings who think one receives more attention than the other. "I want her to be sad about me leaving one day."

I hugged my sister around her shoulders and held her close. Most days I felt as though I were the older one, and often took care of her rather than the other way around. "Don't speak like that. You're not going anywhere, and neither am I. And if we decide to leave, we do it together." I smoothed her cinnamon hair, calming her with each stroke.

"Do you promise, Emmy?" she asked. "Will we always be together?"

"For as long as the moon pulls the tide to shore."

KILLIAN STOOD in the middle of his room surrounded by chaos. He was still shirtless, his tattoos giving off a muted sheen against his sweat-slicked skin. The maps and various trinkets that used to cover his desk littered the ground, and the chairs, bolted to the floor, were missing their arms—the next best thing to destruction he could have done. Dried blood covered his skin, and his chest heaved with exertion.

He whipped his head around at the sound of the door clicking, freezing in place when he saw it was me. I leaned back against the door and crossed my arms, the picture of perfect ease, though inside butterflies wreaked havoc on me. What does one say to the captain of a crew member you just murdered? Not to mention, I revealed my power in front of everyone, though it seemed they already knew all about it. I bought a slave in his name and she was stuck on this ship with us. The entire morning had spun wildly out of control.

Killian flicked his eyes over me, starting with my gore-spattered boots, my pants clinging to my wet body, and the translucent shirt that would have been absolutely indecent if it weren't for the soft leather corset I wore over it. A tick above his brow twitched at the sight of the bruises on my neck. His eyes trailed slowly up to the thin slash on my cheek caused by Kelso's knife. It burned under the heat of his stare, and I clasped my hand to my face, hiding it from his view.

He took a step toward me then back to his original position. "Does it hurt?" he asked roughly.

"No," I answered. "I had forgotten it was there until you looked at it. It's nothing, really."

"It's not nothing. You were under my boss's protection. Under my protection. We broke your trust."

Had they ever actually earned my trust? I knew almost nothing outside of their names, and given the three crew members I wasn't previously aware of, I couldn't even say I knew that much. In fact, I knew nothing about anyone I was stuck on this ship with. "You couldn't have known things would have escalated with that psychopath," I said. Why was I reasoning with someone who nearly murdered a person? Why was I speaking as if *I* hadn't just murdered that person? "Anyways, I feel like I should apologize."

"Don't."

The word rang with finality. A command.

"Do you want to talk about what just happened?" I asked, daring to take a step closer to him. "About what you did to him. Or what I did to you..." I trailed off, allowing the space for him to speak to me about what I was most concerned about. What would he do with me now that he knew I could control some part of him?

"There's nothing to talk about. I did what I had to do. And so did you. I assume it felt compulsive. Like an instinct to protect me?"

My eyebrows narrowed. How could he possibly know that? My face gave away the answer to his question.

He gave a harsh laugh and looked away. "Fucking figures." He looked around at the debris littering the floor then sat down in one of the broken chairs as the fight went out of him. He rubbed his palms over his face, as if attempting to wash away the events of the last hour.

I didn't know what to do, either. The instinct to protect him was still there, though it wasn't as strong. In its place was a need to comfort and soothe. What the fuck? I wasn't his mother. Or his wife. I wasn't even a proper sex partner. There shouldn't be any reason why I felt the need to take care of him.

The same thoughts circled around my head as I headed into the tiny wash closet and grabbed a towel. Next to the tub was a small porcelain bowl I hadn't noticed before. I dipped it in the steaming water, barely pausing to wonder how the water was still hot and clean, then walked back out to Killian.

His head was still in his hands, giving me a close-up view of his back, the muscles stretched taut. The symbols were arranged in a way that seemed as though they were a pattern. The black ink looked like it was lined in silver and gave off the same appearance as that strange netting the other members of his crew were prepared to trap him in.

I slowly reached one finger out and trailed it down the largest symbol closest to his spine. Its whirls and dash marks looked like a language, like it was a story or a song, if only I had the means to read it. They were familiar, and a sense of recognition flowed through me. He stiffened under my touch, then relaxed as I used the point of my nail to trace a symbol. I had the strangest urge to hum as I did it.

Instead, I snatched my hand back, suddenly realizing that I was caressing Killian O'Donnell right after he beat a man to an unrecognizable pulp.

What the hell is wrong with me?

I cleared my throat and dipped the washcloth into the bowl, wiping away specks of blood off his back and sides. He sat up as I circled around him, scrutinizing how injured he might have been under the gore and dirt. He fixed his gaze on me and I tried not to shift under the weight of his stare. Placing the bowl on the desk next to him, I grabbed his hand as I glanced up at his eyes then down at his knuckles.

"One time, when I was young, there was a man who would always enter my mother's dress shop. There was no particular reason for him to be there, but he would go in, look around at fabrics and clasps, then lean against the cutting table as she prepared other customers' orders.

"At first he would go in once every few weeks, walk around, and leave without saying anything. Then it was weekly. Then daily. Every day, she asked him if he needed help with anything, if he was interested in a certain fabric, if there was perhaps something she could try to get for him so that he had a real *reason* for being there." I swallowed, dipped the cloth into the water and squeezed out the excess liquid, watching it turn a light pink. I picked up his other hand and wiped away the evidence of his anger. "It took a few months of this, but eventually, my mother figured out what he wanted." I inhaled and prepared my mind to shut down a little before revealing this truth about my past. About the first time I was truly afraid of a man. "When he leaned against the counter, he could see in the back room where my sister and I would wait while customers were in the store. He saw us playing with each other's hair, or eating a snack. As soon as my mother realized it she told my father.

"The next day, my father left his first mate in charge and waited in the back room with us. He was there the whole day, helping to organize spare fabrics, sort through customer orders, playing with us. It was nice to have him around, and I remember being surprised at how natural it was to see him as a shopkeeper rather than a smuggler. He looked at home, but as the day closed, it seemed as though he stayed behind for no reason. Finally, when the sun was just about to set, the man returned.

"He did the same routine as before, looking through fabrics and fasteners and thread. Then he went to lean against the sorting counter where my mother busied herself and she asked him if he needed anything, same as always. Just as she stepped aside, my father stepped into the doorway. His large frame was menacing in the dying light, and I remember thinking how strong he looked. How fierce of a man he was, to protect his family.

"The man quickly jerked away and started to walk backwards out of the store, but my father didn't let him get three steps before he was on him. An eerie light shone in my father's eyes. It was unlike anything I had ever seen before. Silver, slitted like a cat."

Killian's carefully blank face couldn't hide the pulse in his neck as it ratcheted up a notch. I wet the cloth again then pressed him back against the chair with the other hand, forcing him to relax. Blood was splattered on his cheek, his torso, his legs. I decided to wipe his face so I could assess the damage that was done, and better gauge his reaction to my memory. I wasn't leaving that room without answers.

"A primal rage came over him. He got the man to admit he was there for my sister and I. That we looked like we'd be a good time in a few years. That we could earn him a lot of money down the road. That we would be a useful invest-ment of his time. My mother came to the back room and tried to cover our eyes, but she couldn't cover our ears. I peeked around the grip she held onto me at my father and that man who wanted to steal us.

"His fists pummeled him, but it was the glint to the

tattoos on his fingers that caught my attention. It was the way nothing seemed to get him to stop. It was the way that he didn't stop until he had proven to himself that the man was no longer a threat." I applied gentle pressure to the wound on his mouth, the swelling turning his lip purple.

He inhaled a sharp hiss, the first sound he had made in ten minutes.

"My father left and returned with his first mate and a few others of his crew. They took the body, cleaned the floor, and set everything straight again. After an hour it was like nothing had happened. My father cleaned himself up and came back out with his hair perfectly combed, his pants and shirt settled just so. He smiled at us, and asked if we wanted to go to the tavern for dinner.

"I knew my father got in with the wrong people by the way he and my entire family was attacked and murdered. I knew he wasn't the most trustworthy man. That he sold illegal drugs, and he was higher up in the black market than I had realized at the time. But I didn't know who could have possibly gotten the best of the man who would beat another to death for daring to look at his children the wrong way, and then continue on his day as if nothing happened. I never put it together that the glint of his tattoos wasn't normal, that his eyes shouldn't have changed and contracted the way they did."

My pulse beat rapidly against my neck but I breathed deeply, willing it to calm. I wanted so desperately for him to deny the question burning on my tongue. I stopped wiping his face and waited to see if he would respond or if I would have to come out and say it.

He swallowed hard and bit the inside of his cheek. "Red..."

"It's the same person, isn't it? The person behind my

family's murder is the same man you work for. I ran onto the ship of the man who destroyed my life."

The silence spoke volumes.

"Sven said he couldn't tell me anything. Are you about to give me the same speech? That you don't have clearance or some shit to tell me anything?"

"Red," he raised his hands as if he were trying to placate me, "there's a lot going on that's really complicated and yes, I am forbidden from telling you anything. I don't know what to say."

"Is it the same man?" Each word was forced out of me as a staccato. I slammed my palms against his chest. "Answer me!" Hot tears threatened to fall down my cheeks but I denied their release. My mind was shut down from the horrors of my past, and I refused to let my desire to know the answer to this question distract me.

Killian stood up tenderly, as if his muscles ached to move them the barest inch. He walked his way toward the water closet and stripped. I was too angry to be distracted by the sight of his naked flesh. Did he think he could reveal himself to me and I would pant after him, forgetting what I was upset about? Did he really only consider me as the whore my reputation proved me to be?

He stepped into the tub, his tense body immediately relaxing in the heat. I probably should have looked away. No self-respecting woman stared at a man while he bathed, did they? I didn't care. I marched over to him and stood in the doorway, refusing to give him an ounce of privacy.

He shifted his large body as much as he could in such a small tub. It barely covered all of me, and he was at least a foot taller than I was. He raised his eyebrows in question, probably wondering if I was going to stare at him the whole time. I crossed my arms and leaned against the door. I sure was.

He rolled his eyes and dipped his head under the water. When he came back up for air, the swelling in his lip had gone down and the bruising around his eye socket was rapidly changing from black to green, before almost disappearing altogether.

I wasn't entirely surprised, as my own ailments had healed after my own dip in that tub, though I attributed it to a traumatizing evening.

"He put those tattoos on your body." I didn't bother wording it as a question and he didn't bother answering me. "The symbols are the same that are on the maps and trinkets outside and on the crates." Still, he said nothing. He rested his arms against the sides of the tub and closed his eyes. "They're the same symbols I saw etched on the ship. They're in another language." He didn't move at that. "They're a spell." His pinky twitched, I was sure of it. "A story." His eyes popped open. "A song."

Slowly, he lifted his head and stared at me, more serious than I had seen him in a while.

"Can you read these?" He held up his forearms. His voice held no inflection.

"No, but they seem familiar to me. Like I should know, but I'd never seen them before, except on my father's fingers. And just that one time. They disappeared after and I thought it was just a trick. Trauma, or something that made me believe they were there. But yours don't go away. I know it's related. Don't you dare insult me by saying it isn't."

He stood from the tub and grabbed a towel. I looked away at the last minute, my mouth dry. What was wrong with me? I'd never shied away from nudity before. After a while a body was just a body, but I still felt an immense pull towards him from seeing him lose control on Kelso. It had been intense, passionate, something that I didn't think he was capable of after he gave me such a pathetically pretty speech on why he wouldn't touch me.

A wave of dizziness caused me to lean against the doorframe. Exhaustion overcame me suddenly and I swayed, trying to keep upright. I had such a restless sleep the night before, and purchasing a slave and killing a man in one day apparently took a lot out of me. I collapsed into the door, dark spots blurring my vision.

"What's happening to me?" I wondered aloud.

Killian's firm grip on my arm led me toward the bed. He fumbled with my boots and pants while I untied the leather corset. I was already leaning toward sleep. If I didn't know better, I would say that I was drugged.

"What did you do to me?" I asked him.

"Nothing, Red." His voice was sad, far away. "You're just overwhelmed and tired. Lay here and I'll go grab you some food for when you regain your strength."

I closed my eyes, taking comfort in the feel of the plush blankets tucked around me, and drifted off to sleep.

THE DARKNESS WAS ALL-CONSUMING. *Thick, heavy walls pressed against me, invading my lungs, stealing my joy. It was a collar wrapped around my neck, it was the chains that bound me to one owner after the next, it was knowing I would die without ever experiencing the freedom of choice, of loving without expectation, of commitment without failure. It tightened its grip, reminding me that it had all the control.*

A sound pierced through the vast ocean of nothing before me, a single note that trickled into two and then three. I couldn't understand the words, but I didn't have to. It was enticing, seductive, it was sadness compounded through the assurance that desire would alleviate the pain for just a moment, if given the chance. I knew that feeling well.

I let the melody flow over me, through the blood in my veins, allowing the power to pump through my heart, to take over my organs, to give me a reason to live just a little longer. I breathed easier knowing I wasn't alone.

The contour of the melody shifted. Instead of a haunting song, it changed to one of desperation. Words I didn't understand blanketed me as I felt them seep into the core of who I was. Without warning, the voice was cut off, its echoing notes lingering in the darkness. I was once again alone, fighting against the pressure that was set against me, wondering how I was going to make it out and if this was what dying felt like.

The darkness moved as if it were sentient. Its shadows shifted until a shape took form. I squinted, hoping it would make the darkness clearer, and waited, my breath catching in my lungs and freezing in my throat.

A pulse of power emanated from the shape as it took the form of a body and I knew without a doubt that I would never want whoever that was to come near me. I shifted back a step, the darkness extending its claws to dig into my skin and hold me in place. I screamed and—

I WOKE WITH A JOLT, the feeling of trepidation hanging over me, as if a servant of death waited for my last breath. A heavy heat was at my back, and the thick band of an arm held my waist, as if its only task was to make sure my body stayed bound together. The occasional cry of a seagull interrupted soft snores. The ship still swayed as though it were at a fast clip, and the faint rumble of thunder could be heard in the distance.

Keeping my eyes shut, I waited until my breathing slowed, until I felt like I wasn't being watched by someone other than the person who held me to his front. I turned my head, peering through bleary eyes at the captain. He looked so much younger in sleep, like whatever haunted him couldn't reach him in his dreams.

I wished I could say the same.

It was difficult to decide if I really wanted to extricate myself from him, but him touching me without my consent, no matter how platonic, nearly sent me into another panic. I knew he didn't mean anything by it, but I couldn't shake the icky feeling it gave me that he thought he could be comfortable enough to do that. I might have offered him my body before, but at least I was conscious when that happened.

I slid out of the bed, taking a minute to get my sea legs. The room was cleaned up from Killian's earlier tantrum, and there was a silver platter laid out with delicious fruits, cheeses, and meats. Careful not to make a sound, I crept over to the wardrobe and pulled out another of Killian's shirts then plodded over to the food waiting for me. I wasn't sure how many hours I had slept, but the sun started to dip past the horizon so it would have been nine or ten if it was the same day.

I piled a silver plate with fresh mango, pineapple, and papaya. I hadn't had such treasures since I was a child and went on a small trip with my father to the southern portion of Carnithia. I added a few slices of cheese and a little side of some sort of meat and topped it with an apple chutney. It was food fit for royalty, or at least for one of the seven lords of Carnithia. They were the closest thing to royalty the country still had.

Not caring about the juices running down my chin, I allowed myself the indulgence of eating foods that I had dreamt about for years. It was rare that I allowed myself to steal bits of time to the pleasures of memory, of the way I once was happy and free from care, when I felt that I could be anything I wanted and experience all that Carnithia had to offer me.

I was right, in a sense. I certainly got to know the seedy underbelly, and all the dirty deeds that went along with it.

A soft moan escaped my lips as I bit into the roasted meat. I dipped a sweet bread in a buttery garlic sauce, and let that slide down my throat, savoring the flavors I had denied myself for so long. If I kept eating like that, I would gain all the weight back I had lost in no time.

Good, I thought. I loved my curves.

A rustle in the sheets behind me was followed by the soft groan of a stretch. Killian woke up. I almost paused in my endeavor to get back said curves but decided against it. He thought he could lay with me without my knowledge so he could deal with the disgusting way I ate.

"I could watch you do that all day," he said, his voice thick with sleep from his nap. "What a sight to wake up to."

"You sound like Sven," I said around a mouth full of bread. I stole a quick glance at him, refusing to take in his half naked body stretched out on the bed I had just occupied. "That isn't a compliment, by the way."

His smile faltered and his eyes narrowed. He took in the state of my undress, the fact that I was wearing his shirt, and the smug smirk returned. "You seem to like wearing my clothes." "Is this some sort of macho thing where you feel like a man seeing a woman in your things or something?"

"No, it's just interesting that all of your clothes are laid out right there," he said, indicating a pile of pants and shirts stacked on a side cupboard, "and you still chose to go for mine."

I paused my ministrations, letting the bread plop back down on the plate. A whole pile of clothes? For me? My jaw dropped and I quickly schooled my face, not wanting him to see how much it affected me to have so many items of my own things after having to wear the same clothes, switching with the other girls, never having more than one pair of undergarments at a time.

His eyes softened, which meant I hadn't been stoic enough, apparently. Needing to busy myself, I looked through the clothes and sure enough, there were seven different pairs of undergarments, pants, shirts, and even what looked to be nightshirts. There was also a brush and comb, hats, and scarves—I assumed to cover my hair, so there was no need to worry like I had with Viktor.

The thoughtfulness and care that it took to have these delivered for me was indescribable. It was a foreign feeling to be looked after.

Why would they do this? Are they providing me comfort to catch me off guard? Will they make me pay for it later? Do they fear me, perhaps, because I killed one of their own? Because I killed another man before that?

"Why?" My voice came out sharp, cutting through the haze of appreciation I had started to build up for them.

"Why are you still fighting, Red?" Killian got up and walked over to the platter of food. I took care not to stare or feel the energy pulsating off of him. Those tattoos gave me a new meaning. I now knew who he worked for. The man who murdered my family. And I'd gone and landed myself with someone who took orders from him.

How long would it take for him to find out I'm alive? I had to assume I was a target. Did he already know? Was that where we were going?

"You work for the man who murdered my family. He controls you. How do I know this isn't some sort of manipulation tactic of yours?"

"What is there to manipulate? From every angle, you need us, not the other way around."

My heart sank. "So I don't have value, as you said."

"I didn't say that, Red. You are extremely valuable. I'm saying at this moment, we are far out to sea, you have no idea where we are going, and you can't read any of our maps or know how to use our instruments. You have nowhere to go. There's no reason for us to try to get you to like us. You're stuck with us either way."

He popped a grape into his mouth. All of his bruises were done and he no longer had any cuts or scrapes, either. He looked as if nothing had happened at all.

"How long was I asleep?" I asked.

"Two days."

"Excuse me?" I ran to the window to get a proper look out but of course we were surrounded by water and night was quickly approaching. There would be no way for me to see anything. "Two days? That can't possibly be right."

"June and Clara have both been in and out to check on you. I'm sure they'll be happy to hear you finally woke up." He put his hands in his pockets and turned to fully face me. "I'm sorry you woke up to find me here. The other rooms are being prepared and I haven't slept in days. I just needed a few hours. I was hoping I would slip out before you got up."

"That's creepy." My brain caught up to what he said.

"What do you mean, preparing the other rooms? Preparing for what?"

"We have other cargo we need to get before we hit our destination."

"Are you taking me to him, then?"

He looked at me for a moment then walked to his closet and grabbed another shirt. He took his time fitting his belt then walked to the door. "No, Red. I'm trying to get you out."

8

There is pleasure in permitting.

The first time I ever laid with a man, I was fifteen years old. He was an apprentice sailor, just learning the ropes on my father's small vessel. He wasn't interested in me at first. Father always made it clear I was off limits to anyone, especially if it had been days or weeks since the crew had last been to a brothel. He once sent a man to the deep blue just for looking too long at my body.

So it was natural that this new boy on the cusp of manhood didn't want to spare me a second glance. Or a first glance. But once I had my sights on something, I knew I could get what I wanted. It was a gift and a curse, to sway the opinions of others with little more than a smile and illicit intention.

It had been weeks since he first came aboard the ship.

Gabby had left us when we stopped home for a drop off, but I decided to keep going, taking advantage of whatever time my father allowed for me to be on the open water. Liev was scrubbing the main deck and I just happened to have spilled my cup of ale that I was holding until just the right opportunity. He looked up at me, furious at ruining what I'd just done, but he didn't look away. I'll never forget how his fury melted into something more, something softer.

The following day he didn't avoid looking at me when it was time for supper, and he didn't refuse my help the day after that when it was time for chores. I worked my charm slowly over the course of a week. A lingering look here, a casual touch there. It was a slow progression of me showing him the barest interest, enough to leave him intrigued, that culminated with us laying together. It was the first time I had chosen and done something entirely for myself, and I was grateful to know him. Until my father killed him for touching me.

Insufferable bastard.

Stars glittered like brilliant gems overhead, providing light when they appeared in the breaks of cloud cover. I basked in their light, much the way others do in the sun. There was something about being on the open sea at night. There was nothing but the imagination. The stars that glowed, the vibrant greens and purples in the sky that aren't best seen from land, the way the breeze is quiet, the water lapping softly against the sides of the ship. The ocean sings a lullaby only heard at night, and though there is nothing but darkness to see from any direction, it assured that the possibilities were endless.

I sat on the railing, my feet dangling over the water below. I wondered briefly what it would be like if a shark did jump out of the water and bite me, the way I had seen them do to seagulls and seals when I was younger. I knew I'd be fine, though.

It had been three days since I woke from my extended nap, and short of the endless blue sky meeting the infinite ocean, nothing important had happened. We hadn't stopped at another port, and whatever guests we were meant to pick up, we hadn't done it. June Leona complained for the first day and then realized it was useless and spent her time getting familiar with the workings of the ship. Willy quite enjoyed helping her, it seemed, as I caught them more than a few times standing quite close to one another and whispering softly. It was amazing how quickly relationships could progress when you were in tight quarters with everyone else.

"What are you doing up here, kitty cat?" Clara asked, jumping up to join me.

"Just enjoying the view," I replied. "It never gets old, does it?"

"You mean the suffocating darkness, the water that never ends, the claustrophobia of this infernal ship, and the impossible pressure to keep moving?"

I wondered if I would feel the same if I spent months or years of my life with Killian. It had been only a few days and I hadn't grown tired of him, yet. He came in late at night to lay in his bed, far from where I laid, and every morning he somehow ended up holding me. I would slide out from his grasp, bathe, eat breakfast, and often leave before he got up. We never said anything about it, but more than once I caught him smirking at me across the way.

He couldn't keep the nightmares at bay, though. Every night I felt someone watching me and heard the haunting melody of a familiar voice.

"Where are we going, by the way?" I asked, changing

the subject. "If I'm stuck here with you guys then shouldn't I at least know where you expect to stow me away?"

Clara raised her brow at me. "As if you want to be anywhere other than 'stuck' with Captain Killian O'Donnell." She let out a chuckle then immediately sobered. "We have to go somewhere that will hide you and give Killian something to bargain with."

It was always the same non-answers with them. I'd considered more than once to try to use my gift and persuade any of them to do what I wanted, but even though it worked on Killian in a dire circumstance, I had a feeling it wouldn't work again. I looked down in the water, contemplating my response, when a dark shadow skimmed just underneath the surface. I had an irrational moment of wondering if the sharks really would come to get me and quickly pulled my legs closer to me.

"What is it?" Clara asked, her voice strained. "What do you see?"

"There was a shadow or something under there. Did you see it?"

Her eyes had a look of alarm before she schooled them again. "It was probably just a whale or something. They like to travel next to the ships sometimes."

"It didn't seem like a whale," I said. I turned around and hopped back down to the deck where my feet would presumably stay safely attached to my ankles.

The crates that had been piled high on deck had been moved to the storage area in the hull of the ship, a place I still was not allowed, making the space feel larger than before. The darkness didn't seem as welcoming as it had a moment ago. Gooseflesh rose while I stood there, expecting to feel eyes on me, to hear a voice whispering a heart-breaking melody in my ear.

The triplets, who I had learned had no names to speak of, cleaned up the remnants of dinner on the other side of the deck. June and Willy had served us dinner, although I still wasn't sure if that meant they cooked it as well. No one seemed forthcoming when it came to explaining the food situation. There was nothing out of place, nothing that justified the eerie feeling settling into me.

Clara hopped down beside me. "Anyway, it's Sven's turn to come up with a game tonight. We should probably head down. No doubt it'll involve taking our clothes off."

"I don't mind." I winked, trying to push the uneasy feeling to the back of my mind. "I'm excellent at Devil's Gambit."

"Don't you mean Beggar's Gambit?"

"The name changes to 'Devil's' when we're meant to end up without clothes." I wiggled my eyebrows at her.

"Ah, and are you an expert, then?"

I gave her a mischievous smile. "I've made every effort possible to learn every aspect of the game over the past seven years, and to never lose a hand. I can guarantee I'll win tonight as well and Sven will be the one covering himself in embarrassment."

Clara laughed. "If I know Sven, he certainly will not be embarrassed, nor will he be covering any part of himself."

We linked arms and headed toward the doorway, but a familiar prickle slid down my back. The feeling of being watched. I stopped and turned, searching the deck but found nothing amiss.

But then that haunting melody filled my mind, begging me to listen to it, and every piece of me froze. I knew that sound, the one that played in my mind over again every night in my nightmares. I knew that voice. Why did I know that voice?

"What is it?" Clara asked, trying to tug me along. "Let's hurry or we'll never hear the end of it."

"Do you hear that?" I asked. "That sound? It's like a song."

"No? There's nothing to be heard out here. Is it the whales again? Really, kitty, you gotta spend more time out on the open water."

"I spent my entire childhood on the water and I am telling you, that's not whale song I'm hearing."

Clara tried to push me forward again but I stayed rooted in place, hoping to hear it once again.

"Sven's already three fingers deep," Killian's voice rumbled in my ear. I halted a screech in my throat, my heart pumping overtime. How long had he been standing there? "In whiskey, that is." He smirked and pushed past me, allowing every inch of his body to touch mine in the narrow space.

Clara waved her hand between me and Killian's retreating back. "Listen, if the two of you don't make something happen, we're all going to combust from all that heat."

I rolled my eyes, feigning indifference. "There is no heat. He's just being Killian."

"That's not the Killian we know," she said in a sing-song voice. "Come on. Let's see how long it takes to get me three fingers deep, too."

I chuckled, but I couldn't shake the feeling they were just trying to distract me from what I already knew. That voice in my dreams was real, and it was trying to tell me something. I just wish I understood what it was.

"Okay babe, this is how you play Beggar's Gambit."

We sat in a circle on the floor of one of the other cabins, fluffed pillows cushioning us from the hard ground, because, as Sven put it, it was *cozier* like this. My back protested, wishing it had something to lean on. I had to disagree with his assessment of "cozy".

I snatched the cards from Sven's hands and started shuffling, their movement quick enough to blur. "First of all, don't call me babe." I fanned the cards out then continued. "Secondly, the version we're playing is called Devil's Gambit." I passed the cards out and smirked at his raised brows.

Willy settled in on his other side and shifted closer to June. Killian sat across from me, the heat of his stare burning holes through my skin.

"Thirdly." I grabbed the nearest bottle of whiskey and took a shot, staring back at Killian, a dare and a promise reflected in his eyes. My stomach dipped when he smirked at me. "No one is better at this than me."

Clara looked back and forth between Killian and I and bit her lip, trying to stop herself from smiling. "Well, kitty cat, if you think you can beat us, let's have at it."

June pushed her hand of cards towards me and reached for the deck. "I'll be the dealer this round."

"Hang on, hang on," Sven said. He reached for a bottle of rum and passed out tiny glasses to everyone. Killian pulled from his pocket a beautiful milky white onyx chalice streaked with silver, large enough to hold a double shot of whatever liquid he thought was worthy to be in such a fine piece of art. "A little over the top there, Killian, but I like your style." Sven raised his glass and indicated that everyone else should do the same. "May this night of debauchery result in happy endings for us all!"

A burst of laughter hiccupped out of me, my smile stretching wide and for a moment I felt as though I were floating. *Was this what it was like to have friends? Could I even call them that?*

Silence followed my laughter. I felt as if I were an oddity on display, like they had never seen a woman laugh before. But it was me. I've been with them for nearly a week and that was the first time I had properly laughed. Actually, that was the first time I laughed in months, maybe longer. Killian looked at me with a mixture of awe and curiosity, and I wasn't sure how I felt about it, but my body was aware of his every movement, the way he leaned closer to me before reeling himself back.

"To a night that ends in sin." Killian said each word slowly and distinctly, letting them nestle into forbidden parts of me. Desire coiled through me, stretching awake, yearning to play out the promise in his words.

Willy let out a low whistle. Sven cackled and slapped his hand against his thigh. "Like, Emer*syn*? You dog."

Killian raised his eyebrow at me as if challenging me to say anything different. I schooled the second round of laughter threatening to bubble out of me. The boys were going to lose badly. They just hadn't realized it yet.

I lifted my glass to him then shot the liquid down, wincing slightly as it burned my throat. I welcomed it and poured myself another. "Let's play."

THREE HOURS and four empty bottles later, every person in the room bared their skin—none more than Sven Holstrøm. Of course, I knew it would be that way. Supply him with drink, whisper occasionally in his ear, run my finger around the rim of my glass then suck the water off it for a ridiculous amount of time. His distraction lost him nearly every hand. It was easy and predictable.

Killian, however, didn't play as fair. The more I won, the more he made it his personal mission to make me uncomfortable. Heated glances, licking his lip, maintaining eye contact as he stripped down to nothing but his underwear.

As if that would make me uncomfortable and not more intent on bedding him than I had been when I thought I needed to for my survival.

The breeze whispered against my neck as I breathed in the salty air. The night sky was a blend of deep blues and purples, and the stars twinkled gently overhead. It was warmer, wherever we were headed, and though the wind provided a nice reprieve from the sticky heat of so many bodies in tight quarters, I still felt the humid promise of a more sultry land. We must have been just a few days from the island Killian wanted to stop at.

The ship's railing gleamed in the starlight, and I ran my hand over the handsome wood as I walked a lap around the deck, humming a tune that had been stuck in my head since I awoke that morning. My fingers snagged over a tiny imperfection underneath a piece of wood on the starboard side. I continued singing and pressed against the groove, trying to figure out if it was a natural part of the wood or if it was a carving of some sort.

Thunder rumbled in the distance and clouds quickly closed in. Any light the stars spared for me vanished. A slight ripple shuddered through the ship as if it were stretching after awakening from a deep slumber. Thick rain pelted down, and I ran for the stairs leading to the captain's quarters, the weather having effectively shut down my break from all the tension, though it did little to ease the excitement from earlier.

The door clicked behind me and I laid my back against it, hoping its steady coolness would dampen the heat rising in my blood. It was an ironic twist of fate that allowed me to keep most of my clothes on. Years of whispering sweet lies in my clients' ears earned me a special place to learn various gambling methods of choice for the slummiest of men in Skarsrowe. Card games were my bread and butter, and I tasted the sweetest victory every time I won Devil's Gambit.

I held my belt in my hands, the only article of clothing I needed to remove. My pants fell loose on my hips, revealing a strip of creamy flesh. I smirked to myself, proud that I'd been able to keep it together.

I strode across the room, removing my boots as I went and allowed my pants to fall to the ground. I kicked them away, breathing a sigh of relief as the cool air brushed against the skin of my thighs. As always, there was a platter of food on the table, placed almost precariously on top of various maps of the ocean—this time with decadent desserts. Whipped cream, melted chocolate to dip luscious fruits into, sauces to drench fudgy brownies and cakes that left just the right amount of sticky sweetness behind.

Warm chocolate dripped down my fingers as I pressed a freshly dipped strawberry against my lips, allowing its silky heat to seep into my skin. I didn't know who prepared these platters, but I wanted them to come with me, wherever I ended up.

Awareness prickled at the back of my neck and I turned, mid-bite, just as Killian entered and the door clicked shut. He wore nothing but a thin piece of cloth that did little to hide the sight of him beneath it and I took the liberty of slowly raking my gaze up and down his nearly naked form. He grew under my careful inspection, and a sense of satisfaction filled me as electricity pulsed from my nipples straight to my sensitive spot. I couldn't recall the last time a man made me feel that way with a single look.

I licked the chocolate from my bottom lip, letting my tongue drag slowly along the plump curve. He watched with rabid hunger, his hands clenching into fists then relaxing by his side. He could try to act like he wasn't affected but the evidence was clear, and growing.

Thunder rumbled throughout the ship, and a flash of lightning lit the shadowed corners of the captain's quarters. Rain pelted the ocean, its echo flitting into the darkness in the lantern's glow. The ship rocked against stormy seas, but I had learned in the past week not to worry about storms. June Leona learned from Willy that the ship was protected, preventing anything damaging from happening to it. She hadn't learned how it was protected or who placed whatever enchantment it was on the ship.

At least I wasn't the only person they kept in the dark.

The flame's light danced along the walls as the ship swayed back and forth. Killian took a step forward, his eyes still locked on my bottom lip. He stood inches from me, a look of wicked intention lighting his face. I didn't move, anticipating what he would do. We'd been playing this game all night. Secret glances, stealing caresses against our skin, heated smiles promising lust and sin, if only one of us would give in.

It wouldn't be me. I was done begging for attention. Plus, I wanted to see him take control for once. I wanted him to show me how badly he wanted me, to play out the fantasies his eyes had promised me all night.

What would it be like to be ruined by Killian O'Donnell?

He dipped a finger in the melted chocolate and slowly rubbed it against my lips. Just that one touch sent a rush of liquid pooling between my legs. He inhaled deeply, as if he knew exactly how my body reacted to him. I did the same, allowing his desire to coat me like a second skin, the sweet scent winding its way through my senses. He took his finger and rubbed the remaining down my neck then hesitated for a moment above my breasts, as he read the signs of my body, navigating my needs like a wave.

I dipped my head lightly in encouragement, letting desire flood my features. My skin flushed with his touch and my breathing became erratic as he placed two fingers and trailed them down my breasts. He smirked then dipped his head where his fingers left off and licked the path he made along my body. I tilted my head back, allowing him better access to my neck. He lightly grazed against the curve that meets my shoulder and a soft moan escaped my lips. He bit down and goosebumps erupted along my flesh. I pressed my thighs together, needing some sort of friction there to go along with the pressure he applied at my neck.

Killian noticed, chuckling darkly. He stepped closer and slid his knee between my legs, giving me a barrier to rock against. One hand wound its way toward my scalp, pulling back my hair, forcing me to look at him. His other hand pressed against my lower back until there was no more space between us. My breath hitched in anticipation.

Excitement flooded me. I was allowing a man to touch me because I wanted him to. Because I needed him to. Not because he paid for me. Not because he would get anything from it. I didn't think I would trust someone enough to allow them to do it, but I knew from the moment he caught me when I jumped out of that godsforsaken window that something was different. That he might be one of the good ones, despite the horrors I knew he'd dealt, and despite the murderer he worked for. Maybe I wanted his good heart, but I also craved the way the darkness in his eyes had fucked me before he ever laid a hand on me. And I needed more.

I swallowed, staring into his glassy blue eyes. He chose to act on his desires because he wanted to, not because I was forcing him or needed to prove that I was valuable. He wanted me, just for me. The feeling was foreign to me and I wanted to soak up every ounce of it.

The ship rocked as a particularly nasty gust of wind shook it, and I fell onto Killian, his knee applying the exact pressure I needed upon my sensitive area. I let out a louder moan and bit my lip, the chocolate coating my tongue. Without warning, his lips found mine, and he explored the sweetness left behind, before forcing his way inside to press against my tongue. His hand slid from my lower back until he cupped my ass, grinding me against him.

Gods, it felt so good to let someone else take control, to let him do what felt right and what he knew I would like. I knew I could cum from that alone, so I pushed him hard enough for him to slam against the table, giving myself a short reprieve. He pulled his lips away from me then lifted the hem of my shirt, revealing a lace brassiere Clara had found for me. I meant to use it to tease the boys tonight but I hadn't progressed that far in the game. My nipples were peaks through the thin lace, and Killian bent forward, taking one in his mouth. That same jolt of electricity ignited me again, making me wetter than I remembered ever being for a man.

The booming of thunder shook the silverware on the platters and for a moment the lanterns spluttered. I looked away from his face, wondering for a minute if the walls would capsize around us.

"Are you sure we're safe in this storm?" I breathed as I leaned back, giving him better access.

"As if it were sunny skies," he replied, bending back to continue what he was doing. His other hand drifted between my legs, sliding up the slickness coating my thighs.

He paused and removed his hand, licking his fingers as if he'd just finished an exotic delicacy. His pupils grew to the size of silver coins and a low growl escaped him. He flashed a dark smile before he picked me up and spun me around, the wind from the storm allowing him to toss me against the wardrobe. He tore through the last of my clothes, desperate to get what lay underneath.

Finally. Relief flooded me. *This. This is what I needed.* I needed him intent on destroying every inch of what I had to offer. I needed him to satiate the beast I kept inside, buried underneath the shame I carried for what I'd done to survive.

"You are fucking delicious, Red." He took my legs and wrapped them around his shoulders as he knelt on the floor. The wall at my back forced me to remain upright, as his tongue punished my core. It wasn't like the first time when he did it, taking special care with what I might like or how my body responded. He devoured me as if I were giving him the essence of life and he couldn't get enough, not even pausing to breathe. My release was swift and brutal and even as I cried out his name, I knew once wouldn't be enough.

He stood, his chin slick with the evidence of my desire, and I licked him clean of it, emboldened by the brazen way he took care of me. The taste of me on his skin raised my need, and again I felt myself wanting to see how much more of him I could take, not stopping until I had what I needed. I wouldn't accept his rejection, not this time.

I dropped to my knees and released him before he realized what I was doing, holding the length of him in my hand. I stroked him once, twice, then lowered my mouth to lick the precum beading out of him. I moaned as the salty sweetness hit my tongue then took him in my mouth, not stopping until he just reached the back of my throat.

"Fuck, Red," he hissed through clenched teeth. "That's so fucking good."

I know.

I slowly worked him in and out of my mouth, fisting my hand around what I couldn't fit at the same time, increasing in tempo as I learned what he liked. I licked him from base to tip, circling around his head, then relaxed my throat and took him as far as I was able. His hand clenched my hair again and this time he set the pace with deep, demanding thrusts that made my eyes water.

I grabbed his thighs, digging my nails into his skin as he punished my mouth. I knew he was close to finishing, but I was nowhere near done. I hummed, letting the sensation vibrate through him and he stilled, cursing on a harsh breath as I felt his release flow down my throat and I swallowed it greedily.

His breathing heavy, he lifted me from my knees and smashed his mouth against mine. I gripped my fingers in his hair, pulling him closer to me. I knew he needed more time but I was ready for him to fill me, my body aching for what I desperately craved from him. He walked backwards toward the bed, taking me with him, but suddenly the ship lurched as a powerful gust of wind caused the sea to thrash against the hull.

I broke apart from Killian and glanced outside the window, searching for the force that threatened to break the ship apart. The storm clouds were so dark they looked almost green and ominous as lightning crackled over again through the sky, lighting up the room as if fireflies danced in the air.

"This looks unlike any storm I've ever seen," I said to Killian, attempting a step toward the window, but his arm snatched around my waist and roughly pulled me back to him. I looked up at him, searching his face, wondering where the aggression came from. His pupils were still large, making his eyes almost completely black. My mind turned over the past twenty minutes. I hadn't used my power on him, had I? "Are you sure we'll be alright?"

He dipped his mouth to my ear, his scruff scratching against my neck. Shivers erupted down my spine. His voice was low, desire laced through every word. "I know I won't be all right until I'm buried so deep within you that you forget your name because you'll be too busy screaming mine."

His words unraveled me, but I couldn't let him see how affected I was. I turned away from the window and slowly trailed my eyes down his body. He wasn't ready for another round yet, but damn if I wasn't ready to let him try to prove his bold claim. He thought he could make me scream his name? I wanted to see him try.

My eyes traveled down his face, taking in the scar that marred his left eye, the vein pulsing in his neck, the way his throat moved when he swallowed. I felt like he was my prey and I had to learn everything about him before I devoured him. I smirked and flicked my eyes down once and back up again. "Are you sure you're ready, Captain?"

His pupils shifted to full black and before I had a

moment to be frightened—or more accurately, excited—he crossed the room in two swift steps and slammed me down on his desk, the platter of food scattering, chocolate and whipped cream splattered along my breasts and thighs. My legs wrapped around his waist as he bent and licked me clean. My head hit back against the wood and I cried out, welcoming the pain. I needed to feel the strength of him, to know that he could take care of a body like mine, that he could do what I needed to have him satisfy me.

Another crack of thunder sounded and a louder, more urgent noise rang out on the ship. Was that a shout of alarm? Killian buried himself in me one stroke, growing larger inside me. His eyes were so dark, it seemed as though swirls of deep blue crashed within its depths. I was ensnared in his stare, trapped in the punishing pace he set.

The ship rocked, forcing him deeper into me and I shouted, uncaring who heard me now, if anyone could hear me over the pounding of the stormy seas.

"You feel like sin, Red." He panted as he rocked into me. I felt his breath against my face but I didn't care to hear any more of his words. I wanted him to prove it.

"Faster," I said, biting his ear. He picked up his pace but it still wasn't enough. I scratched my nails against his spine. "Harder," I demanded. "Fuck me like you mean it."

He pounded into me, the wood of the desk digging into my back with every thrust and finally I could feel the need to release start to build deep within me as he kept up his relentless pace.

"There," I mewled, urging him on. My fingers dug into his lower back and I rocked my hips along his, meeting his every thrust, chasing the burst of ecstasy threatening to spill into me. "I'm so close," my breaths came out in short bursts. "More-harder-faster," I moaned, relishing the heat that spread from my core to my fingertips. "I'm so close. Don't stop...there...fuckkk."

My toes curled as desire flooded out of me and I screamed his name. A moment later Killian moaned, following me into a whirlwind of uncontrolled, stormy bliss. He rested his forehead against mine, his breath tickling my face, the sweat from our bodies making our skin stick together where it touched.

"That was unexpected," I said, a small smile spreading across my lips. I felt like I should thank him, but I didn't want to ruin the moment.

Killian's body shook with the effort to get off me, and as he slid out of me, I was surprised to find I'd felt empty where he was just a moment before. He kept his eyes down, then focused at the mess we made.

"I'll have to clean this up later," he muttered, sliding on a pair of pants and belting it closed.

My eyebrows drew together as a familiar hurt stabbed itself in my heart, causing the fissures I'd worked hard to glue together to crack open again. Bile burned in my throat. It was regret. He regretted giving in to me. Or maybe it was shame for allowing himself to fuck Julian's prized whore. I lifted myself off the table, trying as gracefully as I could to not slip in the spilled chocolate spread across the table.

"Hey, Red..." He reached out as if to touch me then immediately dropped his hand.

I scoffed. Of course, if he couldn't look at me then why could he touch me? He was probably disgusted with himself, with my body, with who I was, with what I was.

What I needed was a hot bath and a stiff drink, then I'd be able to suppress the experience until it was little more than a cold memory lying in the shadowed recesses of my icy heart.

9

There is shattering in clarity.

A pulse rippled through the ship, causing a shift in the flow of energy, making it hard to breathe. I looked around, wondering if it was the after effect of some sort of strange ocean earthquake, though it couldn't possibly be. Killian's face paled and he raced to the door without explanation. I swallowed my anger at him and quickly followed, throwing on a long shirt on my way out the door.

The main deck was absolute chaos. The mast broke clean in half, barrels and crates were everywhere, and there was a crack in the railing that continued on to the floor of the deck, as if the ship were cleaved in two. My mind wandered to Kelso's dead body and fixated on the thought of him rolling around the floor of the storage area far below deck. The crates were scattered, some of which were broken open. The wind blew glittering white and black dust through the air in a hazy swirl. *Cassov*, in its raw and refined forms. So they *were* drug pushers, just like my father used to be. The powders clumped together in the rain. That crate alone could have gotten thousands in gold coin in the black market. *Good riddance.*

June Leona wandered over to me, carefully climbing her way through the debris until she stood in front of me. "I have the strangest feeling something isn't right, but can't pinpoint it." She wiped water from her eyes and squeezed out her hair. I shivered as the rain pelted down my body. Why I thought to walk out in only a shift, I'd never know.

"The crew of this ship is basically made up of the mafia," I said, my teeth chattering. "The captain is a dickhead and their boss is the worst person I will ever have the displeasure of meeting. Also, our ship is broken beyond repair in the middle of the ocean. Maybe this is what it feels like to realize I inadvertently sold you into slavery with the worst mob that I could and now we're fucked in the middle of nowhere."

She laughed, surprisingly, but didn't seem convinced.

The triplets stacked the crates, readjusting their lids and resealing them to keep whatever was in there out of harm from the rain. Thick chunks of ice started to fall from the sky, causing small divots in the wood of the ship.

"What the fuck happened to our protection spell?" Sven said as he ran over to us. He took in the state of my undress, of the rain-soaked shirt that surely revealed everything I kept hidden underneath. For once, he didn't make a crude joke, and that had me finally start to worry. "You didn't," he said, his face serious as the rain drenched him.

A huge gust of wind pitched June back against the railing, her arms flying out to her sides as if she could catch herself, but the place where the railing once was went missing and she slipped backwards.

Willy screeched, sliding across the deck and reaching out one long arm just in time to catch her hand, gripping it as the slicked rain made it nearly impossible for them to hang on.

The triplets ran to the broken railing with rope, trying to lasso June onto the ship. June screamed, high pitched with fear as terror marred her face. The lanterns on deck threatened to go out, casting long shadows out into the darkness of the ocean. Lightning flared again, and she was finally pulled back on the ship.

Clara ran over to me, gave me one look, and said, "You didn't."

I feigned indifference, looking at my nails as the storm raged on as if I hadn't a care in the world. As if June Leona hadn't just almost died and I did nothing to save her. As if the mother of all storms wasn't threatening to cleave the earth in two. As if I hadn't given Killian a piece of me that I'd never get back again.

"Why does everyone keep saying that?" I asked. "And anyways, a careless fuck means nothing. I'd fuck you, too. After all, I'm just a prized whore, right?"

The relentless wind froze like a whispered breath, leaving the echo of a chill in the air.

Rain paused where it descended, a curtain of sleet hovering around us. I lifted my hand to the fragile drops and gently dragged a finger through them, watching as they split in slow motion into hundreds of miniscule droplets. More eerie than that, the ocean's waves ceased their relentless pounding against the ship. In fact, we were no longer swaying at all. The absolute silence in the complete darkness rang with a sense of foreboding. It felt familiar and ancient.

It felt dangerous.

"Clara?" I whispered, trying to keep the alarm out of my voice. "Tell me this is a common occurrence for this fucked up magic ship of yours."

"Sorry kitty cat," she whispered back, her eyes wide. "Can't say that it is."

"No one fucking move," Killian's voice cut through the night. The stars dimmed and flickered, but nothing else changed.

Silence, one second then another until *BOOM* something knocked itself against the hull.

"What was that," I breathed. It sounded immense. Significant. Deliberate.

A chilling note sang out sending shivers of recognition and dread down my spine. I looked at Clara, then Willy, then June Leona, but they all were frozen in place. I wasn't sure they were still breathing.

The static notes suddenly ascended in pitch until the exposition of a haunting melody was exposed. It was the song of my nightmares. The darkness undulated and something heavy pounded against the ship again. The voices rang out in the silence, piercing the shock with something more sinister.

Light flickered out of the corner of my eye, and I watched as the ocean lit up in phosphorescent colors. Green, purple, and blue all glowed under the surface as the coral reefs and the currents revealed themselves. Above, the stars glowed brighter, a rainbow of colors swirled in the wind and higher up in the sky, creating a mirror image of what happened below sea level. It was mesmerizing and disorienting, adding on to the haunting effect as more voices joined the first, harmonizing in a symphony of sound and color.

It was overwhelming and entrancing, and utterly paralyzing. The rest of the crew that I could see were unable to move. Clara's eyes were wide and bloodshot, tears streaming down her face as she struggled and failed to blink.

Though moving was as difficult as trudging through a sea of mud, I was surprised to find that I was able to at all. Why wasn't I a victim of whatever magic that took over everyone else?

A final slam against the hull of the ship reverberated through the wood and without warning, the ship tipped over. True panic overcame me as I watched the sky tilt sideways and the deep ocean meet the railing. Still, everything was frozen, and though I could move the rest of my body, my feet were glued in place. I couldn't breathe—refused to breathe—because breathing meant that I was awake and alive and not about to inexplicably tip over into my watery death.

The ocean rushed to meet us and though I'd never been the praying type, I fervently wished that the Lord of Lost Souls would guide me into the next life with ease and not judge me too harshly for the choices I was forced to make as of late.

There was nothing to be done. No way to prepare, no time to be at peace. A wall of ocean hurtled toward me and that was going to be the last thing I saw—

A sultry breeze whipped around my hair, its seductive scent surrounding me. Vanilla, musk, and something floral I couldn't place nestled into every curve, making my breasts heavy and aching with need. I exhaled, trying to control the pant that took over me. Slowly, I opened my eyes.

Deep blues of night were filled with nothing but color: glowing azure trees, rocks covered in neon moss, water that shone brilliant yellows and pinks. Even the fish were electric in the darkened water. The stars were clear, as if millions of tiny suns pierced the black veil, but more than that, endless moons and planets could be seen as if through a viewing scope.

The chilling voices multiplied, and the whisper of a plea I thought I heard underneath in all my dreams was lost in the fray. Though they were beautiful, I felt a piece of me inside want to break. I could feel my blood turn cold, the words I wanted to form turning to ash on my tongue. Pain radiated in my chest, the melody searing through flesh and muscle, tearing my sanity into pieces.

I tore my bread into pieces, utterly bored and wishing to go home. I had just finished a two-week run with father, and we sat at a tavern, his eyes furtively glancing about him. His first mate was there as well, and my mother, though she stood off to the side, speaking to one of her regular customers, keeping one ear turned toward my father. His face hovered over a tankard of ale and he was shivering. "I heard the voices again," he had said. "He's never going to leave me alone or let me out of this deal. I can't think of anything else I could trade that he'd want more than—"

"We've almost figured out how to outrun him."

"His spies are of the sea, and there is nowhere to run, anyway. All souls go to him for the sorting, don't they? He'll find me one way or another. And this fucking brand—"

"There will be others we can trade for her. Other things that he might want more."

"Of all the places in the world, Carnithia isn't one that he'll care to have riches from."

"She'll be safe. We'll keep her safe."

An old singer had sat on the barstool next to the fire, the shadow casting somber licks of darkness across his body. He slapped his hand to his thigh, creating a beat through which he started his song.

> *"When the siren calls*
> *The crew can hear*
> *An inviting path into the depths we fear*
> *But her sweeter song*
> *It is foretold*
> *Will soothe the soul as death takes hold..."*

A thunderous whump resonated as something large appeared on deck, quickly followed by a pressure that forced my crewmates to their knees. When had I started to consider them my crew mates rather than members of the crew? It was interesting how a shared harrowing experience could change the way I considered the people around me.

My gaze flickered over Sven, but snagged on something laying on the ground in front of him. The glow of the sky and plants cast an eerie green light upon the deck, allowing me to see the outline of something that looked vaguely like a body. I recoiled slightly, thinking about Kelso's week-old decomposing corpse somewhere on the ship, and wondered if that were him, somehow. I knew it couldn't be, though. Not by the long aqua hair or the way the skin shimmered under the light of the three silver moons hanging low in the sky.

There was something about it—or her. Them. There was something about them that left me feeling empty, horrified. I felt like I might have known them in a past life. Sadness rippled through me.

"Who is that?" The words barely escaped me, my voice raw with quiet emotion. *Was this what was in the crates they were offloading? Dead bodies?* I know I made a joke about it a week ago, wondering how many dead bodies they were hiding in the hull but the reality was just sick. "Sven, who the fuck is that?"

"That," a rich voice, smooth as velvet said, "is one of my own. Tell me, Captain O'Donnell, why one of my girls is trussed up and dead on my ship."

My ship. The ship belonged to him and that meant only one thing.

A wave of power pressed over the ship and again, the crew quivered and flattened against the deck, leaving me somehow unaffected.

"And you, Emersyn Jane Merona."

All thought escaped me as my mouth went dry at the sight of the man with the musical voice. Man wasn't the right word. Man would never describe someone so utterly inhuman. He was tall, thick through the chest, his forearms covered in tattoos. He was dressed impeccably in all black, his eyebrows arched as if mildly amused. His eyes were the violet of stars, with a silver ring swirling around each pupil.

Those eyes.

Every inch of me stopped and I wanted to scream but the sound froze in my chest. This being, this god, with the sensually musical lilt to his voice and a mouth that promised dirty sins was the same presence that haunted my dreams.

The shock of realization flowed through me. The ship, the way it tilted into another place, the intoxicating scent of the night, the vibrant stars, the exotic plant life, the colors that didn't exist where I was from and certainly never in Skarsrowe...the one he called his girl.

That was a siren that lay dead at my feet. The song, the music, it all made sense. Which could only mean one thing.

The being standing before me was Malakai Barron, The Lord of Lost Souls, Ruler of Vallah: the realm in between this life and the next.

The Lord of Lost Souls killed my family. He owned the crew. And he looked like he wanted to own me.

PART TWO

10

There is splintering in remembering.

Ashes blanketed the ground. The smell of burnt, decayed wood steeped the air through the hazy smoke still rising from the embers. I kicked my way through the debris, shoving away years of memories, of happiness, of love. Gone, in an instant. And for what? What grievous offense did my father commit that could have resulted in this?

Other than the precious seashell, there were only a few scattered coins barely visible across the uneven surface. Scraps that wouldn't last me a day on my own. This was a calculated attack. Everyone knew it; neighbors that once would give me treats when I was a child now had their backs toward me, as if they were afraid to look or step foot on our land because then they would be hunted, too.

Standing in the graveyard of my home, I wracked my brain

as I let the ghosts of my past seep their way into my body, wondering what a girl—a woman, now that my eighteenth birthday had passed—could do to survive.

Someone was after my family, that much was certain, and as soon as they found out I was still alive, they'd try to find me too. Just like the man who wanted to steal my sister and I, just like the countless creeps who leered at us as we walked to and from school, just like the men and women my father murdered for looking at us in a way he didn't approve of.

This had to be retaliation for a deal gone wrong. I knew he was part of a drug operation, was a mule for CASSOV and whatever else needed transporting between ports, but...this? He was one of many of his kind and nothing on this grand scale had happened to anyone else. Not unless they fell in with the wrong boss and made a promise they couldn't keep. And if that was the case, I needed to remain under the radar for as long as possible, at least until I figured out why anyone would be after my family.

There was only one place where a person could hide, if they knew the right people. Only one place where nothing, not even your identity mattered—only what service you could provide. The Tullyhouse in Skarsrowe. It was a tavern that serviced clients of a particular nature, usually sailormen who were known to be too rough for the girls at the brothel next door. I'd gone there once with my father and his first mate when they needed to glean information I was not privy to. The bartender there made decent coin, and that was what I needed if I wanted to barter my own information out of anyone. Or to go into hiding, which was my more immediate concern.

I hired a carriage with the only money I had and once I got to The Tullyhouse, Julian Murphy took one look at me as if I were something he could stick his meaty hands into and keep to himself, to slowly devour me as if I were a special kind of dessert on a menu for one. He said there was only one way I'd make any money with him, and the way he licked his lips as he stared at my body, I knew I'd backed myself into the wrong corner. He'd said he would let me buy out my contract whenever I was able to, but I knew what that meant. He'd put a price on me that would be impossible to pay. And though I tried to reason with him, to tell him I had business sense from working with my mother, I was smart, I was even a decent enough cook that the patrons would be happy with what I provided, he looked at me with his beady black eyes and sneered at my hopeful face.

"I've heard rumors that a young woman with hair the color of fine merlot wine went missing. That her whole family blew up and she was on the run now. You know anything about that?" I had spluttered some answer, but he wrapped his hand possessively around the back of my neck. "I can't seem to recall what the reward was for turning in a gem such as that, but I might remember the second you walk out this door."

"So, what? I have to be one of your sex dolls or you give me over to whoever murdered my family?"

"Now you're getting it." He leered at my clothes, at the dirt on my face, at the curves that my dress couldn't hide. "Sign the contract and prove your worth or else I will tell that person right over there—" He turned my neck, his sweaty fingers digging into my skin, forcing me to shift the direction he pointed in. "Who I suspect you are. And there will be no chance to bargain or escape. You understand, Emersyn Merona?"

He knew my name, which meant he wasn't bluffing. Panic flushed through me. "Briar," I spat out. "My name is Briar Copeland."

Julian sneered at me. "Sure it is, doll."

He took advantage of my fear, making me feel that only my body was of worth, held me hostage while I was forced to sign his contract. But it wasn't him that I blamed. I was the one naïve enough to walk in there thinking I could be a barmaid or work in the kitchens. Considering I'd had men after my body since before my curves developed, it was stupid on my part.

No, the person I would destroy is the one who came after my family, and I vowed with everything in me to break him into as many pieces as I could while I sought my revenge.

The body of a siren lay dead in front of me, her nearly translucent skin glowing shades of greens and blues as the fluorescent light of this realm shone off her. I tried and failed to peel my gaze away from the deadened eyes, the hollow cheeks, the pieces of her torso that were carved out and missing.

I should have been in awe of the place spread out before me. I should have wondered how it was real, how I happened to be lucky enough or had the misfortune of seeing it. Instead, I felt a deep chasm crack open within me as rage and sorrow fought purchase with each other. My hands clenched in fists as I noted the bruises that marred their body, the strange three-pronged markings that looked as though they were from suctions of some sort. What kind of godsforsaken creature could have done such a thing?

It wasn't until the Lord of Lost Souls blocked my view that I finally took stock of him. He towered over me, forcing me to crane my neck back to look up at him. The shadows surrounding him pulsated with a vitality that rendered it hard to breathe. Or perhaps that was just his presence.

Deep violet eyes shone through light brown skin, and his face was covered in dark scruff, as if he hadn't the care to be clean shaven. His dark wavy hair almost brushed his shoulders and his sinful mouth quirked up in a predatory smile. Like he'd finally caught the mouse at last.

That man. God. Creature. That *thing* before me. He was why my life was ruined. He was the reason my family was dead, why I was forced into slavery, why I had nightmares that resulted in me screaming my voice raw every night.

He had been haunting me for years and he was no longer a ghost of what might be, no longer a flicker of a promise of revenge. He stood in front of me, so impossibly perfect, dripping with ego, bursting with sensual energy so heavy it made my breasts ache and my knees threaten to give out. And I hated him for it. He was the one who owned Killian, and judging by the way he looked ready to devour me, it was evident he thought he could own me, too.

We stared each other down, and though I tried, it was a struggle to pull away from the stars reflected in his eyes. They were cunning, as though endless galaxies were buried deep within, and I could get lost for eternity if I wasn't careful.

I would never let myself get lost in him.

The Lord of Lost Souls circled me, sizing me up, and inhaled deeply as if he could taste the essence of my soul through that act alone. Perhaps he could. He reached out a hand and twirled a piece of my hair between his fingers. Disgust overwhelmed me and I recoiled from him, letting the hate I had for everything he stood for in my life to burn through me. His mouth slashed a cruel smile.

With a wave of his hand, Malakai Barron released his hold on the crew members. As one, they crashed forward on the deck, though none dared to complain. Malakai gave me a lingering look before turning toward everyone else. He cocked his head then glided up to June. He moved as if he were on wheels rather than feet, and the image was more than a little disturbing. A long finger reached out, brushing June's cheek.

"Why has another been taken under my care without

my permission?" His voice was velvety smooth, deep like amber whiskey, and caused a thrill to run beneath my skin.

I hated it.

When no one answered he looked around as if he would single someone out. "No? No one care to say why they foolishly broke my number one forbidden rule?"

I narrowed my eyes at Malakai's back, and just as I was about to tell him he could fuck right off, Killian spoke up.

"It was me. My name is on her contract."

"No," I said, giving Killian a scathing look, my blood seething in my veins. Did I appear as though I needed protection? Though I had more than enough rage to tear him to pieces, what could I really do? He was a god, and I was nothing but the lowest form of human there was. "I saved her when her husband tried to auction her off."

"My name is on the contract," Killian said more forcefully.

"Only because I wrote it in after *I* paid for her."

Malakai looked between us and raised an eyebrow. He smiled as though amused, but his jaw clenched in irritation. I'd know that tell anywhere. It was a man holding back on saying what was really on his mind, and for some reason, I had the absurd need to know what it was. Before I could entertain that thought, Malakai shot his hand out toward Sven, who crumpled in pain, clutching his stomach and moaning at the sound of something breaking.

"Why is there a dead body on my ship, Holstrøm?"

Sven curled in fetal position, writhing as the torture went on. It was cruel, barbaric, and unnecessary. It was plain the crew was terrified of him already. There was no need to exert this force upon him.

"Stop it!" I shouted at him as I dared to take a step closer. "Stop hurting him."

Malakai whipped around to look at me with cool shock written on his face. "How interesting." He looked at each of the crew in turn then back at me. "How interesting that you would defend them after they—"

"Our course had to change," Clara hurriedly interrupted him. "We were in a hurry to leave Portsmouth after we were at risk of being discovered by Julian Murphy's right hand man, Viktor Sinclair."

He scrubbed his beard in thought, a decidedly human gesture which made me hate him more. There was nothing human about the monster standing before me.

"Is that where you've been hiding, Syn?"

I bared my teeth at him. "My name is Emersyn."

He turned mocking eyes at me. "Or perhaps you would prefer I call you '*Little Red*'?"

That name. How could he know? The sheer audacity he had to call me what my family always called me when he was the one who murdered them.

"Hmm? No? I didn't think so, *Syn*." Shadows clung to his clothes, to his skin, making him appear as though he were an apparition. It felt almost misplaced in such a beautiful place, which made it all the more sinister. He smirked at me again then whipped around to face Killian.

"Captain?" His voice was whisper soft and deadly, seeping into the darkest recesses of my mind, finding all the hidden truths I kept locked away. He wasn't even speaking to me and I felt myself start to shred apart, echoes of pain rippling through my mind, sending signals of alarm to the rest of my body. I wouldn't want to learn what it would be like if he actually did own my soul. "Why is there a dead siren on my ship?"

"We found one that wasn't completely torn to pieces. We thought you'd want to see the markings on her."

Malakai's eyes hardened as he looked again at the siren. He raised his hand over her body and a dark glow emanated from him. The body rose, and for a moment I wondered if she would come back to life as a reanimated nightmare, but the song of the sirens changed to one of ethereal mourning, and I realized that he was giving her body the respect he believed she deserved.

How could a man—a god—exhibit such empathy, such sadness? In all the old bedtime stories children were told, and later on the more lurid legends that were shared over drinks in seedy taverns, The Lord of Lost Souls was meant to be a murderous, ruthless, fearsome god. I had seen evidence of all that in just a few moments in his presence, but the emotions he showed toward the slaves he owned gave me pause. Did they mean more to him than just harbingers of lost souls? Was he capable of caring or even loving them?

As soon as the body landed on the shore, Malakai whipped his head back around to Killian, all the menace from before dripping from his features. "What happened to Kelso?"

Killian clenched his jaw as if he were debating if the punishment for not answering would be worth it. "You know what happened to him."

"How?" The word slithered out of Malakai's mouth. "How did it get to the point where my Syn delivered me not one, but two souls?"

My Syn. The way he laid claim to me, to the fragments of all I was, drowned me in white-hot fury. Yet, there was a tinge of something else mixed in with the anger, something that made my nipples harden and thighs clench together.

Unbidden, unwanted desire.

Shame at being attracted to the murderer of my family

washed through me in the silence that followed, heating my face, causing me to look anywhere but at him, at the cause to my guilt and my lust. Even the whispers through the trees that surrounded the lagoon stopped their tune. The voices of the sirens, so mesmerizing, melding with the bright lights illuminating the plants and sea life had ceased, the last note echoing around us. The wind halted and the ship no longer rocked on the open water. The crew looked at each other, waiting to see if anyone would tell him what he waited to hear.

A blood curdling scream rent the air as Clara fell to the deck, clutching her head. The scream died down and she writhed in pain. My breath caught in my chest. The next moment, Willy was down, their scream echoing in the night. Then Sven again, then the triplets as one, as if their pain resonated within each other. Then finally Killian, his eyes turned to slits and his teeth sharpened to points. His veins protruded from his neck, turning black as they spread down his arms and chest.

"Stop! What are you doing to him?!"

"Something you want to say, my sweetest Syn?"

"Stop hurting them!" I tried to control my breathing, tried to keep my anxiety at bay, but black spots formed in front of my vision and my heart raced as the world felt as though it were collapsing in on my chest. I wouldn't let anyone else get hurt because of me, because of selfish mistakes I had made. There had to be a reason why no one else told them it was me who killed Kelso and why. What other choice did I have though? "I killed him. He called me a whore and said that was all I'd be good for and then I lost control."

"A...whore?" Malakai's eyes hardened as he looked me up and down. As if he were judging me, too.

A monster, who dealt with tainted souls, who murdered people at whim, dared to judge me. As if I were the vile creature. As if I were worthless.

"Is that where you've been hiding all this time?" he asked, running his hand through the stubble on his face. It was another human gesture, so at odds with who he really was. It was all too easy to forget it wasn't just a man I was dealing with. He cocked his head to the side as he studied me. "Lift up your sleeve."

The attention he gave me felt as though I were being picked apart; all of my emotions and feelings attached to that word—whore—and what I had to do to survive unraveled under his stare. Or rather, what *he* forced me to do to survive. He raised an eyebrow as I made him wait, anticipating when he would turn his magic onto me and make me scream for mercy, too.

"If I want to make you scream for mercy, I assure you, I won't be doing anything you aren't already begging me for."

My cheeks flushed at his implication and a strange thrill of pleasure ran through me before I remembered what he was and the whisper of danger that permeated each word he uttered. I looked down at my sleeve, still wet from the storm before we appeared in Vallah. It clung to me, revealing the shape of who I was, only a thin veil covering the truth on my skin. I was just able to discern the tattoo Julian branded on me, marking me as his. Certainly, that's what Malakai Barron wanted to see. To know which mob boss he'd have to thank or destroy for keeping me away from him for the past seven years.

"The longer you hesitate, the more inclined I am to give you that punishment you're so desperate to see from me."

My mouth dropped open but I failed to string together

any words that would express my outrage. I glanced quickly to see if the crew heard what he just said to me. Judging by Sven's widened eyes and the way Killian bared his teeth at Malakai, I would guess they had. My cheeks flushed. What did it mean that I felt excited over the thought of public humiliation? Especially after living the way I had the past seven years? Excitement mixed with the shame I already felt for having these conflicting emotions.

He continued, his words heating through me like melted wax warming the secret parts of me. "Yes, I know you'd like that. I know everything when it comes to your wants and needs. Now lift. Up. Your. Sleeve."

His eyes narrowed slightly, his fingers flexing as if imagining them clenched around my throat. I could see he was at an end to his patience, and I knew without a doubt that I had no desire—sexual or otherwise—to be humiliated in front of everyone. The impulse to defy him was strong, but so was the unexpected desire to please him. Or at least placate him. I rolled my eyes, one childish act of defiance I thought I could get away with, and slowly lifted up my sleeve.

He was by my side in an instant, his fingertip grazing my cheek. I recoiled in disgust but he acted as though he hadn't noticed. "You, Little *Red*, are quite the bratty one, aren't you?" His eyes drifted to my lips then trailed down my arm until they landed on the tattoo that marked me as Julian's prized whore. A sound much like a hiss escaped his mouth and he launched forward, intending to snatch my arm but he pulled himself short at the last minute, smoothing his hands down the front of his coat as if to maintain an air of control. "May I?" he asked through clenched teeth.

I was so taken aback by his request for consent that I

moved my wrist closer to him to examine without hesitation.

The same finger that caressed my cheek now roved over the tattooed skin. Shivers tore through me as I felt it deep in my core, as if he were stroking another, entirely inappropriate area. I refused to let him see how that single touch affected me, though judging by the cocky smile that sprang on his face, he knew exactly what I felt. It was almost as if he could sense it the way that I could in others, and that thought was more than a little unsettling.

Malakai stilled his finger, allowing it to rest in the center of the design, and heat as I'd never known blazed through me. Fire in my veins. Smoke in my lungs. I choked on a scream as the agony continued, though he merely only pressed his finger to my skin.

"What are you doing to her?" Killian shouted. He tried to move toward me but was held down by invisible tethers. The veins in his neck stood out as he pushed against the forces that bound him. His eyes were wide and frantic. "Let her go!"

"Tut tut," Malakai said calmly, though his mouth tightened and a tick under his eye went off. He was anything but calm. "You know better than to tell your master what to do."

Without looking in his direction, Malakai's magic tossed Killian to the ground as he writhed in pain, a victim to whatever nightmarish hallucinations were being fed to him. I was in my own personal hell and could spare no breath to defend him.

Without warning, a spear of ice ran through the fire in my veins and I released a short whimper of pain before the cold melted in the heat and a moan of pleasure escaped me. My cheeks burned and I looked around with wide eyes to see if anyone heard me. The way they averted their glances let me know they had. That *bastard*!

"What the fuck was that?" I hissed through my teeth.

"That, my precious Syn, was me burning the spell away from your body."

"What do you mean, 'the spell'? Julian just uses special ink to let everyone know who his whores belong to."

"This was not special ink," Malakai spat. "This was an ancient spell that hides the person from detection."

"Why would he do that?" I thought back to when I found him and what he knew about me, the things he threatened. "Was he actually trying to protect me?"

"Protect you?" He gave a mirthless laugh. "I guess from your position it would look that way, but no. He wasn't protecting you."

I looked in his starry eyes, trying not to drown in their depths as I attempted to glean the information he kept from me. What was it he didn't want to share? A painful moan cut through my concentration and awareness returned as I remembered that Killian was still hunched in pain on the ground.

"Will you let him go now? This is entirely unnecessary."

"Oh no, this is necessary and more, but I refuse to look like a murderous brute in front of you any longer, Syn." He smoothed back his hair and adjusted the lapels on his coat as if the screams of those he tortured didn't bother him. They probably didn't.

"Well it's too fucking late for that, asshole."

Malakai threw back his head in booming laughter. "You and I will have lots of fun together."

"Not. Likely."

He took in my stance, the way my wrists were held in tight fists against my sides, the way I scanned my surroundings, as if I were looking for a way to defend myself or find a way out. I would leave that to the softer ones, though. June, perhaps. That wasn't me. I craved a fight with him, needing an outlet for my rage and anguish. The thought of me tearing his eyeballs out with my bare hands was more than a little satisfying. Just as I was about to tell this Lord of Lost Souls exactly what I thought of his alpha bullshit behavior, he spoke.

"Thank you Killian." He waved his hand over the captain and left him panting on the deck but no longer in pain. "You did accomplish one of your tasks, anyway, by bringing her to me."

Blood pounded in my ears to the beat of my pulse and an odd quiet descended. A cold sweat trickled over my body despite there being a breeze that helped keep the humidity at bay.

"Say that again?" I said, my voice drowned by the rising melody of the sirens surrounding us. The waves crashed along the sandy embankment, tossing the ship as I almost lost my footing, or perhaps I forgot how to function like a normal human with my mind so entirely preoccupied by what Malakai said to Killian. I cleared my throat. "Say that a-fucking-gain, please?"

"Oh, you didn't know? I was wondering why you were defending them so thoroughly, but maybe you have a thing for being captured and brought to your Master. Who's to say?"

I looked at each of the crew members in turn, and even June looked away, as if she was well aware of what he referred to. Clara's mouth hung open, as if she wanted to explain but couldn't—or wouldn't. Sven stared at the ground. Willy chewed on their lip, arms wrapped around themself. At last my eyes landed on Killian who stood straight, his own eyes boring back into me, tearing me apart as if he hadn't already shred me to pieces by his earlier rejection.

"One of our assignments was to find you and bring you to him, unharmed."

"Ah-ah-ah," Malakai interrupted. "Untouched. You were supposed to bring her *untouched*." Electricity crackled between his fingers. "Is she untouched, Captain?"

"Bring me...to the Lord of Lost Souls." I shook my head, disbelieving. "But you said you were trying to get me out." Was I really that naïve? Was I no better than my paying customers, who believed a pretty lie I told them just because I had the talent to do so? I thought back to how he was under my window the night I fled Julian and the contraption he had with him that seemed to point at me. Why hadn't I thought that was strange then? Or did I? I couldn't remember. I was in such a rush to get away from the body I left cooling on my mattress. From Julian. From certain death.

The way the ship arrived every night as if it were taunting me, the way it called me *Little Red*. Was it all against my will? Did I just think I needed to be on the ship, that it was calling me as my salvation, because the Lord of Lost Souls willed it to be so?

I backed up a step, and then another. I had no money. No weapons. No idea how to get back to the real world. I sure as fuck wasn't going to stay here with the psychopath who killed my family, and the crew who wanted to turn me over to him. I had just started to consider them as *my* crew. More than that—my friends.

The betrayal sliced deep. More than being called a whore. More than the incessant need to prove my value. And this time, when Malakai turned his sadistic punishment onto the crew again for not discovering who or what was causing the death of so many sirens, I did nothing to stop him.

"Syn," he turned his attention onto me, "I would love for you to have dinner with me."

The casual way he said it was as if we were old friends catching up after months of not seeing each other. "Are you out of your mind?"

"Not at all." He laughed, the sound extremely out of place with the screams of terror from each of the crew members. "At least I don't lie, unlike these rats who would have gnawed off each other's arm just to deliver you to me. At least with me, you know exactly what you get. Now, there is much we need to discuss. Some things to get out of the way before you settle in here."

"I am not settling in anywhere near Vallah. I have a life. I have—"

"You have a life you ran away from. You are accused of murder for not one, but two people. Both of which you admitted to, and even if you hadn't, your name is marked on their souls. I knew the moment you killed them where I could find you. Now I'm a patient god, but I will not be kept waiting any longer."

He grabbed hold of my arm, squeezing it just enough to let me know that there was no chance he'd let me go. "You're coming with me."

II

There is magic in forbidden things.

My mother taught my sister and I from a young age that magic was real, though we should never hope to ever see it. It was reserved for those who angered the gods, or for those who were chosen to follow whatever whim a god fancied. It was for witches. For the mystics. For the sinners who were too stained with the lust of their crimes to ever be forgiven.

She had assured us that we were not part of that elite group. It prevented me from wishing for some dashing prince to whisk me away into a storybook life. It stopped me from dreaming of ways I could cultivate my own magic and brew my own herbs—although that, I think, was more of her fear of the gods. It prevented me from wanting a life

I'd never be able to have. She couldn't have known that I'd end up on a magical ship, owned by one of the most nefarious gods that existed, nestled safely inland in Vallah.

Malakai and I stood upon a hill just past the beach where *Vox in Ventum* was docked, allowing me a full view of his domain. The grass felt soft under my boots, and every now and then a firefly would shimmer as if caught between realms. The stars flashed overhead, along with the swirls of deep blues and purples that afforded us a unique look into the galaxies beyond this earth. The same image could be seen in Malakai's eyes. The sultry ocean air was spiced with the scent of tropical flowers and fresh coconut husks, with an underlying hint of something more earthy, something darker. Something that belonged to the male standing next to me.

The Kingdom of Vallah, if it could even be called a kingdom, was the most entrancing place I'd ever seen. Though the realm was said to live in eternal darkness, the hint of sunshine permeated everything, as if the last golden rays had just dipped under the horizon. It felt warm and safe. Comforting. A part of me even wanted to admit that it felt a bit like home, somehow.

Malakai loosened his grip on my arm and moved to hold my hand instead.

I stepped back, appalled at his audacity. "You dare try to hold my hand after taking me against my will? Have you ever heard of the word consent?"

"Yes, Little Red," he purred, stepping closer to me. His words caressed against my skin, burrowing down to the bone, to the marrow, to the heart of what made me feel alive. They awakened something deep within me, a feeling I should loathe to experience from him, that filled me with disgust, yet I felt a part of me crave his next words, just to see the effect they would have.

His frame towered over mine, though I noticed the shadows no longer played near his feet. Without them, he was nearly like any other man I'd come across. That's all I had to keep telling myself.

"I can feel what you're feeling. I know what your desires are. You would have chosen to come with me. I wouldn't have whisked you away from your captors otherwise."

"You do realize that *you* are my captor, seeing as you sent them after me."

He shook his head and lightly touched the back of my shoulder to get me moving. Heat seared where his fingers grazed me as he led me down the lush hillside and into a valley filled with thousands of tiny flowers illuminating the night. Bright pinks, purples, and blues shone around me, and a yellow pathway lit up the closer we got to the field, as if it were activated by our motion alone. It would have been almost romantic, with the heavens swirling full of planets and comets above us, the beautiful alluring song of the sirens still on the warm breeze, the colors forming an atmosphere of whimsy. I might have loved it, if the circumstances were different.

Butterflies fluttered near our ankles as we strode across the field, his purposeful steps dripping with the arrogance of someone who knew they would be followed. He stopped abruptly and I had to jerk back before walking into him. The less contact we made, the more likely I would be to hold onto my hate and anger rather than play with the idea of something far less responsible that had been churning within me.

Glancing around him to see why he stopped, my jaw

dropped at the awe-inspiring view before me. A huge lake sprawled in front of us. The water shimmered like diamonds in the moonlight, giving off a floral scent, and the grass at the edge of the embankment was soft under my boots, as if I walked on clouds rather than the firm ground. I had never seen such beauty in Carnithia. There was only the harsh coastline, the rocky beaches, the flat fields inland. But in Vallah, a realm that defied all logic, my eyes misted over at a thick forest lining the opposite side of the crystalline lake and a huge ice-capped mountain range in the distance. It was breathtaking.

Malakai waited at the edge of the embankment, and for the first time since entering his realm, I saw another creature other than the monster that stood next to me. A deer walked to the edge of the lake, lapping at the water, utterly unconcerned that two people were standing there. Malakai stepped around me and stroked the deer's brilliant white coat, and to my surprise, it made a noise of contentment.

"This is Mira. Her and her family live in the Druskian Forest across the way."

I looked at him as if he were crazy, which he clearly was if he expected me to care that he decided to name the wild animals that lived in his realm. I was about to say as much when the deer came over and nuzzled my hand, forcing me to acknowledge her. Warm feelings of welcome and joy washed over me, spreading little shocks of happiness that emanated from where I touched her.

I smiled at the doe. "It's nice to meet you, too, Mira."

"Could you hear her?" Malakai asked. His eyebrows drew down in a calculating look.

"What? No. But she felt welcoming. I don't know. Is there something different about her?"

His face remained impassive as he scrutinized me. *How can he make me feel so dumb in his presence with a single look?*

He was the one to ask if I could hear a fucking animal speak in my mind.

It was a swift reminder of the hate I held for him. *Why* I hated him.

"Interesting."

Before I could ask him what exactly was interesting, he dismissed me with a turn of his heel and walked directly on the water. He strode toward the middle of the lake, leaving me with Mira on the bank. It wasn't until he reached the center that he looked back and realized I wasn't next to him.

He pointed in the space next to him. "Now."

"I'm not really in the mood to drown tonight," I called to him. "Not all of us are gods who can walk on water."

Dark amusement rippled toward me. "As much as the sound of you calling me a god excites me, I did no such thing. Look down."

I glanced at the water, noticing a shiny reflection looking back at me. It appeared to be made of glass, or something close to it. Taking a tentative step forward, then another, I was surprised to find that he was right.

Once I reached the platform he stood upon, a spray of water swept over and encased us like a bubble, blocking the outside world under its protective waterfall that surrounded us. It reminded me of the stories I read about the Lord of Sea and Storms' realm. Deep under the ocean, according to the legend, there is a vast kingdom called Kashura ruled by Malakai's brother, Lord Eos, that is encased entirely within a shimmering mirage of spherical essence. It sounded ridiculous, but if a miniature version of it existed in Vallah, I wondered what it would look like on a grander scale.

The platform shifted, jarring me enough to lose my

balance and tip onto Malakai, forcing me to grab his forearm to stop myself. My skin vibrated where it touched his, the tattoos creating a shock where my fingertips laid upon them. He glanced down at me with a raised brow, flicking his eyes between my face and the spot where my hand grabbed his arm as he waited for me to pick myself off of him.

Asshole.

We descended into darkness, the only light coming from the fish and currents that held the same luminescent glow as the ocean. I shifted from foot to foot, growing restless the longer I was alone with him in such close proximity. Sharing the same breathing space as the person who murdered my parents felt like a betrayal to their memory. The urge to obliterate him set fire to my blood that would only be doused when I held his heart in my hands.

"You are quite bloodthirsty, aren't you?" he mused.

"Stay the fuck out of my head," I spat at him, finding the elusive kernel of hatred and gripped tighter to it. "And you're one to talk. Your entire existence is devoted to determining the fate of souls. You could bring people back from the dead if you wanted to."

"That's not how it works, and no, I cannot bring people back from the dead. Certainly not at a whim. Who is it that you are hoping to see alive again?"

I scoffed. As if he didn't know.

The platform we stood upon jolted to a halt and the water around us receded, revealing a magnificent circular room. A large white oak desk stood to the right in front of a wall of books with a beautiful linen couch on the wall opposite. A woven blue rug sat in between with a white coffee table laden with tea and cookies atop it. Opposite where we stood was a wall of windows with a balcony situated just beyond. Curtains billowed on a phantom breeze and a tropical scent hung in the air.

"What is this place?" I asked, stepping foot into the room. As soon as I did, the waterway sealed itself to reveal a plain wooden door instead. "Aren't we under the lake? How is there sunlight? How is it day time in a land of eternal night?"

"Does this room please you?" The deep timbre of his voice and the way he said 'please' sent another wave of excitement through me, and I took a moment to appreciate the way his pants formed to his backside as he walked over to the tea tray and poured me a cup. He extended it, waiting for me to accept his offering. It seemed dangerous, somehow. Like if I accepted it, I was accepting an entirely other thing as well.

I raised an eyebrow. "Do you really expect me to accept anything you give me? How do I know it's not drugged?"

His laughter was cut with a tinge of something darker, like a warning. "I don't need drugs to get you to do what you want. You are curious." He said the word on a whispered breath and I let his honeyed words lazily flow over me. "The danger I present is exhilarating to you, isn't it?"

It was unsettling the way he knew my thoughts and feelings though I'd never expressed them to anyone before. "Stay out of my head."

"I wasn't in your head." He smirked. "I just know your type."

"I'm not a type," I said, irritation breaking through. What did that even mean? I was nothing.

His eyes roamed my body, lingering on my neck before trailing back up to my face. He smirked. "Sure you're not."

Remember you hate him. Remember you hate him.

Exhaustion coursed through me. I had been up for

nearly twenty-four hours, and after a night of drinking, having a regrettable round with Killian, and then the storm that led us to Vallah, I was ready to sleep and chalk it all up to a bad dream.

"This is where you'll spend the night. The bedroom is just through there," Malakai said, pointing at a door to my left I hadn't noticed before.

I narrowed my eyes at him. "You are out of your fucking mind if you think I'm going to spend the night here with you. Wherever this is. And I wouldn't do it if it were the last safe place and the Dracon were biting at my heels. Assuming I would want to is insulting."

His nostrils flared. "This is your assigned room in the Palace of Souls. My home. It is the only safe place for you in the world." Silence hung between us before he gestured to the couch while he leaned against the desk across the way. "Sit. Now. We have things to discuss."

His tone left no room for argument, though denying his request was tempting, if only to see if he really would have punished me like he threatened on the ship.

Remember you hate him.

I obliged him only because I was dead on my feet. Though the plush cushions tempted to draw me in, I kept my back stiff, my shoulders thrown back, balanced on the edge of the cushion refusing to relax in the presence of a predator.

"Speak and then return me to the crew."

"Ah, so you still feel loyalty to them even though they lied to you for...how many days has it been? Nine? Ten?"

"I was only using them as a means to escape. I want to return to Carnithia and—"

"And what? Hide? Be on the run for the rest of your life?" His condescending tone grated on my nerves. And how could he make such a large space feel so small? The scent of him was everywhere. I could feel him on my skin though he was on the other side of the room. He shook his head and folded his arms, causing the veins in his forearms to stand out against the pressure. I found myself mimicking him.

"You are being hunted for murder and judging by the strength of that tattoo, your owner will not give you up so easily."

"What did you mean earlier, when you said it was a spell to hide me?" I rubbed my wrist, remembering the heat that blazed through me as Malakai burned his magic through me. "Julian tattoos all his girls."

"Ah, but you are the only real treasure in his trove, are you not?" He walked over to a sideboard with various liquors and poured himself a glass of bourbon. "Would you like one?"

Surely he was not that dense. If I didn't accept tea from him, I certainly wouldn't accept anything else.

"Suit yourself." He gulped his drink down before pouring another.

"Do gods even get drunk?"

He downed his second glass then leaned against the desk. The silence that followed let me know he had no intention of answering my question. A clock in the next room ticked as the seconds trickled on.

"That tattoo was not made with special ink to let people know you are his special whore." He spat the word as if it were a vile thing, which surprised me, considering he owned countless sirens. They were the epitome of the word *whore*, luring anyone with questionable morals and getting them to do whatever they wanted. That was nothing like me.

Was it?

"That ink," he continued, "was imbued with a spell that hides you from your rightful owner. It's extremely complicated. The key ingredient requires the essence of your owner, which would have been nearly impossible to reproduce. You are kept off that person's radar until the spell is broken. Yours would have been impossible to break without death or someone with my...talents."

"So you just put me in more danger? He can find me now?!" I shot up and headed for the door to...what? To leave? Did Julian have a way to Vallah? Had he made a deal with Malakai?

"Relax." His command shot through me as though a compulsion forced my racing thoughts to calm themselves. I felt my muscles loosen and my mouth went slack. It was almost a pleasant feeling. Yet another he gave me against my will. "This is the only place where you are safe. That vermin is not welcome in this realm and I assure you, if his soul finds its way to me, he will not be shown mercy."

A storm brewed in his violet eyes and for a moment I thought I saw electricity crackle within their depths.

"If I'm safe from him then why does the tattoo remain if the spell is broken?"

"I can remove it." It was another one of those open-ended statements, the kind where if I accepted, I might also be accepting an unspoken offer. Dangerous, from the Lord of Lost Souls.

As he was quick to point out, danger was one thing I couldn't say no to.

I looked down at my brand, the most obvious physical marking of my shame. Of what I felt I had to do to survive. The person I blamed for everything, driving all my choices, was now offering to get rid of it as if the past seven years of my life never happened. As if he could just erase that blemish and I'd be able to move on.

"It would be the first step to reclaiming your power. To help you move forward. Julian, or any other fuck who thinks they can claim you, will never get their hands on you again."

The need to do what he said was a compulsion, something I had wanted to do for years and was only daring enough to do ten days before. But distrust flew swiftly on its heels.

Why did it matter to him if I reclaimed my power, much less through the one who caused me to end up indentured to begin with?

"And what's in it for you? You work in bargains, right? Deals? Do you expect me to give you a piece of my soul just to get rid of one of many scars?"

"I would never take what you aren't willing to give."

It was an annoying non-answer, one that gave me pause. If I allowed him to remove the tattoo, what would that small victory mean for him? If he could sway me, perhaps he would think he could get me to do anything. I would not act as one of his property, to do whatever he desired. But if I didn't allow him to remove it, I'd have Julian's stain for the rest of my life. I'd always wonder if someone was treating me differently because of the brand on my wrist. I'd never believe in the sincerity of others, would never stop to give others the chance at friendship, because who would possibly want to be friends with a whore? And if there was one thing I needed in my new life, it was companionship.

Before I could talk myself out of it, I held my wrist out to him, a silent acceptance of his offer. Of whatever else it was he was asking me. Whatever else he needed my approval of.

I might not have been signing my soul to the devil himself, but what I agreed to give him was worth so much more.

Access to all of me.

12

There is vulnerability in honesty.

As we got older, my sister Gabby and I would get into arguments that would escalate until we'd go days on end without speaking. I never really had many friends outside of her. People in Hammerford were scared of my father, so any friends we did have were the result of forced companionship. Gabby and I were all each other really had. I was devastated when the arguments became more frequent as we got older.

Sometimes they'd start off small. I would take her hair clip without her permission, or we'd squabble over what lyrics were correct in our favorite tavern songs. For whatever reason, they would inevitably grow into something larger and uglier.

One day, when I was fourteen and Gabby was sixteen,

we fought over a secret tryst she'd had with one of the girls from our village. I had just returned from a trip with my father to the northern coast of Carnithia, and had been eager to spend time with Gabby again. I caught her sneaking from our room long after the sun went down and our father's snores echoed in the halls of our home. It was the usual time where we would catch up and share secrets and dreams with each other, and I'd been looking forward to doing it again.

"Where are you going?" I whispered. "I want to come with you."

"Go back to sleep," Gabby responded. "You can't just return home and expect me to want to stay with you."

It hurt when she said that. For years, it was always the two of us. I knew we'd grown apart in some ways, with me always wishing to be on the water with father and her wanting to remain with mother. But she was my constant, the one thing I knew I could always return to.

"Are you seeing Penellope again?" I asked. "Father will go mental if he catches you."

"You're just jealous," she spat at me. "I have someone and you don't. She's a wonderful friend who never leaves me, and she just happens to be interested in me the same way as I am in her."

"Are you saying I'm not a wonderful friend, then? Because I always leave?" I thought she understood how the sea called to me, how the need to be a part of it was inexplicable, and that even then, I was in pain for not being on the open waters. "You are always welcome to come with us."

"You don't get it, Emersyn." *Emersyn.* I couldn't remember the last time she'd used my full name. "For once,

I want people to pay attention to me, to think I'm the beautiful one. I'm tired of competing with you."

The jealousy she had of me was always there, though I never understood it. We were sisters. Why would there be competition among us? "I just wanted to spend time with you," I said, clutching my blankets, staring as the knuckles of my fingers turned white against the fabric. "There isn't anything more than that."

The moon cast a faint light into the room, allowing me to see the curls of her hair, the upturn of her nose, the sneer that marred Gabby's face. "With you, it's always something more."

MALAKAI SLOWLY WALKED over to me as I sat on the edge of the couch, then kneeled on the carpet between my knees. I was suddenly painfully aware of my severe lack of undergarments. We were nearly at eye level, though the submissive position he held while I looked down at him filled me with a different power I'd never felt before. A god was on his knees for me. I smirked, and the earlier shame at the attraction I held toward him changed to something that felt like confidence, like something *more*.

Our breath mingled as he grabbed my arm, treating it as if it were a precious jewel. I looked anywhere but his eyes, not wanting to get lost in their stormy depths, and instead focused on his face, the curve of his full bottom lip, the freckles that lightly dusted his nose. How could he get freckles without sunlight?

My heart thumped in my chest, each beat feeling as though it would break my bones. My mouth ran dry as his fingers caressed the brand on my wrist, and all thought except what it felt like to have him touch me trickled away.

"One day you'll learn to trust me, Emersyn. The only thing I'll get out of it is the satisfaction of knowing that Julian, that sick fuck, will no longer think to have any claim over you."

The day I trust him will be the day the oceans run red and diamonds fall from the sky. Deciding to voice that particular notion to a god was unwise, so I glanced toward the windows where it was clear daylight poured in, and focused on anything other than how attuned he was to every move I made. "How is the sun here? I thought this was the land of eternal darkness."

He swiped three fingers across the ink, brushing my skin as tiny pulses of electricity shot through it. There was just enough pain to make it a pleasurable feeling and I found it hard to focus. "That isn't the sun. I can manipulate the plants to a point where they might glow brighter and mimic something like the sun that you're used to. I thought it would acclimate you better to this realm."

"Why did you steal me away from the crew?" He continued his ministrations as I pelted him with questions. "Why have you been looking for me?" And then the question I wanted to know above all else, "Why did you murder my parents?"

"Ahh, now we get to the root of it. Is that why you harbor such ill will toward me?" He stood from his kneeled position and stared down at me. Everything I felt, the anger, the hatred, the unwanted lust, all competed to be the primary feeling as I craned my neck, hoping to catch a glimpse of honesty on his face. "I didn't murder your parents."

"Bullshit!" I shot up from the couch. Rage won out, stirring a bloodlust in me. The same kind that drove me to hurt Kelso when he was obviously already dead, though I chose not to act on it. I had to keep myself in check. It was a god I was speaking to. He could send me into the afterlife with a snap of his fingers if I wasn't careful. "I spent years, *years* thinking it was just a deal gone wrong. That my father made promises he couldn't keep and the attack on him was retaliation."

"Where did you hear that?" His eyes narrowed to slits but had no other reaction. His calm demeanor did nothing to cool the blaze I felt toward him. "Why would you think I had anything to do with it at all?"

"What?" I was distracted, the buzzing in my veins too loud for me to think clearly. "Julian told me that when I signed my contract with him."

"He told you that I was after your parents? Or that *someone* was?" I wracked my brain, trying to remember. I didn't know. I wasn't sure which...

"How quick you were to believe him, yet every word that comes out of my mouth is an apparent lie?" His features darkened and the shadows he held at bay flowed away from his body, stretching throughout the room. Reaching for me. "You're welcome, by the way."

I glanced at my wrist, unmarred as it had been the day my entire life changed. A tinge of regret swept through me. How easy it was to make something as though it never were. If only darker memories didn't leave an unrepentable stain to the soul. I glared at him instead of thanking him, not caring if my immaturity showed just then. He didn't deserve my thanks.

"There was a deal between your father and I that he made many years ago." Malakai's voice was soft, as if he wasn't sure if he wanted to share what knowledge he had.

My eyes roved over his face, looking for any tell, anything to give away a hint of a lie, but there was nothing to indicate his deception. "He drowned in a storm, and the sirens sent his soul to me. Since he was of a...questionable nature, I had the opportunity to decide what happened to him."

I tried to keep my breathing under control. My father had died? He really did make a deal with The Lord of Lost Souls? I had a suspicion but to have it confirmed was another thing entirely. "What was the deal?"

"He murdered one of my sirens before he drowned. I told him he was to give me one of his daughters in exchange. He told me he'd give his second daughter, who did not yet exist. When it came time for him to deliver, he refused and took great lengths to hide from me. My usual summoning methods with those who gave me a piece of themselves did not work, so I recruited a few I owned to find him. They were meant to deliver him to me alive."

I turned my head toward the balcony windows, not wanting him to see the sudden burning in my eyes as tears threatened. He took a step closer and placed a single finger under my chin, forcing me to look in his eyes. I cringed at his touch, at the way he barely had to crane my neck back at all with how willing I was to look at him.

"The orders were only to bring him to me. Your family was never meant to be harmed. I just wanted what I was owed."

"Why would he promise me to you?" I hated that my voice shook, hated that I didn't know if this was a truth I could handle. There was so much I didn't know about my father, though I'd spent so much time with him. There was so much he'd kept from me. But if Malakai thought for a minute that I believed he wasn't behind my parents' death, he was insane.

His eyes bore into mine as he stilled. I felt naked, every vulnerable emotion on display for him to devour. The stars in their depths twinkled and deep violets and blues swirled together. He looked like a predator as he cocked his head, and a real fear started to seep into me. There was nothing human about the creature standing in front of me and I would do well to remember it.

"You will stay the night," he said, his voice a rumble of quiet thunder through me. "There are clothes and a warm bath through the other room." He leaned closer to the spot on my neck he stared at earlier and inhaled, his canines sharpening at something he smelled. "Wash the scent of him off you before I return."

The door clicked shut behind him.

13

There is terror in remembering.

The first time panic gripped me was after almost a month in Julian's employ. It started off gradual, before coming on all at once. It was the locked door, night after night. It was not knowing whether the hours would be filled with men and women who saved enough coin to spend an hour with me, or if my body was to be used as a way for Julian to fill one of his debts. It was the threadbare sheets, the creak of the hinges when the door opened. The threat of Viktor Sinclair doing to me what he liked to do with the other girls in the early hours of the morning, when everyone pretended not to listen. When no one could do anything to end it.

The first time it happened—the panic—it was the same as any other night. The locked door, the waiting for clients, the threat of Viktor. But that night, the walls had closed in on me. That night, sweat broke out over my body and my heart raced so quickly, it threatened to jump out of my chest. That night, my vision blurred and I just knew my prayers had been answered. I knew the Lord of Lost Souls was preparing to lead me on to whatever came next.

Except I recovered. All of my begging and wishing for him to save me from the hell I resigned myself to, pleading that he send his Dracon after me, to render my soul to him, went unnoticed. And then, the panic set in again with the lock of a door, the quiet pulse that thrummed through my room while I waited to see who next claimed their piece of me, the fear that it would be my turn with Viktor.

And now, after remembering the freedom of the open seas and the promise of salvation nestled on the horizon, I was caged, again. A tsunami of panic crashed over me.

That bastard.

The handle was cold in my grip and refused to turn no matter how hard I shook it. My fist pounded against the door. "Let me go at once!"

Cold sweat trickled down the back of my neck. Breathing became difficult, as my lungs pumped harder to open the airways that threatened to close. My vision spotted and blood rushed in my ears. I tried to keep the panic down. Tried to hold it at bay. Tried to...I tried to...I tried to.

Bile crept up my throat and the room spun as I worked my way toward hysteria. Tears sprang forth from my eyes, the salt of them burning the crack that had formed in my lips from days in the sun. I rested my hand against the wall, my fingers gripping the grooves in the shiplap, curling against the exposed edges. Breathing in for four counts and releasing for six, I repeated the pattern until my heart stopped its assault of punching its way through my chest. I dragged my hand away from the wall and walked on unsteady legs back to the couch and poured myself a glass of water.

Trapped. Again.

The water soothed my sore lungs but my stomach cramped as I realized I hadn't had anything to eat in hours. The tea and pastries looked tempting, but if they were laced with something like *cassov* or worse, I could very well end up passed out for hours and imprisoned in an even worse way. I'd seen it happen all too often with the other whores and I had no intention of putting myself in that position.

My eyes scanned the room and lingered on the billowing curtains and the balcony outside. I'd already attempted freedom from jumping out a window once. Perhaps Eosa, the Goddess of Fate, would be on my side again.

The glass doors stretched open when I approached as if they were waiting for me to make my escape, but I paid little attention to them as my breath caught at the view laid before me.

Lush fields of wildflowers met rolling hills, with streams and rivulets of water dissecting the land as they flowed lazily toward the gleaming ocean in the background. To the left of me were beautiful gardens overflowing with plants and fauna I didn't have names for, each more exotic looking than the last, while the right side gave me a spectacular view of the Druskian Forest and the white-capped mountains beyond.

Two moons hung low in the sky, the full moon providing most of the light while the crescent highlighted the stars surrounding it. Vallah was spectacular, and I longed for it in a way that made me ache with homesickness. It felt as if a piece of me had been missing, but there it was, laid out before me. As if I belonged there.

But it wasn't my home. Carnithia was—and though it offered me nothing, I had nothing in Vallah either, regardless of how much a part of me ached for it.

Steeling my resolve, I walked to the railing and peered down to see how far the drop would be. "Fuck."

My balcony stood at least seven stories up from the ground, not nearly close enough for me to jump. The outside of the Palace of Lost Souls was white and completely smooth. There wasn't a hint of brick or groove that I could use to scale down the wall, not that I would have had the boldness to do so from such a height, and wearing nothing but a shift.

Furious, I stomped back inside and tried to find any other means of escape. The desk was entirely bare, save for paper and writing implements. The drawers were empty and useless. All of the books lining the shelves appeared to be myths from Carnithia and other lands, many in languages I'd never seen before. I couldn't waste too much time there, unless I wanted to find the largest tome to smash over his head when he returned to fetch me.

The bedroom was a dark contrast to the bright sitting room. Black silk sheets and deep red velvet coverings furnished a bed large enough for Malakai and his entire fabled harem. My lip curled in disgust at the thought. A dark netting draped down around the bed and a wooden chest sat at the foot of it. There was an oak dresser filled with various articles of clothing and a large walk-in closet with dresses and skirts and more shoes than I'd ever know what to do with.

Double doors led into the attached private bathroom, marble and gold everywhere. In the center of the room was not a tub, but a small pool built into the tile floor, bubbling with the scent of fresh jasmine and honey. Oils and soaps lined the outside and a pile of hot towels waited in a basket next to the water.

I was overwhelmingly aware of the stench coming off me. Of the ocean water matting my hair, of the sweat and blood resulting from the storm's onslaught. Of the sex still lingering beneath my shift.

A bath wouldn't hurt, I supposed. I would think better if I were clean.

Not needing any more convincing, I stripped my shirt, leaving it heaped on the floor along with my boots and stepped into the heated sunken tub. I sat against one of the built-in seats along the side and reached for a towel, tucking it behind me like a pillow. I almost felt guilty for taking time in such pleasure without knowing what was happening with the crew. I wondered if Malakai released them from his magic's hold, if they were no longer experiencing whatever trauma he thought was best to punish them with.

But they kept so much from me. They always meant to deliver me to him. They knew more about me than I did, and probably still did, which was why the betrayal was hard to come to terms with. Spending days in such small quarters afforded us the ability to cultivate an ease with each other, if not a friendship. The night before, for once, I was happy, despite being on the run for murder.

I grabbed one of the soaps for my hair and worked it into a lather before combing it through my red locks, watching as it took on the color of freshly spilled blood in the water. Death had always surrounded me.

Maybe I was always meant to end up with the Lord of Lost Souls.

Three sharp taps on the door to the sitting room interrupted my thoughts as two people barged in, arms laden with bags and boxes. The first person had translucent skin and I could see the blue blood that ran through their veins. Dark green pixie-cut hair complimented a face with wide-set, matching dark green eyes. Their fingers were long and gripped the bags they held as if they were slippery and were in danger of sliding out of their hands. The other person matched the same features as the first, though they had pink hair and eyes instead of green. Both wore simple dark pants and a white shirt and slip-on shoes. Each appeared uncomfortable as they silently stared at me in the water.

"Can I...help you?" I asked, scrutinizing them as they quietly watched me. I cocked my head, wondering why they seemed familiar to me, until it dawned on me that I knew their kind, I just hadn't seen one alive before. They were two of Malakai's sirens. "Did you need something?"

The one with green hair averted her gaze before her eyes found mine again. "Mal sent us to get you ready for dinner." Her musical voice was soft, as if she didn't want to disturb the air around her.

Mal. The familiarity with which she said it caused an unexpected twinge in my chest.

"We're to dress you and do your hair," the other said, finally snapping herself out of her reverie, heading over to the vanity next to the closet. She dropped her bags down and looked back at me expectantly, waiting for me to leave the tub.

"Yeah, I don't think so," I said. "I wouldn't even drink the tea he offered. Why would he think I would eat anything else he tried to give me?"

The one with green hair cocked her head to the side.

"Why deny what he gives you? He's so generous. He gives us whatever we need."

I stood from the pool, no longer comfortable with bathing in front of them. Climbing the stairs slowly, I let the water trickle down my naked body and tried to press down on the unwelcome feelings that came with her statement. He gave them whatever they *need*? Considering his voice alone made my sex ache with every forbidden thought I'd ever had, I was sure I could imagine exactly what *needs* he provided.

Clearly, they were brainwashed or there was some other strange attachment syndrome that had formed. It was vile, the way he took advantage of these creatures. Even Julian never played with his toys, but it seemed as though Malakai had no qualms about it. And for some reason, jealousy threatened to surge through me.

The siren with the pink hair wrapped a towel around me and ushered me to the vanity bench. "My name is Una. That is our sister, Julep."

"Our sister?"

"My sister, I mean. All the sirens are sisters here," she said, looking at me strangely. "We heard a lot about you. Quite the adventure you've been on, haven't you?"

"Are you hoping I will gossip for the sake of giving him information? If that's his tactic, it's the wrong one." I wiped the water dripping down my forehead and looked at her in the mirror. "I don't mindlessly gossip like other chatty girls I know who have nothing to do but let their insecurities and hatred shine for the sake of putting one another down."

"That's not what we're doing," Julep said, procuring a dress rack from the closet and hanging the garment bags in her hand. "We just have been waiting a long time to finally meet you. We've never had the opportunity to leave Vallah."

"Never?" I asked. "Does he keep you on that short of a leash?"

"It isn't safe," Una whispered. "Only the ones who volunteer will leave and they aren't allowed to stray too far from the entrance into this realm."

"How many of you are there?"

"We are many," Julep said, her eyes wide with the threat of tears. "But our numbers are dwindling. Each loss feels like an ache in the chest, an essential tether to self that has snapped."

"Mal feels it worse," Una said, sniffling. "He's been out of sorts, wouldn't you say, Jules?"

"So, you mean he isn't always a murderous psychopath?" Not that it mattered. It didn't.

"Murderous?" Una gasped, the comb slipping through her fingers. "He would never harm us!"

Julep rolled her eyes at Una. "She wasn't referring to us, obviously. Why else would he recruit nearly every soul he owned to locate the thing that has been killing our sisters?" She shifted through various dresses and fabrics, finally landing on a plain black dress with a deep red stitching running through it.

"I'm perfectly comfortable with what I came here in," I said, eyeing the shabby shift in need of a good washing. Or to be set on fire. "Tell *Mal* I don't need the clothing he keeps on reserve for his lady guests."

"He doesn't have—" Una started, but Julep cut her off.

"You do realize that those clothes you're fine with wearing also came from him? As did the food you ate with Captain Killian. As did the water you drank. As did the money the crew has to spend. As did—"

"Okay, I don't need anymore of his hospitality," I amended. "I don't want dinner. I don't want to be dolled up for him." I shooed Una away as she tried to paint my lips crimson. "I don't need to change any part of me to be in his presence. And I certainly don't need to be here."

I stood from the bench, knocking it behind me as I scrambled away from them. Each step came with more determination to get out. I knew what *Mal* was doing. He wanted to show me luxury and comfort, distract me with pretty things and decadent food and give me whatever I wanted. Except he wouldn't give me the only thing I needed.

Freedom.

14

There is hunger in knowing.

I'd never gotten along with any of Julian's other girls. They were filled with envy from the moment I signed on. It wasn't my looks that did it, or even the special gift that a few of them found out I had. It was that Julian treated me slightly better than them. I was able to bathe first, so I had cleaner water. I was given the option of walking the floor some nights, whereas other girls were stuck to the confines of their room every night. I was given bread scraps while the others suffered through only over-cooked vegetables and sometimes nothing more.

Outside of Gabby, I'd never had a friend or confidante. I never really knew what it was like to trust others, because my former naive self learned quickly that trusting others meant I would get hurt. I didn't know how to form friendships or attachments without suspicion. I had started to with Clara and the rest of the crew, and because I let my guard down, I was left trying to come to terms with the latest betrayal.

But these sirens, Una and Julep, they had a feeling about them that called to me. It was much the same as the call of the land, the emotions it stirred in me. Almost like it was familiar, like it was where I was meant to be. Perhaps it was because I'd seen one of their dead sisters first hand. Perhaps it was because I knew what kind of terror she must have gone through, and the worry and sadness these two felt at losing someone. After all, I had lost a sister once, too.

If I weren't careful, I knew the two of them would find their way under my skin and burrow in the corner of my heart I'd barricaded once Gabby was gone. But they worshiped Malakai, the one responsible for me being alone in the first place, and I had to try more than ever not to let my guard down.

"Emersyn, wait." Una shuffled after me as I walked back through the bedroom, intending to try to open the door. If the sirens came in, then it should stand to reason that I'd be able to get out. Just as I turned to leave, I spotted a note left on the desk, which had been empty prior to my bath. Curiosity got the best of me so I tore open the envelope marked *Emersyn Jane* and read:

> *My sweetest Syn,*
> > *Dinner is in one hour.*
> > *Be a good girl.*
> > *Wear the black dress.*
> > *Malakai Jerohm Barron, Lord of Lost Souls, Ruler of the*
> *Kingdom of Vallah*

Disbelief ran through me at the sheer nerve of him thinking he could command me to do *anything* after locking me in my room with no way to escape. But I did need answers, and there was no way out otherwise. I thought perhaps I'd be able to get a layout of the palace, or maybe I'd be able to map out my own escape route. A cage was still a cage, no matter how camouflaged in marble it was. I tossed the note into the fireplace and watched it shrivel into ash. I wouldn't forgive him.

Taking a deep breath to center myself, I marched back into the bathroom and eyed the two sirens who both looked back at me as though I were a viper ready to attack. "I will wear the silver dress."

"But—"

"Silver."

Una looked between me and Julep then placed her arm around my shoulders, leading me back to the vanity bench. "It's easier to go along with what he says," she said. "He does nothing but take care of our needs. He's an excellent ruler to Vallah."

"This sounds like Skarsrowe syndrome."

"What's that?" Julep asked as she slid a strapless silver gown with dark blue stitching off a hanger. The swish of the silk against the floor grated on my already frayed nerves.

"It's when the indentured servants start feeling sympathetic toward their owners." I gave them each a pointed look. "When they think the owner is actually nice, or a good person, or gods forbid even a potential love match. It's not real. It's your mind's way of dealing with the horrors of what you're experiencing."

"But, we aren't victims of anything." Una tried to paint my face in kohls and rouge. I refused it all except for a blood-red lip stain. "We aren't his servants. We come from this realm and he rules it. He takes care of us like his citizens."

"So, he doesn't force you to bring back souls? Or to tempt the corrupted to get them to follow you back here so he can suck out their essence or whatever it is he does?"

"That's a grossly exaggerated explanation of what happens here," Julep replied as she directed me to step into the dress. "What you're describing is in our nature. It's just a part of who we are."

"You've never—" Una began before Julep cut her off.

"Let's work on your hair, shall we?" The two sisters shared a look between each other before smiling back at me. More secrets. More lies. And they all centered around one male in particular.

Forty-five harrowing minutes later, after much bickering over whether or not I would allow jewels and rhinestones in my hair, a knock sounded at the door.

The siren sisters looked at each other with raised brows then back at me. I'd had nearly an hour to come up with what to ask him and what to do. I smiled at myself in the mirror, steeling my reserve for contriving a way to trick the Lord of Lost Souls. "I'll let him in," Julep said as she headed for the door, but I put my arm out, barring her at the entrance to the sitting area.

"You'll do no such thing. I'm perfectly capable of doing it myself."

Smiling, I looked between the two of them as the seconds ticked on until finally, Una whispered, "What are you waiting for?"

"Absolutely nothing." If he wanted to demand my presence, I sure as hell could try to take back some level of control of my situation and make him wait a few minutes longer.

The sisters tried to keep busy as they cleaned up, but I caught them sneaking glances into the sitting room as if they could see him through the wall. Once the silence grew uncomfortable and it was clear either Una or Julep were preparing to tackle me to the ground to answer the door themselves, I rolled my eyes and headed to the entryway.

The door whooshed opened on silent hinges, revealing the Lord of Lost Souls casually leaning against the wall across the hall. He wore dark blue pants made from a material I wasn't familiar with and a black shirt with buttons down the middle. His sleeves were rolled up to his elbows, giving me a delicious view of the tattoos that swirled down his arms. He stood with his hands in his pockets as he took his fill of my body. Or my dress. Both, probably.

His face remained passive though the stars in his eyes twinkled as if he were amused. I suppressed a scoff as he nodded his head at me and turned on his heel, leading me down a blue carpeted hallway to a grand staircase.

I counted the number of doors between my room and the stairs (nine) and how many windows there were (seventeen) and which ones could be opened (four) as we descended down the stairs and into what looked to be the main entryway. Anything I found could provide my salvation.

Escape, make it back to the ship, and then figure it out from there.

Malakai led the way, making no attempts to speak to me, although I did catch him looking at me out of the corner of his eye a few times. I ignored him as well, instead putting most of my attention to counting all the exits (three patio double doors, one large front door) and seeing if there were any other people around that may stop my attempt at escaping (there were two sirens who quickly found another route to take).

The palace was quite beautiful. It wasn't filled with gilded trinkets or statues as I suspected. The most lavish part appeared to be silver-veined white marble floors, though the paintings on the walls depicting scenic landscapes of Vallah seemed like they must have cost a fortune.

We turned right down another hallway (passing four more sets of double doors leading out to various patios and gardens) before entering a large chamber with arched ceilings and wood beams crossed along the top. The wall to my right was made entirely of glass and gave me a view of the glimmering lake I walked across earlier that day along with echoes of a restless ocean in the background.

It was strange to look out into perpetual night, but the fluorescent glow emanating from the plants, through the ripple of currents in the water, and on gently floating pollen in the breeze all gave a cozy, enchanting atmosphere. I longed to go out and explore, to figure out what made those colors appear, and to lay back in the billowy grass and stare up at the cosmos for hours.

But I wasn't there to enjoy the beauty of my prison. I needed to leave, even if it meant I had to strike a deal with him.

The dining hall was surprisingly empty, and though I couldn't tell what time it was in the endless night of Vallah, it couldn't have been more than three hours since he whisked me away to his palace. I wondered briefly if time moved the same way in his realm.

"Where is everyone?" I asked. The emptiness of such a large home felt eerie. "Shouldn't there be more slaves bustling about, ready to do whatever you command?"

He continued across the empty dining hall and opened a set of glass double doors leading outside to a patio with a single table for two. A stone wall separated the patio from a garden filled with black roses with glowing purple veins running through them. The warm breeze shifted through trees that looked as though they were weeping vines of white daisies. In the distance, I could hear the ocean crash against the shore and a beautiful low humming, as if the land itself were seducing me, ripening me to the possibilities and intrigue of being in a place so romantic and mythical. A molten feeling like hot wax pouring over me allowed my muscles to relax as I fell into the magic of Vallah.

The scraping of a chair against the stone brought me back to the moment and it took a minute for me to shake off the sultry wantonness of the place and instead focus on the task at hand. I needed to get away from the one who sought to control me. His powerful, alluring land was as tempting as a siren song, and I refused to be seduced by it.

"Sit," Malakai said, his voice as velvety as the air surrounding us. "Relax, Syn. Let me take care of you."

Let me take care of you. The words were innocent but the way he said them was absolutely filthy and a rush of liquid pooled in my core. I fought to keep my face passive, not wanting him to catch on to the way he affected me, but a quirk of his mouth told me all I needed to know.

"Where is everyone?" I asked again as I sat down. "I find it hard to believe that a palace this big would have no one here besides those two worshipers."

"I've sent them away." He poured us each a glass of wine as a server came out with our first course of food. "I wanted you to myself, and I find I'm distracted with the others around."

A bowl of a chilled creamy soup was placed in front of

us, topped with a delicate hibiscus flower. I stared at the server as he placed the other bowl in front of Malakai. He wore a similar outfit as Julep and Una, except his pants were a linen gray to go with a flowy white shirt. His skin was darker, though somehow still translucent. Blue blood ran through his veins as well, and his eyes glowed a bright orange in the darkness.

"Are you a siren, too?" I blurted out. I didn't think it was possible, but he appeared the same as the others. "I thought only females were sirens."

The server looked questioningly at Malakai, as if seeking permission to answer my question. Anger coursed through me. Was everyone so afraid of him that they were not able to speak out of turn?

"Do you like this control you have over them?" I asked, nodding toward our server. "Does it excite you knowing they don't speak unless you allow them to?"

"One could argue that it's a trait you'd benefit from," he replied. "However, he was not looking to me for approval to speak but rather how much he is able to share with you."

"Does he have a name?" I looked back at the server, whose eyes shifted between me and Malakai. "He said you do not need his permission to speak. So, do so."

The server bowed at his waist. "I am called Sufjan. There are both male and female sirens. We often raise the young, when there are any."

"The young?" I asked. "You mean sirens aren't just created?"

Sufjan cocked his head like a predator would to his prey and I wondered if the male sirens had something more dangerous than seduction as a weapon.

"See to the next course, Sufjan." Malakai dismissed him and set to work eating his soup. I refused to partake in the food, my stomach protesting my reluctance, when he said, "If you don't start eating, I'm going to force it down your pretty little mouth and will relish the sounds of you gagging on it."

My jaw dropped before I could catch it. That he even implied that he could get anything near my mouth, much less down my throat, was so absurd, it was laughable. Except I could never laugh with the person who murdered my family.

Reluctantly, I picked up my spoon and dove into the creamy soup, surprised as the cool flavors and a hint of spice overwhelmed my tongue. I tried not to look pleased at the taste, but I was ravenous and had just finished the soup course when Sufjan came out with the next.

A slow smile built on Malakai's face as he watched me finish the last spoonful. "Good girl."

I felt the skin on my neck flush as a different kind of heat rushed to my core at his praise. Disgust quickly followed. How could I want to please this god who spent his time making deals with vulnerable human souls? If I let my thoughts stray too far, I might end up forgetting that I wanted to leave him, rather than bask in his presence. I had to stay focused, resist his charm, and figure out how to get out of this place.

"I have ruled this land for eons," Malakai said in between sips of wine. "The sirens are of this land, same as the deer in the Druskian Forest, same as the fish in the Baronian Sea. Not all are created by me, though some may be, depending on the magic the deal requires and the terms of the arrangement. I have made many over the centuries, though more often than not, they are born within these lands."

I nodded my head, contemplating what he said. It was

different from the legends we grew up with. I only knew of sirens created by him. I hadn't realized they were born, that they had young. I shifted topics until I could properly consider what other information I might have been incorrect about. "Where is the crew?"

Sufjan placed a mini tray of assorted fruits and cheeses in front of me. A different bottle of wine appeared on the table along with fresh glasses.

Malakai popped an olive in his mouth and chewed slowly. "Which crew are you speaking about, exactly?"

"You know which crew. My crew."

"Ahh, so you still consider them yours? How interesting."

"Do you always give non-answers?" I stabbed a fork through a piece of cheese. "It's unbecoming for a god."

He cocked his head to the side and bit into a strawberry, letting the juices drip down his chin. For an absurd moment I thought to reach over the table and lick every last drop that escaped his mouth. Before I could do exactly that, he trailed a finger through the slick wetness and popped it into his mouth, sucking on it slowly. He raised a brow as I continued to stare. "Do you always ask so many questions?"

I quickly downed a gulp of wine, desperate to wet my suddenly dry mouth and tried to focus. Seducing him back as a means of retaliation would only serve his purpose instead of mine. Besides, it would be incredibly stupid of me to try to manipulate the Lord of Lost Souls through seduction, especially when he raised and bred the sirens to perform in exactly the way he taught them. I'd never come across anyone who dripped sex the way Malakai did.

"The crew are on their ship and will remain there until the morning when I decide what to do with them. As for you, after we have this meal you will return to your room while I see to the needs of my sirens."

Something green slithered through my chest, threatening to break through the cavity and expose all the feelings I'd rather keep buried down in the dark sea where no one would ever find them. "Exactly what needs are those?"

As if on cue, the patio doors slammed open and a whisp of a siren fell to her knees and bowed her head at Malakai's feet. She had a blue tinge to her translucent skin and hair darker than the Vallah night sky, but the rest of her face was covered in shadows.

"Master," she whispered, keeping her gaze to the ground. "It is supposed to be my scheduled time with you."

The twinkling lights in Malakai's eyes went out, replaced by a foreboding storm. I thought I saw lightning bolts within their depths, and I casually sat back, wondering what the fuck was happening. I knew her type; I had to play that submissive role many times with my own clients. In fact, I recognized some of those qualities she possessed in myself, particularly the eagerness to please. What I didn't understand was why she was interrupting my dinner and what the hell she meant by it being her scheduled time.

I watched as Malakai transformed from a calm, egotistical god to one filled with the promise of punishment. His shadows that he kept to himself all evening flowed outwards and lashed out onto her, binding her wrists in place behind her back.

"You are disobeying my instructions, Seraphina." His voice was laced with violence and I was reminded that he was a powerful god and I was just a human trapped in his lair. I couldn't find the voice to defend Seraphina, nor did I think I wanted to. Their relationship was between them, but that didn't mean that I liked it.

"It's our time," she repeated before casting me a vicious look, a red swirl reflected in her eyes. "You never miss our time. I thought I was special."

"You are being insolent. Return to your room immediately and await your punishment."

"Good. Maybe I want to be punished by you."

"Not tonight, you won't."

A collar of shadows appeared around her neck, nearly choking her, though she looked like it caused her far more pleasure than pain. He gripped his hand in the air and the shadows tightened, causing her eyes to widen in surprise.

She scurried back to her feet and returned to where she came from before he could say another word. "Really?" I asked as soon as she left. "You fuck them, too? It isn't enough that you own them. That you control what they do. But this? Even Julian never touched his girls."

"Do not speak about what you do not know." The violence he kept barely leashed started to leak through. His tattoos glowed and his canines lengthened, similar to what happened with Killian on the ship. "Dinner is over. Julep will return you to your room."

"Fuck that," I said, shooting into an upright position. "You haven't given me one answer all night. You demand I play dress up for you. You demand I spend the night against my will. You demand I eat dinner with you, which you are now demanding I not finish. You are tossing me around like a marionette."

"Do not think to disobey me, Little Red. I will come to you when I finish with her."

"When you finish fucking her, you mean?"

He chuckled darkly, his eyes hardening. "Jealousy does not become you."

"That is one emotion I will never feel when it comes to you." I hissed back at him. "You disgust me."

"Come on, Emersyn," Julep said, appearing from the garden beyond us. Had she been standing there the whole time? Her hand clasped around mine.

I yanked my arm back out of her grasp. "I will not go back to my room until I have answers."

Malakai approached on silent feet, so quiet that I hadn't really noticed he stood inches away from me until he was right there. Power radiated from him along with a seductive violence I knew well. It was the same that flowed through me when anger took control. He cupped a hand against my cheek and I felt my muscles immediately relax, and wanted to listen to anything he had to tell me. Somewhere in the back of my mind, I was aware that this was similar to my singing ability, and the words Killian spoke to me my first night with him about not having control over his body came to the forefront of my mind, yet I couldn't bring myself to speak.

"I know you don't like this, love, but I need to take care of this problem. I will attend to you shortly."

Julep gave me a sympathetic look and a small smile, the kind one gives when they feel sorry for another, and led me back to my room, where the spell didn't lift until the door locked once again.

15

There is achievement in bargaining.

The rest of the dinner feast was waiting for me when I returned to my room, though rage poisoned my insides and the sour taste of bile crept up my throat. I didn't know what I was more upset about—the fact that he made me dress up for a dinner that he didn't see fit to see through to the end, that he clearly took care of whatever sexual needs his sirens desired, which was what I suspected but also felt like an absolute abuse of his power and their reliance on him, or the fact that even though I was filled with nothing but disgust, a pang of jealousy swiftly coursed through my veins.

I ripped off the dress and scavenged through the chest of drawers against the wall, grabbing a fresh pair of soft navy pants that conformed to my hips and a plain white shirt. The closet contained an endless row of shoes, sandals, slippers, and boots. I grabbed the first sensible pair I laid my eyes on. It didn't escape my notice that everything was exactly my size, and I filed that information away until I could process what that meant.

"Would you like me to fetch you a tea?" Julep said from the corner of the bedroom. I'd been so wrapped up in my haste to get dressed and leave that I'd completely forgotten she was there. "Or a whiskey? Something to help the feelings?"

"I'm feeling a murderous rage, Julep. Do you have something for that?"

Her wide green eyes flickered strangely in the shadows from the fire and her pupils dilated. She approached with her hands out and hummed a single note, then two. Her fingers trailed up my arm then slowly grasped around my neck as her humming continued. She squeezed gently, then more firmly, and I felt the rage trickle out of me as she applied more pressure.

"What are you doing to me?" I asked.

"Our siren gifts are all different. We don't all seduce. Some of us heal. Some of us harm. Some of us can dissipate emotions, or some combination. We have evolved over time to perform as a functional society. Malakai's power in this realm grants us the ability to use these gifts. I'm a healer."

"I'm not broken. I don't need to be fixed."

She looked at me with sad eyes as the last of the fight drained out of me. "Oh, Emersyn, no one is saying you're broken, but we could all use some healing." She took a step back and rubbed her hands down her front, her green hair wild in the flickering firelight. "Our powers don't always work on our sisters but sometimes they do, when the need is strong enough."

I looked sharply at her. "What does that have to do with me?"

"Nothing." She went to get a cup of tea from a tray next to the bed and handed it to me. "You were curious about sirens earlier so I thought perhaps you'd want to know a little bit more."

I nodded my head and blew on the steam, taking small sips at a time. Though my anger had dissipated, I still felt nauseous from the evening's events. "What goes on around here? You two practically worship the ground he walks on, Sufjan doesn't speak without permission, and that other one comes in begging for her time with him and getting excited about the punishment he's no doubt giving her now. Do you realize how much he has manipulated you all?"

"No." Julep shook her head. "Things aren't as they seem, Emersyn. I wish I could explain it to you, but it'll become clear soon enough. No one is doing anything against their will. He doesn't tell us when to speak. He does not force himself on us. Malakai has all of the powers. He seduces, yes, but it is not us that he puts those powers on. He heals, he feels the emotions from others. It's compulsory. He has no choice but to provide. Really, if anything, it is us that control him."

"He said he sent everyone away because he would have been distracted."

"Yes, if someone is feeling a particularly strong emotion, he knows. He's a god and this is his realm. There isn't anything that happens here that he doesn't know about."

I had to keep reminding myself of that. He was a god, I

was in his world, and there was nothing I could do that he wouldn't know about. It certainly explained why he could sense my desire for him, but it also meant that he could tell when I wanted to tear the skin off his bones as well. I was too exposed in Vallah.

"What does he want with me? Why is he keeping me locked here?"

"I am keeping you here because I can tell how tired you are."

His voice was a thunderstorm and I felt pieces of electricity flow off of him as he appeared behind me.

Julep took her leave and left me alone in the bedroom with him, the door clicking shut behind her. The sound was swallowed by the crackling fire and I became extremely aware how close he stood.

"I am keeping you here because I can feel that you've been fighting for too long. I'm keeping you here because you are malnourished. I can sense the things you need and I am compelled to care for you."

"I don't believe that you didn't kill my parents," I blurted out, ignoring his declarations of caring for me. "I also don't know why you have the idea that I want to spend any amount of time with you. I want to go back to my realm. Return me to the ship."

Danger flowed off him but I breathed it in and allowed it to fuel me further. I didn't care that he didn't like the way I was speaking to him. He probably fucked the other siren before daring to sneak into my bedroom and telling me that he now wants to take care of me. Did he think I would just comply with whatever he wanted? He knew nothing about me at all.

He scrutinized me then casually placed his hands in his pockets. Alarm bells went off. My experience with men was that the calmer they try to appear, the more pain they want to cause. "I have done nothing but care for you from the moment I became aware of where you were. I have only good intentions toward you. When will you see that?"

"I don't know, maybe when you remove any illusion of intention you have with me." I walked toward the door, intending to follow the path I laid out earlier, but then I turned on my heel and spewed out more words, losing control entirely. "You expect me to believe that you only have good wishes toward me? That you don't harm for no reason? What about the crew? You put them all through hell, torturing them just because they didn't answer you quick enough. There are women on that crew, Malakai."

"That crew all sold a piece of their souls to me in one way or another. They are bound to my will and if someone under me is insolent, they will be punished." His voice was dark and for a moment I saw where the legends I grew up on came from.

"And your sirens? Do you do the same to them?"

"Would I send people hunting for their murderers if I had wanted to see them harmed?"

"I don't know, maybe you're too much of a sadistic fuck and believe if anyone were to murder them it would be you."

"You clearly know nothing of me, nothing of the legends that came from this place, nothing of what it is to rule Vallah." He took a deep breath, his control starting to slip.

Good, I thought. I wanted to see how far I could take him, what sort of punishment he thought he could dole out on me.

He walked toward the wall of windows and looked outside, smoothing down the front of his shirt. The corded muscles of his forearms clenched and relaxed. Once he retained his calm, he turned back to me. "Those sirens are extensions of me. They are the veins that pump blood to my heart. I need them to survive and I do whatever is necessary to make sure they are well taken care of."

His teeth elongated into sharpened points, similar to what I had seen on Killian and I wondered how alike the two of them really were. Was Killian a god as well, or did Malakai share power with him since he owned his soul? I should have been terrified, and maybe I was a little, but it also fascinated me. I would not be intimidated by him, whether he was a god or not.

"It is an abomination to my very nature to harm anything that would disrupt the balance here. I will peel off the skin from whoever is in charge of those heinous murders and use my magic to keep them alive while they watch me suck the marrow from their bones."

Heat went through me and pulled at my core. The bloodlust in his eyes, the death promise he made, the ferocity with which he spoke sang to the darkest parts of me I tried to keep hidden. Was I just as bad him, then, to relish in the future murder of a stranger I hadn't met yet? I suddenly wanted to see who really was in charge of the murders and I wanted to watch this smooth, dark, mysterious man lose every ounce of control on those responsible for the crimes against his precious sirens.

"And if I made a deal with you?"

The fire in the room died down to embers as the luminescent light from the plants dimmed until we were in almost total darkness. Thunder crashed and the electricity I felt a moment ago turned sticky and static in the air.

Malakai's eyes changed to inky, bottomless pools as the

stars flickered out. "Do not utter those words here. Unless you wish to bind yourself to this realm. To me."

I swallowed through the thickened air, willing myself to stay calm in the sudden change. There were so many rules I didn't know. There was so much I didn't understand. "The way you feel is the same burning vengeance that I've felt in my blood since the day you ordered my family's murder. Send me back to the crew. Let me help them find who it is."

"If you're still stuck on the belief that it was me who wanted your family murdered, why are you willing to help?"

Why *was* I willing to help a monster? After he took me away, locked me up, ordered me to do what he said when he said it. Perhaps if I helped him, he would do what I wanted in return. He'd allow me to roam free, regardless of what he said about Julian. Without the tattoo, I could change my appearance and go by a different name. I could finally assume the identity of the person I longed to be, of the girl from the past I mourned each day.

Or maybe it was because seeing the body of the dead siren ignited a fire inside of me that I wasn't aware existed. The thought of something like that happening to Julep or Una, though I had only known them for a few hours, filled me with an overwhelming sadness. The strange mutilation on that siren's dead body screamed of torture and agony. I wanted to hurt whoever had done that to her, and I let that rage fuel me as I closed the distance between myself and my family's murderer.

"No one should have to die the way that siren did. No one should know that type of abuse or suffering. I will go after the revenge you seek, if only to protect innocent lives from that abominable fate."

Malakai circled me, his strange shadows licking and

trailing along my legs then further up the curves of my hips and breasts. The way they caressed my body, learning every line, every dip and swell, felt as though The Lord of Lost Souls were whispering exactly how he'd take care of me if given the chance. As if his shadows discovered my darkest secrets and relayed them back to him to use at a later time. Perhaps that was part of their function. Or maybe they fed off the bloodlust I felt just then. I refused to react, choosing to glare at him instead.

He smirked when he stopped in front of me, though his shadows still explored my body. Blood rushed through my veins, heating my skin, flooding the most sensitive parts of me. Goosebumps threatened to expose the desire rapidly building in me, and when a shadow stroked the exposed area low on my stomach, it was all I could do to bite my lip and hold back a moan.

"Interesting," he murmured as his pupils expanded and he inhaled, undoubtedly smelling my arousal just as Julep said he could.

"You really need to learn the concept of consent. It isn't freely given, you know." I threw him a disgusted look but he wasn't fooled. The only person I was kidding was myself.

I tried to remember the stories of the gods and their powers to see if perhaps Julep left something out. Surely mind reading wasn't one of them, though I felt him take up every space inside of me with the weight of his stare alone. Malakai Barron, according to the legends, created sirens to lure souls to him. He had two brothers, one of whom ruled the ocean and another that ruled the underworld, where souls were sent for their next journey. He also had a sister who ruled the sky and they all worked in tandem, though I had seen no evidence of that so far. But what else? What was the full extent of his powers, and most importantly, what weakened him?

"If you did not consent, the shadows would not have gone to you in this way."

"As if I want any part of you touching me," I scoffed.

He raised an eyebrow. "Don't you?"

Did I? I was confused. I spent so long hating him, spent so long at the mercy of people more powerful than me who would abuse their position to seek what they wanted. He was no different. So was some part of me intrigued by him, or was he simply that good at manipulation that I failed to see it before it was too late?

Immediately, the shadows retreated, leaving me cold and filled with an unfamiliar desperation for them to return.

"You have been mistreated for far too long, Little Red. We have much damage to undo."

His voice was etched with concern, as if he actually cared. Another manipulation tactic, I was sure. That's all seduction was, anyway. Manipulating someone else to feel what you wanted them to feel.

"Will you let me go, or not?"

The silence stretched on and I watched his throat as he swallowed, his chest as he inhaled, his heart pulse through his neck. Finally, he extended his hand toward me in an offering to take it and I didn't hesitate like before.

The room melted away from us and I had the distinct feeling of something oozing over me, as if honey were being poured slowly out of a jar. It was a sensation I didn't pick up on the first time around because I was so frazzled, but it was disorienting and oddly soothing.

Drizzle pelted my face, my hair immediately frizzing in the balmy night air. The scent of coconut and ocean whispered through me, and the rocking of the water against the ship was a gentle hug as it returned me back home.

As soon as Malakai appeared next to me the rain stopped, and it was only then that I noticed the crew were still plastered to the floor of the deck, shivering from being wet for so long.

"You kept them like this?" I hissed at him. "For hours? You really expect me to believe you take care of those that are yours?"

"There is much you need to learn about our world," he murmured to me before he snapped his fingers and the crew shot to their feet, completely dry. I didn't like the way he said *our* world, as if I had a place there with him.

Clara stepped forward, seemingly unaffected, as if she hadn't been writhing in pain or soaking wet the entire time I was gone. "Are you okay kitty kat?"

Then Sven. "Babe, tell me you didn't do something stupid."

June Leona. "I'm so confused."

Willy, murmuring softly, "I'll explain it to you later."

But Killian...Killian said nothing.

I eyed each of them, wondering how I should respond. They had lied to me. They knew Malakai had some sort of claim on me, that they would eventually have to answer to him. They knew I wouldn't really get away at all. They spent days treating me as if I were one of them, accepting the strangeness about me, willing to take on my baggage. They treated me as if I were a friend.

More than that, they kept me in the dark. I knew they had their secrets, and I could now safely assume that Malakai had them under some type of spell that prevented them from spilling any details, but they knew about me, much more than I did.

Malakai put his hands in his pants pockets and casually strolled in front of them. Immediately all eyes were on him, a mixture of fear and what might have been awe on each of their faces. Except Killian's. His were filled with nothing but resentment.

"Syn has offered to aid you in the mission that you have all been failing miserably at."

Killian looked horrified at that, his eyes immediately finding mine. "Tell me you didn't make a deal with him." When I didn't say anything, he took a step toward Malakai instead and frantically said, "What do you want? I'll give you anything to release her from the contract."

Malakai laughed, its sound a mix of dark delight and a threat. "There's nothing left for you to bargain, Captain. Your whole soul belongs to me and you know I only bargain with souls."

A mixture of emotions ran through me. Confusion for why what happened to me mattered to Killian when he betrayed me so thoroughly. Anger for him thinking to defend me, as if I wanted to owe him anything. But there was still a piece of me that wanted to come to his rescue instead, to make sure that he was taken care of and no harm would come to him. An offer to give my soul to ensure his safety was right at the tip of my tongue, the words ready to launch themselves out of my throat when Malakai whipped his head over to me.

"Do not speak those words," he said, his voice filled with fury and command. As quickly as the impulse came, it faded away. "Your words are binding and there will be no way out of them. That is the second time I've had to warn you. There will not be a third."

Frustration poured through me as I realized that my actions, my emotions, even the words I was allowed to speak, were all out of my control. Fury was a mighty sword and I was ready to behead the Lord of Lost Souls for taking all of my agency away from me.

Malakai's eyes softened. "The protectiveness you feel is because you're connected to me through a different bargain, and it's all part of the same binding magic for you to do whatever it takes to protect me. Because I own Killian's soul, you want to keep him safe because you know it will keep me safe."

What the fuck. "So, what? I wanted to fuck Killian because of some twisted hold you have over both of us?"

The planes of his face sharpened and his shadows shot out of him, twisting themselves around Killian as though they were a python, constricting his movements, suffocating him as they would themselves tighter around him.

"What are you doing? Stop hurting him!"

Malakai growled at me in warning to stay back, but I grabbed his arm anyway, forcing him to face me. "Let go of me, love."

"No! Why are you hurting him? Leave him alone."

"Babe," Sven's timid voice spoke up. He raised his hands in a placating gesture to Malakai, not wanting his wrath to turn on him instead. "We aren't allowed to touch his girls. Anyone that belongs to Malakai is under his protection. Killian crossed a line with you. That's why this is happening."

"Are you out of your fucking mind?" I turned back to Malakai. "I am my own person and I will fuck whoever I damn well please. You will not get a say in it. No one will ever tell me who to have sex with or when ever again."

The shadows writhed tighter against Killian and he let out a moan of pain. For a moment I saw red as rage burned through me and all I wanted to do was murder whoever dared to harm him. But when I looked at Malakai, the rage simmered down and nothing but confusion was left in its wake.

"Let him go. Please."

Did I just fucking say please to this sadistic asshole?

Malakai rubbed his temples as if I were the one having a childish outburst and not him. "This binding magic is going to be a pain in my ass until you're both taken care of."

He waved his hand and the shadows retreated, although reluctantly, and the rest of the crew were left with stunned looks on their faces.

"You have three weeks to figure out what is happening to my sirens. If you fail, I will be collecting what each of you have promised me." He looked at each in turn, even June Leona, and then his eyes settled on me. I promised him nothing but the name of the murderer so I had no problem delivering on my end.

"Let me bargain something else," Killian said, his voice raspy from the weight of the shadows. "Please. Don't take her."

"By *her*, I hope you don't mean me." I refused to let any of these men think they could own me or tell me where to go.

"Syn, you have been promised to me for far too long. The deal is done, twofold. There is no way out of it." Malakai almost looked reluctant except for the way his shadows turned their attention on me as if they wanted to caress me again. Those eager assholes were no better than the male they belonged to.

"I have no interest in being owned by anyone ever again. And I will *never* go to you willingly, so I hope you're ready for a fight in three weeks."

I was no stranger to murder. First a drug lord, then a

dirty pirate. I could add on a sadistic, blood thirsty god to the list. I would, if it came down to it.

Malakai gave me one last smirk. "We'll see about that."

He snapped his fingers and the world was plunged into darkness.

16

There are answers in abandoning.

At first, there was nothing. I was an endless floating mass without a body to tether me to the earth. There was no sound, no feeling, no pain. Just blissful detachment in an unending echo of darkness.

Blazing heat from the sun burned my skin as I squinted against the sudden brightness. The scent of brine and seaweed invaded my nostrils, the wind non-existent.

"Fucking hell," Sven said as he walked with his eyes tight shut and arms outstretched. "He couldn't have left us somewhere a little less fucking bright?"

"That was absolutely terrifying and I never want to go back there," June said as Willy rubbed her arms up and down in a sign of comfort.

"You get used to it," they said. "It isn't always that bad."

"I thought it was beautiful," I said, though I didn't really know why. My opinion shouldn't matter to them, especially since my feelings, wellbeing, and freedom didn't.

The crew looked at each other awkwardly, except for the triplets who got to work trying to get the freshly repaired ship to move, but we were on dead water so there was nothing to be done except to tread until mother nature decided to work in our favor.

"Red..." Killian made a move toward me, but I held up my hand to stop him.

"I'm not ready to speak to you. To any of you." I set my sights on the stairs leading toward the Captain's Quarters. "I'm going to take a bath. Then I'm going to sleep because I've now been up for a day and a half. Then I'm going to eat. And then maybe after that, I'll demand answers from you."

I left the crew with awkward silence between them, sighing in relief when I made it safely behind the door to the captain's quarters. There was no evidence left of what happened between Killian and I the previous night. The chocolate that had spilled across the table and floor were gone, the bed was made and replaced with fresh sheets. The desk was covered in maps and the odd instruments just like the first day I stepped foot in the captain's quarters. No doubt Malakai had something to do with it. He seemed to like erasing the past as if it didn't exist.

At least something was explained. The magic aboard the ship was from the Lord of Lost Souls. The food, the fresh water for baths, the protection that Killian claimed was on the ship. Except, for some reason, that part failed during the storm.

It was a question I should have asked when I had the chance, but it was distracting being in Vallah and surrounded by such beauty that made me ache with the need to be a part of it.

I wanted to clear my head and push the memory of that place behind, starting with a hot bath and food.

As soon as I had that thought, a tray appeared with tea, fresh tropical fruit, and chocolates. A note rested on the stop, the name Emersyn written out in sprawling blue ink. I rolled my eyes, fully intending to ignore it, but that just wasn't in my nature. Not since Vallah was confirmed as real and that I was sailing on the Lord of Lost Souls' ship on a mission for him.

My dearest Emersyn —

I hope you find this to your liking. It's chamomile tea with mint, my personal favorite when I require a proper sleep. I believe this should satisfy your needs, for now.

-Malakai Jerohm Barron, Lord of Lost Souls, Ruler of the Kingdom of Vallah

I scoffed before tossing the note back on the table. He really had the nerve to not only send the same tray of tea I refused earlier in the day, but also to sign his full name like that, *again,* as if I wouldn't have known who he was.

I stripped my clothes, ignoring the tea entirely, and headed toward the golden tub. Steam rose from the water, and I sank in with a sigh of relief. I'd been tense the entire time I was in Vallah, and my anxiety caused my muscles to lock up. The warm water soothed me, lulling me into a sense of security.

Well, I was secure for the next three weeks, at least, then it seemed as though I had a fight with a god to worry about if he still had the absurd notion that he would own me.

My eyes burned with exhaustion. There was no way I'd last a moment longer, so I climbed out of the tub and dried off with a warm towel left for me. Not wanting to fully dress, I shrugged on an oversized sweater and trudged toward the bed, snagging a cookie on my way. The blankets welcomed me, hugging me tight, comforting me as an old friend, and soon consciousness escaped me.

Darkness. Nothing but floating, thick, immense darkness.

It surrounded me, held me down, suffocated me, made me want to beg for mercy if only I had a voice.

A sound pierced the silence, its melody one I was well acquainted with by now. Though I still didn't understand the words, it was a song of sadness. Of longing. Of wanting to be rescued.

I knew it well.

The fear that enveloped me soon gave me a reprieve and I breathed deeply, or what I imagined would be considered deep breathing if I had a body.

I waited.

Seconds rolled on but the voice never wavered, never paused for a breath. It was beautiful and profound. I longed to find the owner of it so that I could thank them, embrace them, grab their hand and run away from this life forever. To live free with them.

"Emmy," a voice echoed inside the chambers of my mind. "Find me, Emmy."

"Who's there?" I called out into the void, but no one answered.

Soon, the darkness changed shape and became shadows. The outline of a figure formed, though I wasn't filled with the same fear as the last time I'd had the same dream. Instead, I felt rage sprinkled with lust. I felt heat and fire. I felt like the figure who haunted me was exactly the type of danger I longed to throw myself into.

"Syn," a deep voice rippled out to me, melting me down to the essence of who I was. "Can you hear me, darling? Can you feel me?"

The darkness wrapped itself around me and instead of suffocation I felt nothing but elation and joy and freedom.

That word. Freedom. Finally I could taste it, the sweet nectar running down my tongue, satiating a craving for promises fulfilled.

Yes, I tried to say. I feel safe. I feel complete.

A rumble of laughter promising forbidden things settled deep in me, awakening a deep-seated desire that I had long forgotten.

A moan escaped me before I could stop it and suddenly I wished for something more—

"You dreaming about me, babe?"

My eyes flew open and I kicked out on instinct. A grunt met the end of my foot and I finally focused on the person who was either brave enough or stupid enough to wake me from my sleep.

"Why?" Sven squeezed out in a pained voice. "Why would you do that?"

I groaned and put a pillow over my head, ignoring his deep breathing as he fought through the agony. I would have apologized, but maybe he deserved that and more for pretending to be my friend.

"The boss sent me to get you."

I flung the sheets off myself, barely conscious of my state of undress. "Malakai? He's here?" Smoothing my hair was an impossible task, but I didn't want to look a complete mess when I saw him again. Not that I cared what he thought of me.

"Uh, no," Sven replied, looking at me as if I'd just asked if we landed on the moon. "Killian. He wants us all on deck so he can tell us his plan."

My cheeks burned as I slowly rose out of bed and casually walked over to the desk, now with a pile of tea sandwiches arranged on a silver platter. An envelope with 'Emersyn' written in calligraphy waited for me next to a pitcher of iced tea with lemon. Rolling my eyes at it, I grabbed a mini sandwich filled with cucumber and cream cheese and poured myself a chalice of iced tea, since apparently he only thought to leave chalices as drinking vessels. I was acutely aware that Sven stood with his arms folded across his front, waiting for me the whole time.

I sat at the desk and crossed my bare legs, noticing how Sven took in his fill of my skin before finding the wall much more interesting. I smirked and opened the envelope, in no rush to read what The Lord of Lost Souls had to say, but keeping Killian waiting as long as possible amused me.

My Dearest Emersyn,

Please, eat today. You will need your strength in the coming days.

-Malakai Jerohm Barron, Lord of Lost Souls, Ruler of the Kingdom of Vallah

Cryptic.

The second sandwich I grabbed, one with peanut butter and honey, stuck in my throat as I thought about the note. *Why will I need my strength? Does he anticipate something happening to me?* Chewing slowly, I pondered on all the ways he would think of my strength sapping away when a throat cleared.

Sven shifted on his feet, clearly uncomfortable with the slow pace I was setting.

I gulped down some iced tea, a bit of liquid spilling from the wide brim of the chalice, and sloppily wiped my chin. "You're awfully impatient today."

"We're on a mission, doll. Time is of the essence. We need to hurry."

I turned my back on him and removed the oversized sweater, feeling his stare boring into my bare form. "I'm not stopping you from leaving," I said as I reached for a pair of pants, fully aware that my scantily clad body was on display. I peeked over my shoulder, watching as he drank in the sight. "Could you stare any harder?"

"Honey, if you're putting on a free show, I'm not gonna say no."

So predictable. "Of course you're not."

Sliding on a pair of black pants and a white cotton shirt, I finger-combed my hair then went to the washbasin in the corner of the room to brush my teeth. Sven held my boots out to me in offering, and I sighed as I snatched them from him.

"I don't like to be rushed," I said. "Your crew has kept countless secrets from me for days. Ten extra minutes isn't going to put you out too much, is it?"

"Let's just go."

The blazing sun shone down on the deck and there was no wind to speak of. The air was dry, without the sound of any gulls to signify us being near land. I rolled my sleeves up, wishing I had something to wear other than long pants, and tied my hair up with a piece of scrap leather.

"Sleeping beauty awakes," Willy said, smiling at me.

They stood next to June at a table erected in the middle of the deck and covered with various maps and instruments. Clara, the triplets, and Killian all hovered over it, leaving little space for me and Sven to join. They each looked a little worse for wear, with their hair unkempt and clothes wrinkled, as if they hadn't gotten any rest since returning. I still hadn't forgiven any of them, not that anyone had bothered to apologize, but the longing I felt to be part of the crew warred with my pride.

"What's the plan?" I asked, keeping my face neutral. They didn't have to see how badly I wanted their friendship or how much I was hurt by their betrayal.

Clara cleared her throat. "There are a cluster of small islands we want to explore. They're difficult to get to, but they're unusual enough to warrant a closer search."

"Why?"

"There's a strong current that encircles the entire area," Killian said, avoiding eye contact. He placed his finger down on the map to indicate the area, then put a round instrument made of glass and gold on the map where his finger was. The glass amplified the image and allowed it to spring to life. The water flowed outward from the islands, and there was a deep purple woven underneath layers of blue ocean.

"That purple line indicates the current. See how fast it flows? I've been staring at this map all night. There are certain times when it slows or even seems to reverse, though I can't figure out how or why. That's when we have to try to get in."

"Are you saying it's too strong to just sail through? With a magic ship?" I found it hard to believe that there would be anything that Malakai's magic couldn't break through, but

I also didn't know what it was like to do a god's dirty work, either. Maybe there were limitations.

"That's exactly what I'm saying. The current keeps everything out. Look at this." He switched the device with one that looked like a small square of fabric made from some type of luminescent jelly. "This lets us see under the water, so we know its depth and any dangers that might lurk beneath us. Lean in closer and tell me what you see."

The map suddenly burst to life, revealing a sweeping, brightly colored coral reef, schools of fish, and magnificently jeweled crustaceans. I'd never seen sea creatures like them before. They were almost otherworldly, expected of a different land or realm. It seemed as though that piece of earth was sliced away from Vallah and existed peacefully without the corruption of humans.

"That's incredible," I breathed. "I've never seen anything like that before."

"Now look around the islands." He shifted the device closer to the drawing of the land on the map. "Notice anything?"

I peered in, eager to see more of what lay in that beautiful ocean, but nothing appeared. It was just deep, dark ocean. No signs of life were to be found, not even a different shade of another current running through. To see that was unsettling, especially directly next to the land. It seemed as though the sand bank dropped down into a void of darkness.

I reared back as an uneasy feeling crept over me. "It's as if the two pieces of ocean are reversed. The coral should be much closer to the islands, shouldn't it? How is there nothing there?"

"Exactly what we've been wondering. This is where I intended to take you, so you would be—"

"Trapped?" I interrupted him, the fury I tried to swallow swiftly slicing through me. "On a set of islands with no way out? You thought to cage me?"

"I wanted to keep you out of his reach until we could properly explore the islands so I could trade you for what he really wanted."

Two opposing thoughts hit me at the same time. He thought he could trade me as if I were a piece of hide that might be useful to someone else? The second thought was more disturbing.

Malakai doesn't really want me?

I gave voice to the safer thought of the two, unwilling to dwell on why I cared about the other. "Trade me? You thought to keep me caged on an island with no way to escape only to *trade* me afterwards? Because on this remote island that is seemingly impossible to get to, you thought you would find something that would have more value to him than my *life*?"

"Red, I don't think you understand your situation here."

"Oh, really? That's strange, seeing as how forthcoming you've all been with me."

"I think we're getting a bit off topic," Clara said, staring me down. "We need to figure out what's special about those islands."

June spoke up. "Why would they have anything to do with what's happening to the sirens? Where's the connection?"

"Besides this looking like it came straight from Vallah," Killian replied, "there's something unnatural happening here, where the current divides the two pieces of the sea. For all we know, it could be the lair of whatever hell spawn is harming the sirens. Red, can you feel anything different about the island?"

Though Killian looked at me expectantly, I had no idea what he was hoping I would feel or sense. I looked at the largest island on the map along with the smaller clusters surrounding it. After a moment, I felt a tingling, like an awareness. It seemed similar to when the *Vox in Ventum* drew me in from The Tullyhouse, like it was my beacon to salvation. I suddenly had the urge to spring into action, needing to heed its call.

Still, I hesitated to voice what I felt. I saw no reason to be quick to respond when they withheld their own answers for as long as they had known me.

Something on my face must have revealed my thoughts because Killian then continued, "Whatever is harming the sirens is unlike anything we'd ever seen. Malakai has no idea what could be causing those markings on their bodies, and he's been alive since the beginning of creation. I think it's worth exploring."

"So, what's the plan for getting the ship past the current?" Sven asked. "That seems like one barrier I'm not sure I can break through, if you know what I mean."

Clara shot him a disgusted look then asked a question of her own. "I think the better question is, how long will it take to get there?" She pointed to a spot on the opposite side of the map near the edge of Carnithia. "We're somewhere around here, based on last night's star chart. It would take us a week or longer to get there, and that's if we went non-stop on a good wind."

"Really, the question is how are we going to get the ship moving at all since we're sitting on dead water," Willy chimed in.

Killian put the first instrument he used back on the map to the spot where we were, then dragged it around the surrounding area. It looked as though he were using it as a magnifying glass to search for the answer to our problems.

"Here," he finally said. "Look at this current. It's going in the same direction we need to be, and it's faster than our hull speed. We should be able to make some progress if we can maneuver the ship that way."

The triplets, who stood in the only patch of shade from the mast on the ship, peeled away from their post and opened up compartments in the deck floor that I hadn't noticed, removing long oars from their hiding place.

"You want us to row our way to a current in the middle of nowhere and hope that it takes us closer to the middle of nowhere?" I shook my head, unable to process that thought. The ship was massive and more than that, it was owned by the Lord of Lost Souls. If a ship that a *god* gave us that was imbued with his magic wasn't capable of taking the crew he hired where they needed to go, then I seriously questioned what kind of power he actually had. And they were out of their minds if they thought I would row a ship in the blazing hot sun for gods knew how many hours.

"Of course not," Killian replied as if what I asked was absurd. As if on cue, the boat lurched forward, changing direction of its own accord.

I peered past Killian, looking for the source of the ship's movement, but nothing seemed out of place. Walking over to the edge of the railing, I peeked over the side of the ship, now bobbing up and down as it glided over the sparkling water, and saw three oars attached on the outside, all cutting through the powerful water and leading us forward. I ran over to the other side and saw three more oars. *Well played.*

Sven's voice carried over to where I still stood against the railing. "We still need to figure out how we're going to get past the current, and how to protect ourselves against whatever we might find on the islands."

"I'm cooking in this sun," Clara complained as she fanned her face. "Maybe we should discuss specifics once we're sure we can even make it over there. Plus, I need a bath and a nap."

The others murmured their agreements, so Killian relented. "We'll pick this up later in the afternoon."

I turned away from him and started to head below deck when his voice carried over to me. "Hey, Red. Can I have a word, please?"

Curiosity got the best of me as I stopped on the top step and waited for him to reach me. He approached with his arms full of maps and instruments, so I walked the rest of the way and opened the door to his room for him, assuming that was where he would lay them down.

The door hadn't had time to shut behind him before he blurted out, "What did you and Malakai discuss after he took you away?"

I raised my eyebrow at him, wondering why he wanted to know. Hesitation filled me as I thought about where my loyalties were supposed to lay: with the captain who claimed he wanted to rescue me, as if I were a damsel in distress, or the Lord of Lost Souls, who I still believed was behind my parents' murder, though he seemed willing to do whatever it took to prove it wasn't him.

"Why does it matter?"

"Did he mention me at all?" His stare penetrated through me, its intensity making me uncomfortable.

"Oh, you're interested in knowing how much of your betrayal he revealed?" I wondered where his need to have that question answered came from. "Or are you a lover, scorned? Jealous, perhaps, that he wanted to spend time with me instead of you?"

"Don't be ridiculous," he grumbled, tossing his belongings haphazardly on his desk. He shifted a map over and gazed down at something. He turned, revealing the notes from Malakai in his hand. He shook them accusingly in my direction. "What the fuck is this?"

I cocked my head, wondering if it was in fact jealousy, or something else. "Notes," I replied, dragging the word out as if he were slow to comprehend.

"No fuck, they're notes. Why is he sending you notes now? What exactly happened between you two?"

"If you read them, you could see that he wants me to eat. To keep up my energy." Killian's lip peeled back at that, but I continued. "As for what we discussed, he spent most of the time either keeping me locked in my room or else trying to say that things aren't always what they seem."

His shoulders relaxed a bit at that. "Anything else?"

"What else is he meant to have said to me? I didn't want to speak to him at all."

"Nothing about...you? Why he wanted you? Why he believes he owns you?"

"No one fucking owns me," I spat, "and all he said was my father made a deal with him years ago and never paid. That's it."

"So there's nothing going on between you two?"

The question threw me off guard. I didn't want to mention his shadows and what they did to me, or the dream I had where I admitted I felt safe with him, safe enough to want to do whatever it was he asked me to. Or all the ways I thought about what I'd allow Malakai to do to me. His seduction was alluring, impossible to escape.

"I offered to help him find out what's happening to his sirens. That's all."

He nodded his head but the look in his eye said he didn't believe me. *Fuck what he thinks. I gave up on that last night when he rejected me after getting what he wanted.*

Killian stripped off his shirt before donning another one and splashed his face in the basin off to the side of the room before returning back to the desk to eat the finger sandwiches that remained, downing each in one bite. I stood awkwardly off to the side, no longer tired enough for sleep but not wanting to explore the ship and risk running into anyone else, either.

"Love, maybe we should—"

"Killian!" Sven's voice barked through the door. "You're gonna want to see this."

The captain groaned as he stood up. "What is it, Holstrøm?"

"We've got sights on another ship. And um..." his voice trailed away.

Killian shook his head as he looped his scabbard and a holster through his belt. "And fucking what?"

"It's...well, it's *her*."

Killian paused what he was doing, thinking so loudly I could almost decipher what was on his mind. Whoever this "her" was, she had great meaning when it came to the captain. He crossed the room in two steps and threw open the door to find Sven with his dark hair tied back, a hatchet attached to his belt, daggers in holsters along his arms and legs, his sword hung loosely in his right fist. Seemed a bit like overkill to me.

"Are you sure?"

"Positive. Same sized vessel, same flag. She's coming in

at a nice clip. They'll be starboard within the next twenty minutes, I'd guess."

"Probably fucking sooner than that," Killian spat out as he shoved past Sven. Curious on who they were so up in arms about, I quickly followed them back into the blinding sunlight. "This can't be a coincidence. He must have sent her on the same job as us."

"And, what?" Sven said. "She's been following until we looked like we had a lead? That seems unlikely."

"That bitch has her ways."

"Who are you talking about?" I asked, hoping I could get answers this time around.

"Another crew your precious Lord of Lost Souls owns," Killian growled. "The captain of that crew is psychotic. And dangerous. And a bloodthirsty bitch always looking for her next fix."

"They have history," Sven whispered to me.

Envy trickled through my chest, but I dismissed the feeling right away. What did I care?

"Fuck off." Killian snatched a spyglass from next to the wheel to see for himself. "She has a larger crew than last time. I count eight...nine on deck."

Willy ran up from below deck, Clara close on their heels. "Look what just came through from the boss." She held out a piece of parchment that appeared to have smoke rising from its edges.

Killian scanned the parchment then fisted it, a low growl sounding from his chest. His nostrils flared as he breathed deeply, no doubt in an attempt to control another angry outburst. My skin flushed and it had nothing to do with the heat from the sun. I almost wanted to see it again. Almost.

His eyes slitted like a cat's, a silver gleam coming

through and his skin had a light glow to it, although that could have been a reflection from the sun. He focused that eerie gaze on me but it changed quickly back to normal. "She can't harm us. We'll see what she wants."

"No choice but to do that, boss," Sven said. "She's too close to do anything about it now."

A ship that seemed the mirror image of the *Vox in Ventum* sailed through the ocean though there was no wind, undoubtedly aided by whatever magic Malakai imbued in his ships. It slowed as it approached our starboard side. As one, Killian, Willy, and Clara all lined up in front of me, the triplets and Sven standing on either side, fully encasing me.

"Um, I can't see anything," I said, poking Killian in the back. "Move aside."

"Not a chance, love," he replied. "Not until we know what she wants."

A loud groaning noise rumbled toward us, disturbing the calm of the waves against our hull.

"What in the seven hells does she think she's doing?" Willy said.

"She can't be serious," Sven said as members of the other crew shouted orders to each other. The triplets tensed and shared a look between each other. I wished they would speak so I would know what everyone was so concerned about.

"Aren't we protected by Malakai's magic? His people can't hurt each other or something, right? So we're fine."

"Those cannons are pointed at us, Killian," Clara said. "What are our orders?"

"Hold. She can't possibly think we would run from this idiotic threat."

A boom echoed as the ship rocked, wood splintering as a cannonball hit its side.

"I told you she's fucking psychotic," Killian shouted as his body slammed me to the deck in an attempt to keep the wayward debris from falling on me. His eyes returned to slits and with a mouth full of sharpened teeth, he said, "You need to leave. Now."

I scoffed, refusing to balk from the monster he showed me. "Excuse me?" I threw my arms open wide. "And go where?"

"Take her," he implored Clara, climbing off me. "They'll finish the job."

"Finish what job? What are you talking about?"

"Come on, kitty kat, this way." Clara grabbed my arm and started pushing me toward the edge of the ship, pressing a mechanism on the underside of the railing once we got there. The ship vibrated under my feet, causing my teeth to slam together as the wood groaned. Willy and Sven arrived with two bags and tossed them overboard.

The triplets appeared in front of us, each wearing their own set of weapons and holding various other instruments I didn't recognize. Killian turned the wheel of the ship, willing it to change in the current it was currently stuck in.

"Where are we going?" I peered over the edge, surprised to see a large rowboat resting in the water. A rope ladder spilled over the side of the ship, waiting for us to descend.

"That bitch is bad news babe," Sven said, offering me his cupped hands to give me a leg up.

"Okay, and I repeat, where are we going?"

"That set of islands over there," Willy said, pointing off in the distance. "They're the ones we were aiming for."

"How the fuck did we get there already? Didn't you say it would be a week's journey?"

"Severe miscalculation, now move your ass!" Killian yelled. The other ship prepared to fire again, and I realized he turned our ship to hide us escaping from it. His eyes held mine as he said, "I'll come find you as soon as this is taken care of."

I accepted Sven's help and put one foot then the other over the railing, finding purchase on the ladder. Its thick rope was rough on my soft hands, rubbing them raw with each step down. I couldn't believe I was abandoning the ship in the middle of nowhere and heading toward a set of seemingly unexplored islands that may or may not have some sort of creature that killed sirens.

My feet found safety on the boat, and I was grateful that at least I wouldn't get eaten by the sharks that Killian always threatened everyone with. Clara arrived immediately after me and reached for the oars.

"Let's hurry. I don't want to be caught in the crossfire."

"Why isn't Malakai's protection spell working?" I rummaged through the bags, noting small knives and rope, some snacks, and a canteen with water. The other bag held more food and spare clothes.

"I don't know, but she's dangerous. Her and Killian—"

"Have history, I know," I interrupted. "What the fuck do I care if they used to fuck?"

"It's more than that. He used to be her first mate and he sabotaged a plan she had and she's been hellbent on destroying him since then."

Interesting. "Doesn't Malakai protect him?"

"That type of magic doesn't work the same against other people he has contracts with. The only beings who get his total protection are the sirens. Everyone else is just as mortal as they were before they bargained a piece of their soul, but we aren't allowed to cause mortal harm to each other. She never should have been able to attack that ship." Clara started to breathe heavily with exertion and sweat beaded on her forehead. The sun was relentless in the clear blue sky, but at least the hint of a breeze was a welcome reprieve the closer we got to the islands.

"Do you want me to have a go at that?" I asked, feeling badly for how much she was doing while I sat completely useless.

"No," she said. "I'll need you once we hit the current."

A shriek rent in the distance and I whipped my head around back toward the ship. I couldn't tell who was on the deck, but I wondered if it was the captain of the other ship who made the noise.

Two loud booms echoed, trailing over to us and Clara froze, her eyes wide, jaw dropping at what lay behind me. I turned fully and saw a hole clear through the *Vox in Ventum*.

"Oh gods," I whispered. "What happens now?"

"We hide, Em." She renewed the vigor she rowed with. "And we trust that Killian's plan works."

17

There is truth in discovering.

The ship was little more than a pinprick in the distance. I couldn't take my eyes off it, though the sunlight made it difficult to make out its exact shape, the way the sails still billowed in the wake of the explosion and the hole that shot straight through the hull. I thought she still stood proud, even with the damages she sustained. Hope was all I had to hold onto.

Clara grunted, struggling with the oars as we neared the current, if it could be called that. I looked down, the water clear enough to see straight down to the bottom. The tropical fish swimming in and out of the brilliantly colored coral, paired with the glowing pinks and blues of the crustaceans trailing along the ocean floor, were mesmerizing. Off in the distance, the water shifted, as if an impenetrable wall was erected. Its buzzing energy filled me with trepidation. It didn't feel right. Malakai's magic felt warm and seductive. The wall ahead felt cold and foreboding. I shivered as we approached, our boat rocking to the side as if it were being warded off by the current.

"What do we do?" I asked Clara as I grabbed hold of the oars to help her keep them steady. "We're going to either be pushed back the way we came, or we're going to tip over. And I don't want to get pulled into there." I grunted, the pressure of the water almost too much.

"Can...you...swim?" Clara asked, breath no longer available to her. "If we go under?"

Could I swim? It had been more than seven years since I'd last had the pleasure of feeling the saltwater coat my skin, but it wasn't something I was likely to forget. I was practically born with the ability to swim and the water made me feel as though I'd come alive, including all the dormant pieces of me that I'd had to keep hidden for so long. But the current was unlike any other I'd seen before and the possibility of drowning increased the closer we got.

Before I had time to answer, the boat tipped over and the cold fingers of the ocean snatched me from the surface and slammed me into the wall of the current. My eyes burned as I tried to see through the dark water, reaching out my hands to find purchase against anything. I spun too fast and was dragged further down into the cyclone of the rushing water. My lungs were fire in my chest and as I reached out to the rushing torrent, a sharp pinch on my finger drew out a silent scream.

At once, the world around me paused and a quiet calm spread through me. Time felt suspended and a serene floating sensation encased my body, allowing me to drift through the still current. My mind cleared of all thoughts except of Gabby, and how I wished she were alive so I could tell her of the crazy adventure I'd had for the past week as my lungs finally gave out and I welcomed the reprieve of unconsciousness.

THE DARKNESS WAS a heated blanket warming my icy bones. Shadows drifted over me, their soft tendrils smoothing over my face, my neck, my hips. I welcomed them as they licked at my cheeks and fingers as if they wanted to play. Sleep felt right, though. Sleep was a break from the fear and anxiety that came with the unknown.

But what was unknown? I couldn't remember anymore. Sleep was working in my favor already.

"*Little Red...*" a voice came from the shadows. It melted into me, pouring more heat into my body, building an aching desire between my legs. "*Wake up, Little Red. You are safe now.*"

"No," I whispered back. "Not safe. Never safe."

"*You are with me.*"

"Where are you?" I reached as the shadows retreated, as the cold threatened to seep into my bones again. "Please stay with me."

But the darkness retreated and I woke with a gasp, spluttering and coughing salt water, choking on it as it cleared from my lungs. Matted hair clung to my face, obscuring my view of my surroundings. My wet clothes molded to my body, the sand scratching at my exposed skin. I shivered despite the heat and another wave of nausea threatened to overtake me.

"Fuck the Dracon and the seven fucking hells," Clara coughed next to me. I blinked rapidly, trying to clear the black spots from my eyes. She looked worse than me as she attempted and failed to peel off her shirt and pants, succeeding only in tangling them up tighter around her.

"What in Eos' name just happened?" I asked, cursing the Lord of Storm and Seas for almost drowning us. "How did we get past the current?"

Clara huffed her breath as she continued her struggle. "You got us through, kitty. I'll explain later. Just please for the love of fuck, help me out of these gods damned wet clothes."

My body was still too weak to stand, so I grabbed onto her sleeve from my prone position and held it in place as she peeled her arm out of it. Shirtless, her breasts were exposed to the sun as she sighed in relief, allowing the heat to dry her body. A warm breeze gusted along the water, aiding her. She sat up and removed her boots then tried again to force her pants down. She let out a cry of frustration.

I laughed at her as she threw herself back on the sand in an angry huff. "Just let the sun dry you off a bit more and then it'll work."

"I hate the feeling of wet clothes," she complained. "But I'm just too fucking weak right now to do anything about it."

"Do you think we're safe here?" I asked, remembering why we were there in the first place. "What if whatever killed the sirens are here, watching us, waiting for our moment of perfect vulnerability to strike?"

"Sven could be dancing in front of me butt naked and I wouldn't even have the energy to dick punch him. I'd say we're as vulnerable as can be right now."

My head pounded from the thrashing of the current and the abuse of the sun and I found it impossible to do more than flop on the ground as I started my own attempt at removing my clothes. The effort proved easier for me, and I soon laid naked on the sand, willing the deep aching chill in my bones to recede.

The feeling of being watched crept over me, so I turned toward Clara, shielding my eyes to better see her. "You see something you like?" I asked, calling her out for her blatant staring.

"As alluring as you are, I was just lost in thought." She rummaged through one of the bags next to her, withdrawing the canteen of water. She took a tentative sip then bigger gulps as she drank her fill.

"Save some for me," I whined, well aware of the sand caught in my raw throat when I swallowed. I tossed my arm to the side, unable to find the strength to lift it again. "Hand it over."

"It refills with fresh water," Clara said. "Here, do you need some help?"

I didn't want to accept her offer to help but I was unable to sit up on my own. The weakness that flooded my entire body was foreign to me. Bruises had started to blossom along my skin, everything painful to the touch. "Yeah, I can't sit up."

Clara scooched over to me and pulled my arms, rolling me into a sitting position. My face fell onto her chest, and she laughed despite my frail desperation. "You could at least seduce me before you get intimate with the girls."

"I could seduce you in my sleep," I grumbled. "Just give me some water, please." I was starting to see double, the spots wavering in front of my vision an omen that I was on the verge of passing out again.

She tipped the canteen over my lips and glorious, fresh water spilled down my throat, soothing the ache. Already, I felt my headache diminish and strength return to my muscles. "What is this magical gift of life?"

Clara laughed. "It's just water. Here." She handed me a dry pair of linen pants and a loose shirt. "Put these on. We need to get out of the sun."

I marveled at the dry clothes and decided not to question what was undoubtedly another gift of the Lord of Lost Souls. I wanted to learn what his magic was and how he was able to use it on so many inanimate objects. The thought of him sent a shiver through me. His shadows had embraced me after the water. Did he know I was in danger? Was that his way of making sure I was okay?

Grabbing the other bag, I finally took a look at our surroundings. White, powdery sand stretched across the wide expanse of a beach, with palm trees swaying in the breeze a few dozen feet from where we stood. Beyond that was lush tropical forest, the scent of mangoes and something floral catching on the wind. Seagulls soared overhead and we could hear the tweeting of more birds in the distance. Tiny gnats fluttered around our faces, though I couldn't be bothered to swat them away. It was a beautiful paradise and I was grateful we'd arrived safely.

We stumbled our way across the sand, sliding as our steps gave way under the powder, and didn't stop until we were well into the vibrant forest. Plants I'd never seen before sprang from the ground and large red and purple flowers decorated the trees. Vines hung every now and then, reminding me of the danger of snakes and other potentially harmful creatures. I took special care to keep my eyes open for any animals or predators, but it seemed as though we were the only ones on the island.

"Shouldn't we stay near the beach so Killian can see us?" I asked.

"It's going to take at least a day for that ship to repair itself, possibly two, and we don't want to remain in the open for anyone else to catch a glimpse of us if we can help it."

Clara led the way, slashing through low hanging branches and carved a path through the rain forest. I didn't know where we were headed, but the further inland we went, the more humid it got and the crankier I became. I needed food. And sleep. And to just sit somewhere away from the mosquitoes that were now attacking every exposed part of my skin.

Clara stopped abruptly, causing me to bump heads with her.

"What is it?"

"Do you hear that?" She cocked her head to the side then whipped it around to face the direction we just came from. I turned and looked down the path we cleared but didn't notice anything different. "Something is walking towards us."

"Like an animal?" I whispered, as if that would somehow prevent whatever it was from seeing us though we stood open in the forest. After waiting a few minutes and still not hearing anything, we continued on until we reached a lagoon with a beautiful waterfall rushing down a rock cliff.

"Oh, thank fuck," I sighed, removing my boots and walking toward the water. "I'm so hot." Cool water rushed between my toes and instantly my mood lifted. I peered eagerly into the water, hoping to see a beautiful array of fish and other inhabitants, but the water seemed devoid of life. My stomach rumbled, reminding me that we'd have to find something to eat soon. "This is a little slice of paradise, isn't it?"

"Hmm," Clara hummed. "Well, it's beautiful, but still unusual. That current keeps almost everyone away from these islands, so it begs the question of who is using them and if what we're looking for is here."

"Maybe we should find some shelter," I suggested, a creepy feeling coming over me at her words. "I'd feel better with some sort of protection."

Clara pointed to a depression in the rock cliff just to the right of the waterfall. "That looks like a cave of some sort. We can investigate and make sure no wildlife lives there and commandeer it for the night."

I nodded my agreement and reluctantly stepped out of the water. "Fine, but we're definitely going for a swim after we're done exploring."

18

There is shock in revelations.

The moon hung low and heavy in the sky, its brightness eclipsing the stars that shone overhead. The lagoon glowed brilliant violet, and the trees surrounding the cave flickered with green lights. Tiny blue worms clung to the ceiling, creating a soft atmosphere. The temperature cooled greatly—not enough that would require a fire, though I still wished we had one.

This island was so much like the Kingdom of Vallah, I expected the Lord of Lost Souls to wander through any minute. No matter how hard I tried, my thoughts kept returning to him.

We had spent the evening collecting fresh papaya, guava, coconut, and mangoes and were quietly eating, only the sounds of slurping interrupting an otherwise peaceful evening. I hummed as I ate, allowing myself to relax my body until I became one with the earth. This was the freedom I had craved, though I was still trapped on an island and there was a potential murderer on the loose. But I was able to eat what I wanted, explored where I wished. I was no longer chained to the confines of one room.

"Can you tell me more about the captain of that other ship?" I asked Clara as we ate. "Why was Killian so against her seeing me?"

Clara scrunched her nose. "You mean you don't know? Hasn't Malakai or Killian told you anything?"

"What does Malakai have to do with anything?"

"What does Mal—! Fuck me, I don't think I'm the one who should be telling you this." She tossed her scraps of food in the lagoon outside the mouth of the cave then came back in to sit across from me. "But maybe there are some details I can spare, if only so you start to understand things a little more."

"Like why you all lied to me, and why you were hunting me to begin with?" The sting of betrayal still picked at me, tearing me into tiny shreds the more I thought about it.

"I'll try to tell you as much as I can," Clara said, "but Killian or Malakai will need to tell you the rest."

I nodded, letting her know I was fine with that. At least I would get some type of answer.

"I joined Killian's crew almost eight years ago. My parents died when I was young from sickness and it was just me on my own for a while. I took odd jobs when I was a teen, like selling newspapers or running errands for the older folk in the village I grew up in, and even started to learn more about new technology that started to come out. Learning how to take photographs and develop the film, for example. I actually like that a lot.

"But then the doctor in town got sick and my neighbor went into labor and she was terrified. I held her hand and told her when to breathe, when to push. It felt like the most natural thing in the world. I helped deliver four babies that summer, all of which survived—which was a miracle. But then the doctor healed and he sneered at me for thinking a teenager could take over his job, for daring to think I could do it better. The next few weeks, all the new mothers died under unusual circumstances and the only thing connecting them was me. The doctor fueled rumors that I was the culprit, and I was on the run.

"I ran to the docks, much like you did, and came to the *Vox in Ventum*. She was just sitting there as if she'd been waiting for me my whole life. Sven stood at the railing and indicated that I should go up. He thought I was dirty, that I'd been working for one of the slum lords and running so I wouldn't get caught, and he was willing to hide me for a price."

"What was the price?" I interrupted, praying that she wouldn't say that Sven or Killian required sex in return.

"Help on a dangerous job. If I got through it then I'd have a permanent place with them, if I wanted, as long as I was still willing to do the dirty work. I'd had nothing at that point. So I agreed."

"What was the job?" I felt like she was trying to tell me something significant, but I didn't understand the connection between what she went through and the woman on Killian's ship.

"I had to place a charred skeleton in the remains of a burnt down property."

"That sounds...grim. What was the purpose?"

"So Killian could convince his boss that the job was done, and the person he was after was dead."

"What does that have to do with the other captain?"

"Jana was employed by Malakai to search for your father and force him into complying with the bargain he made years prior. It turned out that Malakai hired several crews for the same job and in the chaos that ensued, your parents ended up dying. Killian thought it might have been her to give the kill order, even though it was against Malakai's wishes. He'd ended up abandoning her ship once he caught on to what she wanted to do. Killian tried to save your family, and Jana never forgave him. Not for leaving, not for the betrayal, not for trying to protect you."

"The remains you had to leave...was that at my family's house? Why?"

"To make it look like you died as well. And Killian's punishment for it was his entire soul rather than a piece, like his crew."

"Are you telling me he gave up his entire soul for me? Why would he do that? I never even heard of him before."

"He never really spoke about it, but Killian is a good guy. Despite him murdering those who turn against him, and for his reputation of bedding whatever pretty thing comes his way, he has a strict moral code that he always sticks by. Either that, or he felt protective of you since you belonged to Malakai once you came of age."

Anger seethed through me again. The revelation that Killian knew who I was, that he wanted to protect me, that he knew who really did murder my parents—all that was on the backburner while I thought about her "owning" comment.

"No one owns me," I said through clenched teeth. "Because of Jana, I sold myself into the worst form of slavery a young, innocent woman could have sold herself into. My ignorance nearly killed me. It was only sheer luck that Julian found me valuable."

"He considered you valuable because of your special talent. And you have that special talent because of the way Malakai worded the deal he made with your father."

"What does that mean? Malakai didn't mention anything about the way he worded the deal with my father."

"That's where I can't say more. Not because I don't want to, but because the spell prevents me from spilling that secret before its time. I'm sorry."

My mind reeled with the overflow of information. Killian knew who I was? For seven years he'd known me. Did he ever check up on me? Did he ever learn of the depraved things I'd had to do, or did I fall off his radar just as surely as I'd fallen off Malakai's?

"And now she knows I'm alive because Malakai removed my tattoo." I rubbed the spot where it used to be. "Because I'm somehow connected to him."

"That's the theory. And she likely either wants to finish the job or get revenge against Killian. You know this line of work. We have to be ruthless, cunning, unafraid to get our hands dirty."

I let that sink in. There were too many questions I still had that would have to be asked of Killian or Malakai but if what Clara said was true, then I owed them both an apology. To think Malakai murdered my family...he was still a dick who wanted to own me but if he really hadn't murdered them, then that shed new light on him. What did he even want with me, anyway? And Killian...he had been protecting me in his own way all that time.

It still didn't explain how he was able to find me if the special tattoo Julian gave me hid me from Malakai, because that would have hidden me from everyone else in his employ. What was it about that instrument he dropped the night I fell on him that was able to lead him to me?

"What does this mean for me?" I asked the question I really longed to know. "Why were we able to gain access to this piece of paradise? Why do I feel different? It doesn't make sense."

"Are you really that dense, kitty? You're a siren. When your father made that deal with Malakai before you were born, you were destined to become one of his. It was part of the magic. It's why you have that special gift. All you have to do is hum and you have everyone wet and panting for you, ready to do whatever they say. It's why you have control over Killian when he turns into his Dracon form, and why Malakai has a direct connection with you now that he broke that spell."

A siren.

I was a siren.

Some revelations in life act as though a missing puzzle piece has finally been placed and the world could breathe a sigh of relief at converging lines balancing again. That was what it felt like when Clara voiced what I should have known all along. Perhaps I knew but wasn't ready to acknowledge that I was made from legends. I looked nothing like the creatures I'd seen. My skin wasn't translucent and my blood didn't run black in my veins. And yet, something felt right when she said that, like it was the most obvious thing in the world for me to be.

It made sense, why Una and Julep kept giving me furtive glances, why Julep's magic was able to calm me down, why I was able to seduce at will, simply because I wished it to be so. And, knowing what I did about Malakai's connection to his sirens, I was starting to understand the madness it must have caused him to not know where I was, to have no confirmation of my death, to not have seen my soul pass on into the next life. Something nagged at me.

"Sorry—did you say his *Dracon* form? As in, the guardians of the seven rings of hell?"

"Yes, they're Malakai's creatures. Killian's form is just a shadow of what they're really like. There are only seven true Dracon, but I suppose for Malakai's purposes, he can choose what Killian should shift into depending on the threat level."

That was...interesting. I'd spent the past seven years trying to discern how the black market worked, who the key players were, ways to keep Julian happy so he wouldn't suspect my wanting to run away from him. It seemed I should have spent more time reading fairy tales and legends my mother used to tell Gabby and I as bedtime stories.

"Can I ask you a question now?" Clara said, her voice unusually timid.

I sat up and turned to fully face her, bracing myself for what she might say. Would it be something about Malakai? Did she want to know details of my life before? I raised my brows at her while she seemed to gather her thoughts.

"Can you teach me?" A blush rose on her cheeks. "To do what you can do, I mean."

My mind blanked out, unsure of what she was referring to. "Um, teach you what, exactly?"

"You know. How to make people want you."

My mouth opened but no sound came out. I tried and failed twice more before I managed, "What?"

"Never mind, that was dumb. Forget it."

Clara, who had been nothing but a strong, feisty woman, sat before me completely vulnerable and embarrassed, and I did nothing but stare at her like she was insane.

"No! No, that wasn't dumb. I'm just surprised. You're an attractive woman with a killer personality. Surely you don't have any problems with finding someone."

"I'm nothing but a dirty pirate, Em. I pay for what I need, same as anyone else. It isn't like we're at port long enough to go on the hunt. Nor would anyone on the ship want to give me the time of day, either."

The way she said that, with a tinge of bitterness in her voice, made me feel that perhaps something had happened with someone on the ship, but she didn't want to discuss it.

"You and Killian never...?" I trailed off, not really wanting to know the answer to the question but I couldn't help asking.

"No, gods no. He's good looking but he's had so many rotating through that it's just gross at this point."

I nodded, understanding what she was saying. I, of course, was part of that category. So many rotated through my body, using me until they'd had their fill, some demanding more, others putting me down for what I did while they picked an opening to shove themselves through.

My resentment must have shown on my face because she quickly added, "I didn't mean that about you. I know you were just doing your job and you had no choice. It's different when you have a choice."

"And if I still chose to be with more than one person? Or two?"

"If it makes you happy, if you're being safe, then I have no problems with it."

I nodded, wondering if she would feel that way if I did in fact get to choose for myself more than just Killian. I looked at where Clara lay on her side, facing me with her eyes turned down toward the earth. Her long, wavy hair covered half her face and the glow from the cave gave her an ethereal appearance. Her tanned skin shimmered when she moved, her eyelashes curled slightly.

She was beautiful, there was no doubt about that. And she trusted me enough to teach her something she clearly longed to see.

I trailed my fingers down her bare arm, lightly grazing her skin. Her eyes flashed up to mine and I gave her a small smile and cocked my head to the side, assessing her for any tells. For a quickened pulse, an unsteady breath. I leaned over, taking care to leave a slight gap in the collar of my shirt, so she could peek if she wanted to, and rested my hand against the curve of her hip.

"You're beautiful, Clara." I lowered my voice a little, as if what I said to her was just a secret between lovers. "I'm sure you don't need my help with this."

I waited a moment, my hand resting upon her while she looked at me and *there*, a quick lick of her lip, a subtle glance down my shirt. I smiled wider at her, showing her that I liked her reaction.

Clara shifted to sit in front of me with her legs crossed. My hand trailed from her hip to her thigh, my other joining her as I rubbed them up and down slowly, letting her get used to my gentle touch.

She licked her lip again and said, "You've hardly done anything, yet I feel special, like I'm worth looking at for more than a few moments."

I frowned at that, but kept my hands in motion. "You *are* worth looking at for more than a few moments. But this is what you need to know. To seduce anyone, they *have* to feel special. Like in a room full of hundreds, they are the one person you're gravitating towards. The only one that matters. They're the one that can make you feel good, that can give you what you need. If they feel that coming from you, and they're interested, they'll reciprocate in kind."

It was her turn to frown. "But I don't have the type of allure you do. I don't have that natural potency that sirens have. You exude nothing but that. Even when you're just standing on deck looking out to sea, eyes are drawn to you."

I caught her gaze then lowered my eyes to her lips as I placed her hands on my ribcage, encouraging her to trail up and explore if she wanted to. Her fingers trembled against me as they lightly brushed my sides. She inched closer to me and I leaned in, letting her know she had my permission to do whatever she was comfortable with.

The outline of Clara's body was encased in a green glow from the lagoon and her eyes reflected the soft blue light from the cave. She looked ethereal as her blond hair shifted in the breeze and her breath smelled of tropical fruit as she leaned in and gently placed her soft lips against mine. I deepened the kiss, opening my mouth wider and allowing her the chance to explore it. Her tongue tentatively roved over mine until her strokes became more confident.

She broke off after a moment and smiled at me. "You are so beautiful, Em." She placed a loose piece of hair behind my ear and looked in my eyes, biting her lip as she stared at me. "I hope I can make Sven feel half as desirable as you've made me feel."

"Um," I reared back, biting my lips against the laugh that bubbled up my throat. "I'm sorry, did you just say *Sven*?"

Clara's cheeks glowed a rosy pink. "I know, I know...we spent a night together when I first joined the crew but we just never talked about it again. And I just can't stop thinking about him." She lowered her voice. "And between you and me, I have *never* seen a more perfect—"

"Okay, okay," I laughed, cutting her off. I definitely had no desire to think about how perfect or not his dick was. "You know, all you have to do is walk past him and he'll be interested."

"It feels like too much time has passed! If he was interested in me, he certainly would have made another move, right? Sent me some sort of signal?" She ran her fingers through her hair and gave an exasperated sigh. "And anyways, he's one of my best friends now. Maybe it's a terrible idea."

"Perhaps he's just waiting for you," I suggested. "Men like to feel like they're desirable just as much as women do. You both are on the same crew so being open with each other is most important. If all else fails, just talk to him. Communication is the basis of the best sex, and is probably the same for a successful relationship."

"I suppose you're right," Clara sighed. "Let's try and get some sleep. We have to see if there's a killer lurking on this island."

I laid on the floor, watching the light blue glow of the insects on the ceiling and felt at ease for the first time in a long time. I might have had a mob boss after me, a pirate who wanted to kill me, another who wanted to claim me, and a god who wanted to own me, but in that moment, I had a friend, and that was worth more than anything I could have dreamed.

19

There is beauty in brutality.

The darkness surrounded me again and I waited as it pressed against my chest, squeezing the breath from my lungs, unfurling in my belly like a demon ready to claw its way out. It felt wrong. They weren't the shadows I was used to. They were cold, vicious, and it felt like drowning, as if the weight of the ocean held me against the darkest depths and I would never be free. I would remain trapped, caged in never ending pain as it shredded through me, as it tore away every essence of my being until I forgot where I was, until I forgot my name, I forgot...

"Emersyn!"

Hands shook me but it wasn't enough to bring me back. Nothing would ever bring me back. I was lost to it; I was nothing. *I'm nothing.*

"Emersyn Jane!" A slap across my cheek stung me back to awareness but it was still so dark, so cold. "Em. Fuck!"

I shivered uncontrollably, my teeth clacking together as I convulsed.

"Shit." Clara tossed a blanket over me and hugged my body to hers as I thrashed against her. "What the fuck is happening?" She sounded frantic which did nothing to ease the pain racking my body.

"S-so dark-k and c-c-cold," I stammered, biting my tongue. I whimpered in pain as I tasted blood.

"Don't talk!" She hissed at me. "Gods you feel like a block of fucking ice."

I squinted my eyes at her, peering through the darkness only to realize it wasn't dark anymore. Daylight streamed through the cave opening and birds squawked in the forest beyond the lagoon as everything came alive in the morning. That's what I needed. Light to chase away the dark. The warmth to warm my bones.

"Outs-s-ide," I stammered. "Need sun."

Clara jumped up and tried to help me stand, but when that didn't work, opted for dragging me out the cave mouth. I didn't mind since I couldn't feel anything anyway, other than painful, mind-numbing cold. She stopped once we reached the grassy embankment and the heat attempted to do its only job as I waited and hoped to melt away from the agony.

It was a slow process as I laid there, willing myself to stop shivering. Clara muttered to herself and paced back and forth, cursing Malakai, cursing magic. Something about being stuck between realms. I didn't understand much of it. All of my focus was concentrated on coming back from wherever I was.

Finally, I regained feeling in the form of pins and

needles and winced against a new pain on my scalp. I gingerly reached up and rubbed the offending spot. "Did you leave any fucking hair on my head as you dragged me like a barbarian?"

"Oh, fuck me. Thank you, thank you, thank you." Clara leaned down and helped me sit up. "Oh gods, I didn't know what to do for you. You were moaning in your sleep all night but then the piercing scream. I thought someone came to murder you."

"It fucking felt like it."

"What happened? Where did you go?"

"I don't know. I felt like I was drowning. Like a darkness seeped into every part of me and stripped me of all I was. I didn't even remember my name—just pain and nothing. I could see nothing."

Clara stared intensely at me, her eyebrows drawn to the middle of her forehead. "We need to figure out where Killian is."

The sun reflected off her bright blond hair, leaving an impression of her behind my eyelids every time I blinked. "We didn't even see if the thing killing the sirens was here. We have to keep looking."

"Well now I'm concerned that it is, considering what's happening to you. We need to get moving."

She ran into the mouth of the cave to grab our bags while I sat next to the lagoon, allowing my toes to dip in and out of the warmth. A swim would have been nice, if I didn't fear bodies of water, thanks to first almost drowning when we arrived, and then my nightmare. The ocean always soothed me, always made me feel I was whole, but I could hardly stand the thought of being near it. It was unsettling.

A ripple flowed from the middle of the lagoon. I

squinted my eyes, eager to see what caused it. We hadn't seen any fish yesterday, not even when we took a quick dip. There was nothing but birds and insects to be found on the island.

Another larger ripple came from the other side, as if someone dropped a stone from a distance. I looked up at the cliff, checking if anything fell from there but it was still. Nothing but a promise of another humid day this far inland.

"Ready?" Clara asked beside me.

"No, something weird is happening. Watch toward the center of the lagoon, tell me if you see anything."

"I don't think we should—what the fuck is that?!"

Long, thin, tentacles peeked through the surface of the water, undulating as if tiny muscles rippled underneath their skin. I was so focused on the speed at which they came at me that I nearly missed the head that poked through the water.

A beautiful male stared back at me with eyes as blue as the Baronian Sea, onyx hair, and tan skin that shimmered as he moved. He had lush, full lips. He looked like sin, which was even more disturbing considering the tentacles were surely coming from his body and heading towards me as if they were torpedoes or magnets finding their polar opposite to cling to.

"Em, move your ass!" Clara tried pulling me back but I was caught in his stare. A calm feeling swept through me, paralyzing my body as I wondered how a creature both so beautiful and terrifying could exist.

Clara jumped in front of me as the tentacles latched onto her skin instead of mine. She let out a piercing scream, her eyes rolling to the back of her head before she crumpled to the ground. I grabbed one of the daggers from a bag and chopped through the slimy gray masses in one swoop. The thing shrieked in pain and shot himself out of the water. I closed my eyes and aimed the dagger in his general direction but he snatched it out of my hand. His eyes were slitted in anger and his mouth revealed row after row of tiny sharp teeth. It was much more frightening than any sharks Killian threatened the crew with.

He wrestled me to the ground as his bleeding tentacle stumps flopped around me, sloshing me in a foul-smelling, inky mess. I wrapped my thighs tightly around his middle and flipped him over, punching him in the throat before he could sit up and tear a hole through my neck.

The hilt of the dagger he stole from me glinted a few inches away from his head but he was too distracted by bloodlust to notice. I launched for it and smashed it against his head just as he reached a hand out to choke me. The strength in his fingers felt like the power of the current that protected the island. Like the promise of a swift death, or the threat of a slow one. Black spots floated in front of my eyes but I refused to let that be the end of me. Emersyn Jane Merona would not go out by a psychotic being with tentacles.

I smashed his temple again with the hilt of the dagger then stabbed him straight through the eye. His strength still did not waver so I stabbed again, and again, through his cheek, his other eye, his mouth, his neck, over again as black blood oozed out and soaked into the grass beneath us. I didn't stop alternating between stabbing and smashing until his skull cracked and brain matter spurted everywhere.

Clara moaned, her voice weak and cracking under the strain of her pain. "Take these fucking things off." The tentacles from the beast were still latched deeply under her skin, but no matter how much I pried, they wouldn't come off.

"I'm going to have to try to work these off one by one," I said as I rummaged through one of the bags of supplies. I frantically searched as her whimpering increased. Clara's skin was pale and she started to sweat. It was a reaction similar to those who consumed too much *cassov*, and I had the irrational thought that the creature had released it into her bloodstream. Finally my fingers landed on tiny twin daggers, and I used them in tandem to dig under her skin to pull each sucker off until finally one of the tentacles came loose.

Clara screamed again as I pried it from her arm, revealing a purple bruise in the exact shape as what was found on the dead sirens. A closer look at the tentacle revealed dozens of sharp, miniscule needles protruding from the sucker. We looked at each other in alarm.

"Fuck me, Em. I think that would have killed you."

I swallowed hard against the lump in my throat as I realized how lucky I was to be alive. Clara had saved me and she was in complete agony because of it. I worked as quickly as I could to remove the other five tentacles still latched onto her body. Judging by the look of the scars that remained, along with the knowledge of how the other sirens died, I feared my assumption of a toxin was correct, and knew I had to be careful not to accidentally prick myself in the process.

Finally, the last of the tentacles fell away and I gathered them off the ground, careful not to touch any of the needles, and stuck them in one of the bags. "What are we gonna do about him?" I asked.

Clara's rapid shallow breaths had me worried, but she shoved off the help I tried to give her. "We have to take it with us for Malakai." She tried to bend over as if to grab for the creature but wobbled on her feet, nearly losing her balance.

"Whoa, careful," I said. "I'll drag this thing, but I won't be able to do that and help you walk." I handed her the water canteen. Clara was feeling the effects of whatever poison might have been slowly working through her blood and I was still weak from the dream that almost killed me, but fuck if I was going to let either of us waste away in the middle of some weird ass paradise.

I grasped the creature by the ankles, surprised at how light it was. The heavier bag with the tentacles sat on my back and Clara wore the other as we slowly began our walk back to the beach. I kept a dagger in my hand just in case anything else decided to pop out at us, but the walk remained uneventful.

The sun was high in the sky as we shuffled toward the water's edge. I was exhausted, famished, and in desperate need of a proper bath. Tiny flies clung to the sweat soaking my skin and my clothes felt tight from the humidity.

A ship loomed in the distance and relief poured through me. A ship meant the crew was okay. A ship meant we would get off this island. But then I remembered what it took for us to gain access to the paradise of hell and what I presumed it would take for us to leave again. *If* we could leave again. I had a feeling the island's only purpose was to ensnare, not to release its prey.

Even if we could leave, Clara was trembling and her skin had taken on a gray sheen, and I had a dead body to worry about. Even if I could swim out to touch the current, even if it let me pass, how could I possibly hold the weight of Clara and the creature above water?

Clara sank onto the sand and with shaky fingers,

removed the water canteen. It pained me to see her that way, to know what she did to protect me was slowly killing her. She took a sip of water with most of it sloshing down her chin, before bending over and hurling it all back up. Bright red and black mixed in the pile of sick and she looked up at me in alarm.

"Shit!" I exclaimed. Panic raced through me. "We need to get back to the ship. It can heal you right? A bath in one of those tubs or whatever the fuck kind of magic Malakai has on there will heal you right?"

"I don't...I don't know." She laid down on her back, shivering. "It's c-cold as fuck though. Any ideas on how to m-make it back?"

The sun beat down on us and perspiration flecked all over my skin. I was ready to pass out from heat stroke and she shivered as if we were in the northern mountains in the middle of a snow storm.

I turned back toward the ship, which appeared to be closer now. If Killian could sail as close to the current as possible without scraping the hull against the reef, I thought I might be able to make a few trips to get Clara and the creature on board.

Feeling like an idiot, I flapped my arms around in the direction of the ship, hoping someone was looking through a spyglass for us. I ran back to the edge of the rainforest and grabbed a fallen palm frond and dragged it back to the water's edge, using it as a flag to make it easier to be seen.

The ship sailed closer to us and relief flooded through me. It looked in perfect condition; the holes that had blasted through her were now repaired, and I marveled at how quickly Malakai's magic worked.

"Clara!" I turned to look at her, suppressing a gasp at the black veins that now ran through her face. "Clara?"

Her eyes shot open and she tilted her head in my direction. "I'm s-so cold, Em."

"Hold on, Clara. Killian is here. It's going to be okay."

I shouted in the direction of the ship, willing them to hurry, needing Clara to survive. I refused to let her die for me.

"Em," Clara croaked. "Em, no."

"Shh," I said, kneeling down next to her and wiping her hair back from her face. I didn't know how to soothe her. The bruises across her body were a dark purple and the black in her veins was spreading down the length of her body. I just knew once they covered all of her, she would be dead. "They're almost here. It's okay. It's going to be okay."

"No," she moaned again. She tried but failed to sit up. "Not him."

"Not him?" I looked at the ship again and then back down at her. "Of course it is. That's the *Vox in Ventum.* It's almost here. We're going to be okay."

"That's...not...Killian." Her breathing was labored and her eyes seemed to be out of focus. She was confused. She had to be. There was no one else it could be...except.

I recalled what I learned earlier. That all the ships of those Malakai employed looked the same. And the one that had attacked the *Vox in Ventum*...it looked exactly as ours did. And that ship...

No.

The ship was right at the boundary of the current and I watched as a body launched themselves off the side and splash into the water. A few moments later, the ship continued on. *It continued on* through the current.

If Clara and Killian's theory was correct, then the only way the ship could make it through the protective barrier to the island was if they had a siren on board. And I knew that there were no other sirens on the *Vox in Ventum*.

"Hide," Clara rasped, her grip surprisingly strong. "Leave me here and hide somewhere until Killian can save you."

She was still trying to protect me. My only apparent friend since well before I signed my contract with Julian was using the last of her strength to tell me to leave her. But I would stay with her until the end. I released myself from her grip and stood, ready to take on whoever was coming for us. I would not falter. I would not break. Never again would I appear weak, even with the odds against me.

There was nowhere to go, nowhere to run or turn to. Clara was moments away from taking her last breath, the body of the monster was festering in the heat, and we were spotted. I had no chance of dragging Clara to safety without sacrificing the body, and even if I did that, we would never make it before Jana showed up.

I had to trust that she would not kill me, for surely she would not want to bring down Malakai's wrath more than she already had. He must have known it was her who murdered my family, since all deaths left an imprint on the soul. What could possibly have been her excuse that he let her live?

I wish I knew more about her, other than that she was Killian's former lover. What drove her to turn against Malakai's wishes? Why come after me now, seven years later, when I never even knew she existed?

Gods, the ship was close enough I could see at least fifteen bodies on deck. Even if I had the skill, I could never fight them off. My ability couldn't work on more than one or two people at a time, depending on how much I concentrated.

Clara's gasps rasped in my ears as my blood pounded and the ship that was once impossibly far away suddenly dropped anchor.

I raised my chin and swallowed against the lump of fear that threatened to suffocate me. It didn't matter that apparently the captain of this ship wanted me dead, that she might have orchestrated the death of my entire family. It wasn't the first time I'd had to handle myself around a criminal and known murderer. I was the same as her, wasn't I?

But there was one thought that kept circulating through my mind, one thing playing on repeat. I let it strengthen my nerves until I felt it within every part of me. Until I knew it to be true.

"I don't need a man to save me."

PART THREE

20

There is envy in betrayal.

I was no stranger to chains.

Sometimes Julian would put me on display in the morning market, collared and chained as he paraded me around, showing everyone what a good pet I could be, if that was what they wanted.

Several clients enjoyed chaining me to the bed, or "lightly" smacking me with them. They were allowed to do anything, so long as I wasn't bruised for the next person.

One client enjoyed watching me slide a length of chain across my body, and I was forced to watch him pleasure himself while I did.

It came as no real surprise that I once again found myself in chains, bound to the mast of the ship. It was a first for me, at least, not that I wanted to cross that particular thing off the list of things to do before I died. Why they chose to use metal instead of rope, I didn't know, but it was uncomfortable and my wrists were already raw from the cold steel rubbing against my sweat-slicked wrists.

My eyes squinted open against the bright sunlight and I used what strength I could to lift my head and rest it against the mast. My moves were sluggish and I felt as though my muscles were not quite mine. My throat felt like I'd swallowed sand.

The last memory I had was a ship approaching that I'd realized was not Killian. No, that wasn't right. There was a smaller boat that came out to the island. Wait, was there? No. There was a woman with bright red hair and dark gray eyes. Yes. That I remember. Her thick lips were painted in a cruel smile and...what? *What did she do?*

There was a powder, some type of substance. That must have been why I didn't remember. She drugged me with something. Drugged...toxins...Clara.

I tossed my head from side to side, looking for the blonde powerhouse that I had come to consider my friend. Boxes and crates were stacked in the corners, giving a resemblance to Killian's ship, but the similarities stopped there. Jana's ship was covered in grime, as if no matter how often they swabbed the deck, the salt of the ocean still split the wood and allowed mold to rot it from underneath.

A woman came into focus. Hair the color of fire fell down in luscious waves against a curvy frame. Her gray eyes were lined in kohl and her lips were painted a blood red. She wore a tight, black one-piece suit. She looked more like an assassin than a captain of any vessel. That was who Killian used to have a relationship with?

"She awakens."

The sultry voice that came out of her mouth promised

nothing but desires fulfilled. She was temptation and sin. There was something about her that captivated the attention and it had nothing to do with me having nowhere else to look but at her.

"What do you want with me?" My voice was gritty. "I don't even know you."

"But I know you, the elusive Emersyn Jane Merona. You have been hard to find, you naughty thing." She trailed a pointed nail down my cheek, the sting of it piercing through my skin. A drop of blood welled on her finger and she placed it in her mouth, sucking it clean.

"What do you want with me?"

She leaned in, her nose lightly grazing my neck, and inhaled. "What is it about you that they all seem to want?"

"Where's Clara?"

"Ah, yes. Unfortunate what happened to her. Luckily we had an antidote. Couldn't have her dying in our care."

Relief pressed through me but I couldn't help but ask, "Why not?" It seemed like something the bitch would do.

"Are you dense, girl?" She sneered. "We can't let a soul belonging to Malakai die in our hands. He would know something had happened. And his wrath would be unending."

I tried to focus my gaze on her, finding it hard to speak clearly against the thickness of my tongue. "Are you afraid of him?" I looked her up and down.

"Only a fool would find no reason to fear him," she said. "I've seen him split humans in two with a flick of his hands. He can tear souls apart or disintegrate them with a snap of his fingers. A mere thought and you'd be tortured for days." She said it as if she had personal experience with the last point. She tilted her head, examining me. "Or is it just the other side of him you've seen? Hm? The way his shadows lick your skin, creating a dark desire with the slightest caress? The sharpness of his bite soothed away by a slow swipe of his tongue? The way he fits inside you as if he was made for your body alone?"

I let out a snort. Did Malakai fuck every female he came across? I frowned at her, unsure of how to answer. Of course I hadn't known Malakai that intimately, but the way she looked as if she wanted to flay my skin from my bones suggested jealousy and something else, something stronger that brewed beneath her. Was it wise to let her believe that something happened between us? It didn't matter. Something more pressing concerned me.

"What happened to Killian?"

Wrong question. Her face changed from one of jealousy to one of murderous intent. The gray of her eyes iced over and she bared her teeth at me as if wishing to tear out my jugular.

"Don't worry, girl. He got what he deserved."

Fury ripped through me but I swallowed it down. If Killian were gravely injured, I would know it, wouldn't I? Because of the connection we shared through Malakai? I narrowed my eyes at her. "Then I'll ask you again. What the *fuck* do you want with me?"

"Such a dirty mouth to go with a naughty girl. No wonder they all want a whore like you around."

I smirked at her. "What's the matter...what's your name again?"

"Captain Jana Leary."

"Okay, Jana," I said, refusing to use her title. "Are you jealous that they pay me more attention than you? That they crave the things I do to them?" I might have been crazy for baiting the bitch but I didn't care. If she wanted to call me a whore, I'd play right into it.

Jana's lips thinned and a muscle above her eye twitched. "You are lucky we can't kill you, girl, or else I would take great pleasure in watching you bleed."

Her crew moved in behind her. I quickly counted eight men, all looking worse for wear. It didn't surprise me that she had no women on board. She obviously didn't know how to play nice with other females. Each of the men held swords and daggers at their sides, ready to make a move at a signal from Jana. I decided to change tactics. The more I knew, the more I'd be able to plan my next moves.

"How did you get to that island? I thought only sirens could enter." I fished for information. "Is there a siren on board?"

"Oh, so she does have half a brain." Jana looked behind me, beckoning to someone with the point of her knife. "Come over here, darling. Let's have her take a look at you."

Hard steps thudded across the planks toward me. A pair of black high heels attached to long legs in a leather mini skirt and short leather crop top. Long hair was pulled back in a high ponytail and a sneer marred her face. I tried to keep my features neutral, though I lifted a brow. I'd seen her just a few days before. It was the submissive wench that interrupted my dinner with Malakai, the one he chose over me.

"Seraphina." Jana's voice was like honey as she placed her hand on the back of Seraphina's neck in a sign of ownership. "I believe you know her?"

"I know her type," I replied. I wanted to dislike her, but it was the truth. I'd known many submissive men and women. They all loved it for various reasons, each of them as valid as the next. That one, however, I didn't understand. The other night she looked at Malakai as if she worshiped him for the god he was, and now she was with the woman who tried to kill me seven years ago?

"This pet came to me quite a while ago. She has been instrumental in your capture, I must say."

"Where are you taking me?" I asked again. She might have worked for Malakai but to have her capture me when Malakai and I agreed to work together didn't make sense.

"To the boss."

"To Malakai?"

She smirked. "You'll see."

The lack of an answer threw me. There couldn't possibly be anyone worse than the Lord of Lost Souls, could there?

21

There is malevolence in creating.

Two details from the memory of my parents' attack never quite added up.

I remembered being on the edge of town rather than on my father's boat. I remembered my family and my father's crew waiting for me. I remembered a storm rolling in, swift and violent. I remembered the shouts of alarm before the blast of a cannon went off, and my father's ship in pieces.

Throughout all the chaos, the bodies in the air, and the sea turning red with their blood, I also remembered two specific thoughts that ran through my mind. How were there so many ships that arrived in a storm at once? And the other thought, the one that haunted me for months after I fled for the illusion of safety under Julian, the one that kept me in another state of mind while I had to allow men and women to do what they wanted with my body: who did the flag on the last ship, the one that gave the killing blow to my father's ship, belong to?

As I raised my eyes toward the sky, I saw that beacon of demise. I saw the one symbol that haunted me night after night for months. The one that gave me the strength to go on, in the beginning, if only to seek the answers I needed. A navy blue flag with a black trident slashed through with white x's and a star cresting along the top.

I glanced around, nobody paying me particular attention. Why would they? I was chained to a pole with no visible way out. Jana stood off to the starboard side with Seraphina, the latter of whom shot me scathing glances every now and then. The other crew members all worked in sync, occasionally sliding along the filth of the deck until the ship began to plummet.

After my time on the *Vox in Ventum* and then on the island of horrors, I was starting to become immune to the workings of magical ships, but the plunge into the deep blue was still filled me with terror.

It was different to when Killian's ship completely rotated into the Kingdom of Vallah. Jana's ship simply tilted downwards and the ocean parted ways as if an invisible tunnel opened its mouth and swallowed us whole. What seemed to be a protective oxygenated layer encased the ship, allowing us to sail down into the depths while the water was held at bay. Scores of fish swam to the outside of the shield, nipping ferociously at it and I was quickly reminded of a few days ago on the *Vox in Ventum*, when Killian accused me of being the cause of weird fish behavior. Surely they weren't viciously trying to penetrate the protective layer because of me?

If Killian was somehow right about the fish, I wondered

what he meant by tossing people overboard to the sharks as punishment. I swallowed hard. Now that I was down here where it felt more likely to happen, I didn't want to find out.

A muffled silence replaced the wind in the sails as the ship steadily creaked its way into the depths. It was eerie and suffocating. My brow prickled with sweat and nausea overcame me as my breaths came out in short spurts. My dream from the other night felt similar. Like there was a sense of something wrong. I used to love the ocean but it felt antagonistic to my life, rather than the familiar embrace of a loved one. Lamps flickered on in the descending darkness as the crew stood like sentinels, waiting for something I couldn't decipher.

A tingling sensation shimmered over me, as if my body were numb and just regaining feeling. It was painful, in a way, and it heightened my belief that something was off about where we were going.

The ship finally leveled out and hovered at an underwater dock. It wasn't until the anchor dropped that the crew sprang into action.

Jana walked up to me with Seraphina close on her heels. "You will not speak unless spoken to. You will refrain from snark. You will answer any questions asked of you. Understood?"

"Where's Clara?" I felt the chains around me loosen as I searched for her. "You said she was fine."

"And she is." Jana snapped at someone behind her and Clara was dragged up the stairs that led to the various quarters. Her blonde hair was dull and her skin was pale and sweaty, but she no longer had black veins running through her and her eyes had a sense of clarity that they had not when I last saw her. One of the crew members hurried her along until she stood next to Jana. She gave a subtle shake of her head, though I had no idea what that was in reference to. I barely had any friends, much less knew what their signals meant.

The last of my chains came undone and my arms prickled painfully as feeling came back into them. I rubbed my chafed wrists, remembering the last time they'd been rubbed raw by steel. The time when I'd escaped one hell and landed in another. Still, something Malakai had said to me replayed in my mind the deeper we drifted. Nothing was as it seemed and what I thought I knew was wrong. That fact was evident the second I turned around to view where we docked.

Thick, black coral reefs ascended from the ocean floor, screaming as if starving for sunlight. Beyond that, few bodies moved in and out from between various ships and whatever lay beyond the dead coral forest. Everything had a dark blue hue to it, emanating barely enough light to see just a few feet away, and the entire area was encased in the same protective barrier.

Clara sidled up next to me. "Don't say anything about Malakai," she whispered. "Not a breath about him or his realm, no matter what you see or hear here."

I stole a glance at her then shifted away, as if she hadn't said anything to me.

"I will never betray him." The words surprised me as they left my mouth, but I realized they were true. Malakai was many things, but whatever he was, pure evil wasn't one of them. At least, I didn't think so. All he'd claimed to want was to take care of me. Vallah felt comforting, like home. It brought me a sense of peace. The place before me, however, brought out a true sense of unease, trepidation, and fear.

Jana led the way off the ship, not bothering to look back to see if Clara and I followed. Why would she need to? There was nowhere for us to go. We were at the bottom of the Baronian Sea, at some type of...port? Town? I wasn't quite sure what it was meant to be, but the imbued magic allowed for a safe area of dry, breathable air. Our steps were muted as we descended. There were no sounds of any type of creature that might call such a place its home. It was a desolate chamber of darkness and nothing.

Absolute dread wound through me as we traveled past the blackened coral forest. Though the faintest blue light shone through the darkness, Jana seemed to have our path memorized. Clara clutched at me, her fingers gripping into my arm. A small part of me noticed the strength that had returned, and I was thankful, but it left me wondering what type of nightmares she survived to witness.

A scream pierced through the muted quiet, its anguish filled with pain and whatever horrors befell it. Jana's crew didn't seem particularly disturbed, though I did notice Seraphina wince at the sound. She looked back at me then flipped her ponytail with attitude when she caught me staring at her. Clara's grip on my arm sent a numbing pain through my fingers.

"What was that?" Her voice was almost swallowed in the empty darkness.

I had no answer for her. Another pained moan tore through the air, much closer. It sounded as if it were coming from the blackened coral forest surrounding us. Jana continued forward, gripping her sword tighter as the other crew members stepped closer to each other. A rustling in the distance heightened into a frenzy.

We rounded a bend in the path and came across a series of caves that appeared to be carved into a rough cliff wall, giving it a dilapidated appearance. The scent of iron clung heavy in the mist that started to roll in, as if blood were spilled so often there it had become part of the ecosystem giving it life.

"Walk quicker," Jana barked at us. "You don't want to be left behind where we're going."

Members of her crew removed a small device and as one, pressed a button in the center. A pulse rippled around us, and the frenzy halted, as if something stopped whatever it was from approaching.

We continued on into the network of caverns, complete darkness rushing over us, ensuring that whatever plan of escape I might have come up with surely wouldn't work. A steady drip of water echoed along with our steps. It was moist, surrounded by rock, the scent of blood thicker inside.

"Stay close." Jana's voice was low and laced with warning. "Touch nothing. Say nothing. And if I were you, Emersyn, I would try to make myself as small as possible."

I didn't know what she meant, but I didn't have time to ask. The further we went on, the sharper the floor plunged and deep caverns with bars fitted over them came into view. I wondered why Jana would bring us in through their dungeons. If the lack of people and the feeling of complete hopelessness hadn't instilled fear in us, that creepy coral forest with whatever creatures lurked within it would have done it. Going through the dungeons was utterly unnecessary.

The ground turned uneven and felt like undulating waves. No matter how hard I tried, I couldn't keep my footing even and kept tilting into either Clara or one of Jana's men. It was freezing; our breath crystalized with each exhale and I could feel any droplet of perspiration on my skin turn to ice.

We approached the first barred cavern and my heart thudded in my chest. I didn't know what would be imprisoned, what type of creature needed to be locked up. It was too dark to see inside but long, slurping sounds played nightmares with my imagination.

White hands gripped the iron bars of the next cage, and in the fire from the torch held aloft by one of Jana's crew, I could see black veins running just underneath the skin. Wide eyes stared back just beyond the flickering flame, and a mouth of cracked lips was held open in a silent scream. The terror on the creature's face raised my heartbeat and my footing stumbled again on the undulating ground, this time landing me against the bars. I grabbed hold as I quickly tried to correct my stance, but a strange sound held me frozen in place. It sounded musical—beautiful, even, but no matter how hard I tried to look into the depths of the dark cavern, I could not see what made such a sound.

A feeling slithered down my spine. It crept like a shadow, weighted with the power to suck the hope and joy from me, not that I had much to hold on to. Though I was frozen and drifting off to a dream state, I felt a distant prick on my ribcage as something latched onto me. A scream built itself from down in my belly, crawling up my stomach, piercing through my throat and terror unlike any I had known burrowed into me, fueling the need to panic and scream, to do anything to free me from the hell I was thrust into.

Suddenly the pressure eased, and the despair I felt creeping into my soul slowly leaked out, leaving an echo of hopelessness behind. On the ground next to my feet lay a gray tentacle with black suckers along the underside of it, reminding me of the creature I killed on that forsaken island.

The soft whine of a sword sliding back into its scabbard drew my eyes to Jana, whose face was filled with fury. "What the fuck did I say? You're not dying on my watch."

She bared her teeth at me then whirled around, continuing to lead the group past more cells. Clara grabbed hold of my arm and helped me walk. Her hand was clammy and cold friction helped it cling onto my sweat-soaked skin.

"Are you okay?" Her voice was low, hardly a whisper in the darkness.

"What in the ever loving seven rings of hell happened?"

"These creatures," Clara responded, "they seem to be torturing the sirens. You're lucky Jana stepped in, Em. I don't think any toxin got into your system."

More screams rang out from the cells as we walked on, the terror level palpable. I didn't think myself capable of feeling such insanity as I did walking down that cursed hallway, but it was almost indescribable. To know such fright, to be utterly helpless against the physical and psychological torture made death seem like a welcome reprieve. I had only known seconds of it; how long had the other sirens been subjected to the monsters? How long had they been wishing for their deaths to finally free them?

Finally, the ground rose on an incline and we ascended into a seemingly innocuous hallway. Black stone made up the floor and walls, with a thin gold lining through it. Glowing blue orbs hung in the air every few feet, and the ceiling was high enough that I couldn't make out where it actually ended. The walls were bare of any art or photograph and there were no windows or doors leading outside, though I knew from having just been there that it was no better than being inside.

The halls twisted and turned in ways that didn't make sense, and with the lack of any adornment on the walls, I knew that even if I escaped, I wouldn't know where to go. My hand found Clara's and I intertwined my fingers with hers as a wall next to us slid open, revealing a giant throne room.

The cavernous room felt well-suited to the castle of hell that we'd just walked through. Huge columns ran down the middle in two rows, creating a pathway to the raised dais at the other end. There were no windows, but the blue lighting from the hallway floated near the ceiling as well, casting shadows that gave the appearance of being underwater. Or, perhaps the fact that we were underwater added to that effect. The corners were shrouded in darkness and I felt eyes on us, though it was impossible to see if that was my imagination or not. My heart faltered at the thought of what could be lurking in the shadows and not for the first time, I hoped that whatever claim Malakai thought he had on me meant that he could track me wherever we were. Our footsteps echoed as we walked through the center of the room and it was the first time I realized that sound had returned to normal. Chains protruded from the ground, as if whatever spectators were normally there were held against their will.

Jana and her crew paused in front of the dais and bowed low to the ground. Clara quickly did the same, but I refused. I could see nothing of who they offered their reverence to other than the outline of a face, his features undefinable. If I was meant to go on my knees for a male—some supposed king—I would at least see who it was I was bowing to.

A dark chuckle rumbled in the cavern, pouring itself in the hidden crevasses of my mind. It was deep, sensual, invasive. It made me feel exposed, like I was a dirty thing that needed to be washed and wrung out. It made me lose all sense of self, reverting back to the ignorant young girl I used to be, desperate for a way to save myself.

"Such a stubborn little thing, aren't you?"

Power tore through the space between where I stood and where the supposed king sat and I felt it all at once— the suffocation, the sensation that I was drowning, the hopeless despair of my nightmares that haunted me night after night for years.

It wasn't Malakai, who I thought was the villain of my dreams. It wasn't the god I thought was responsible for the death of my parents and my sister, for my father's entire crew and countless other innocents. It wasn't the power of the male who had been searching for me for the past seven years. It was something worse, something wholly evil, something that I would never be able to claw my way out of.

My knees buckled under the intensity of the pressure bearing down on me and they slammed against the marble floor. My teeth clacked in my mouth and I tasted blood.

"Good girl."

My eyes burned in fear and defiance and I stared at the male. Slowly, he shifted forward in his throne until his face could be seen. Deep, ocean blue eyes shone with cunning and intelligence from a tanned face. His nose was straight with a slight hook at the end, his lips perfectly lush and sensuous. Dark, wavy hair fell to his broad shoulders. My breath faltered at the resemblance he bore to another god, another king to his own realm.

"Welcome, Emersyn Jane Merona," he said. "Welcome to the Kingdom of Kashura."

That name evoked a terror in me greater than any other.

Greater than the possibility of my soul being stolen from Malakai Barron. The Kingdom of Kashura was one that was whispered among all who sailed the seas; its legend was enough to make every sailor fear the unknown of the deep blue. It was the kingdom of the undead, a place where those who were unlucky enough to find themselves there were punished for eternity.

There was one being who was said to rule the Kingdom of Kashura. One god, who happened to be the brother of another. Sitting before me was Eos, the Lord of Storms and Sea.

22

There is bliss in ignorance.

At once, the shadows receded into the walls and the eyes I felt staring at me became apparent. A scream caught in my throat, clawing its way out. Though I was certain he knew the depth of my emotions, if his powers were anything like Malakai's, I refused to let terror be the main one he focused on.

He stood and slowly walked to where we were bent in deference, a half-smile tilting his cheek. He wore all black, similar to his brother, in sleek pants and a shirt with buttons down the front, his sleeves rolled up. His eyes were similar to Malakai's, though where his swirled with colors of the night sky, Eos' undulated with the dark depths and currents of the ocean. There was nothing to do but drown in them. I tore my gaze away and stared at the creatures watching from the sidelines instead.

Chained every few feet were beings similar to the one I killed on the island. Identical, achingly beautiful faces, all with dark hair and eyes stared directly at me. They were tall and muscular, and their vicious smiles promised to relish in my death. They each bore tentacles that hung at their sides. The memory of the tiny needles that released their deadly toxin filled me with fear. My stomach clenched as I realized I was surrounded by deadly weapons, dozens of them, all of whom looked ready to feast on my flesh.

"Yes, Emersyn, they all know what you did to their brother. So bloodthirsty, aren't you?"

Eos stopped in front of me and I could do nothing to stop the trembling that overcame me. Never had I felt such fear with Julian, with Killian, not even with the only other god I knew. Each man with power I came across had the ability to kill me within seconds, but it was the beast before me that filled me with dread. He raised a finger and trailed it down my cheek. Bile threatened to rise as I felt nothing but violation at his daring to touch my body. Somehow, I knew I wouldn't be able to free myself.

"The truth is beginning to dawn on you, I see. Yes, there is nothing you can do to save yourself." He grasped my hair, forcing me to my feet.

"Why?" My voice cracked with a whisper. "Why do you want me?"

He raised his brow and smiled wider. "Didn't anyone tell you not to speak to me?" His face lit up with absolute joy. "You do know giving me the sound of your voice allows me to hold power over you, doesn't it?" He leaned in closer and I felt a flicker of his wet tongue against my cheek. "That it will allow me to do whatever I wish to you, and you will have no choice but to comply?"

Clara silently sobbed next to me, her fear fueling more of my own. I didn't know what he said to be true. Yes, I'd been told not to speak unless spoken to and I spoke first but why hadn't anyone told me the consequences? There were no legends that told of such things.

"Well, the damage is done now, isn't it?" he whispered in my ear, his nose trailing down my neck as he inhaled my scent. "Since you were so generous, I shall answer you.

"My brother owes me a debt, and as one who deals with souls, he knows how terribly important it is to follow through. And if not, there are consequences. You, my dear, are what I'm owed and what will hit him most."

I struggled not to respond. It didn't make sense. I thought my father made a deal with Malakai that he could have me when I come of age in exchange for his life. Now another god had been after me the whole time, as a way to get back at Malakai for not fulfilling his end of a deal?

"I've waited quite a while for you," he continued. "It took years to come up with the proper toxin to kill the sirens, to weaken my brother and his realm. Do you know how incompetent humans are? Pathetic, all of them. But no matter. I gained control of the black market, allowed *cassov* and other manner of drugs to circulate. It's because of me that you were hidden from Malakai for so long, why all the other sirens sold into sexual servitude are hidden from him. They are such a *nuisance*, stealing the corrupted souls I need to make my plans work. It was an arduous process of trial and error before I came up with the perfect toxin. You saw the consequences of my efforts, I'm sure."

He paused, waiting for some sort of response from me. The only thing I wanted to do was vomit with the sick truth behind his words. Everything we passed on our way, the horrors we saw, were just his experiments until he created the perfect weapon.

"You were simply the missing link. Without you, my brother will be weak enough for me to destroy him." He smiled wide enough to reveal razor sharp canines. "And I will finally be ruler of land, sea, and the beyond."

He whipped his head around at the sound of a chain clinking behind him.

"Ahh, I almost forgot. I do have a gift of sorts for you."

I didn't want it. Whatever his sick idea of a gift was, I wanted nothing to do with it.

"Oh!" Eos' face lit up with glee, his voice taking on a crazed edge of delight. "Oh, my. This is better than I thought it would be." He placed a cold finger under my chin, forcing me to look up at him. The gesture was so like what Malakai had once done, except then I was filled with heat and forbidden promise instead of trepidation and disgust. "My devious brother turned one of your own into a siren. And, fool that he is, he lost her some time ago."

No. It couldn't be true. I refused. But there would be no reason to lie to me about that. Realization swept through me. The voice. The voice from my dreams. The one crying out for help, begging me to save her. Over and over I heard her pleas, and I knew, I *knew* the familiarity in it.

"Come closer, pet."

At his command, the woman moved closer, the chain clinking with each step she took. Slowly, she came into what little light there was. Her long, pale legs were bare, right up until her hips which were covered in a gold cloth, barely held together by any stitch or string. Her midriff was bare, exposing the ribs that protruded from her sides. Her chest was covered in another piece of gold cloth that did little to hide what was underneath. Long rivulets of black hair fell down past her shoulders. Shifting black veins flowed beneath her pale skin. She looked nothing like how I last remembered her, deep golden tan from hours in the sun, bright mahogany hair that gleamed without trying.

"She *is* a tough one, isn't she? It took a while to break her. A deliciously long time of punishment and reward. But I did break her, eventually. She is actually the reason I was able to experiment to find the right toxin. The blood that runs through her veins helped me devise the perfect poison to kill them all. My brother is foolish. He thought he got the best of your pathetic father, but instead, I got the best of *him*."

Then the woman spoke, her voice raspy either with disuse or years of screaming for mercy as my heart shattered into a million fragments. "Hi, Emmy."

"Gabby?"

END OF BOOK ONE.

SIREN SONG

Siren Song
When the siren calls
The crew can hear
An inviting path into the depths we fear
But her sweeter song
It is foretold
Will soothe the soul as death takes hold

Now a sailor tried
To rescind the deal
Fear gripped him
In its spinning wheel
So he told the lord
Who had the soul he lost
I'll do anything
At whatever cost

Ah
Into the underworld we go
And our souls scream far below

So the lord did have
A furrowed brow
Crafting cunning deals
That he could disavow
So he said, I know
A fair exchange
Your second born daughter
When she comes of age
And the sailor
Unbeknownst to him
Didn't feel love
At the time for such things
So he signed with blood
And he sealed his fate
Never knowing the toll
Of his mistakes

So the years they passed
And the sailor found
The greatest love that would know no bounds
A heavenly lass
Two daughters fair
And the kissed the sun
And the salty air

But the time had come
And the lord appeared
From the darker depths
That all sailors feared
He held out his arms
And the waves, they crashed
The bow did bend
And the sails lashed

But the sailor fought
For his family
And kept them safe
At least as safe as could be
But hidden and cramped
Like snails curled
They were found and dragged into the
*   underworld*

But the sailor tried
With all his might
To distract the lord
As the second born took flight
And she soared the skies
Away from the sea
Red waves were what remained
Of his family

But to this day
The lord he seeks
The soul that flew
Over blood red seas
She sang a haunting song
Of liberty
But soon she'll sing
To him for eternity

ACKNOWLEDGMENTS

Writing can be such a lonely venture, and this journey in particular was unique in that I had more people supporting me than ever but it still was a solitary experience. The idea for this story was created when I first felt the winds of change approach my life. Drafting was when the cyclone had arrived, and publication was when I felt completely lost at sea.

This book saved me in more ways than one and there are so many people to express my gratitude for. "Thank you" never feels like enough, but it will have to do.

First to my developmental editor, Quinn Nichols. You have this amazing superpower of being able to see the story I'm meant to tell when all I give you is scraps to work with. Thank you for hacking away at that first draft and giving me the stepping stones to move forward.

To B.N. Laux, my line editor. I understand how chaotic it is to work with me. Thank you for taking the time, especially on your days off, to talk me out of rewriting this book and for talking me out of postponing publishing at all. You are a true gem.

My Whimsies: Britt, Jesse, Jessika, Jenn, Chelsea, Holly- I know I've been absent from the writing group for so long, but thank you for reading the first draft of my book and discovering Syn, Killian, and Malakai with me. Your input and support kept me going in the beginning. And thank you for the support and positivity in times where I felt like I was drowning.

My beta readers: Kiraka, Peter, Lilian, Tanya, Kim, Victoria. The hype, the positivity, the attention to detail! I cannot express enough how much I appreciate you all reading and giving this book a chance. Each one of you brought me new insight into what I've written, and the absolute cheerleading you all provided encouraged me to try harder and keep going. Thank you, thank you, thank you.

JP: how many ways can I thank you and show my gratitude? These words will never be enough. You have been one of the greatest influences when crafting this novel, from working out that first scene together (I am impatiently waiting to do it again), to encouraging me every time I felt like I was putting too much of me on the page. The constant support, the way you didn't think to hesitate when I asked you to help me with the siren song (which came out absolutely perfectly, you musical genius), to helping me figure out the plot holes and names and language usage and description. Pieces of you are bleeding all over these pages, which makes sense, in a way, as you've given this story life when there was none, and it would not have been nearly a fraction of what it is without you. Thank you for anchoring me and the endless support and patience you have while I navigate these waters.

Finally, my family, for always believing in me even when you don't entirely understand what I do or how I do it. And to Oliver, for reminding me that there is more to live for and to never stop trying. I love you.

About the Author

Emmie Hamilton is forever inspired by the "in-between" moments. You know the ones - the empty spaces between the chaos of life. The conversations that are never said, the days filled with waiting, the silence after the emotion calms down; those are what Emmie's stories are built off of.

In her free time, Emmie likes to fulfill her passion for "life" whether that's writing emotional connections, reading addictive novels, traveling the world, or trying new food.

Emmie received her MFA in Creative Writing in 2019 and has since had poems and essays published with Scary Mommy and Pure Slush Press. Her debut novel, Chosen to Fall, was released in May 2021. Its sequel, Fated to Burn, was released November that same year.

Keep up with Emmie's life on Instagram and be sure to check out the shop on her website for fun book merch related to her novels.

www.emmiehamilton.com

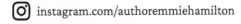 instagram.com/authoremmiehamilton

9 781736 699492